BOOGER MCCLAIN OZARKS DETECTIVE SERIES BOOK 3

GONE IN THE NIGHT

THE STORY OF THE SPRINGFIELD THREE

ALAN BROWN

BRIAN BROWN

This is a work of fiction. Names, characters, places, and incidents are products of the author's imagination or are used fictitiously and are not to be construed as real. Any resemblance to actual events, locations, organizations, or persons, living or dead, is entirely coincidental.

World Castle Publishing, LLC
Pensacola, Florida

Hardback ISBN: 9798397786676
Paperback ISBN: 9781960076922
eBook ISBN: 9781960076939
First Edition World Castle Publishing, LLC, June 26, 2023
http://www.worldcastlepublishing.com

Licensing Notes

Cover: Karen Fuller
Editor: Karen Fuller

CHAPTER 1

THE DISAPPEARANCE

Springfield, Missouri, is Hometown USA. From the most populated Springfield, Massachusetts, to the home of Lincoln in Illinois, 35 states in the U.S. have a "Springfield" or a related name, such as Springfield Township, Michigan. The one in Missouri is the third largest city in the Show-Me State, with a population of about 150,000. It rests comfortably on the Ozarks Plateau in the southwest corner of the state, where nothing changes quickly but the weather. Springfieldians have been known to say that one can experience all four seasons in a week. The "Queen City of the Ozarks" is a family stop on Route 66 between St. Louis and Tulsa, Oklahoma. It was the boyhood home of Brad Pitt. Bob Barker went to college at Drury. "Oh, oh, oh, O'Reilly's!" was born here. Fast food is at every major intersection.

Crime is low, and neighbors are friendly in Springfield. Parents rarely worry about their children riding their bicycles around the block. People look out for each other. Most have either grown up here or choose to stay here, having escaped the fast pace and headaches of larger communities. The cost of living is low. Church and family are the priorities. Springfield is a slice of the American Pie, a little piece of the American Dream with a white picket fence. It's a community where people feel safe.

Or they used to be.

This wasn't supposed to happen here. The Springfield Three.

But on a warm day in June, it did.

June 7, 1992, is the day Springfield changed forever. It is the scar that forever altered its psyche. It marks a day of lost innocence. Nearly 30 years later, if one just mentions the "Springfield Three" to any longtime area residents, chances are they will recall in great detail what they were doing and how they reacted when they heard the news.

The day before was graduation day at Kickapoo High School. Nineteen-year-old Suzie Streeter and her friend Stacy McCall along with nearly 700 other graduates, walked down the aisle. Janis McCall and her husband, Stu, were in attendance, along with siblings and other relatives, to watch their daughter Stacy graduate. Stacy, a good student, had plans to attend the hometown university, what was then still called Southwest Missouri State. Her best friend, Suzie Streeter, was considering following her mother's career path as a cosmetologist. Both were looking forward to a relaxing and fun summer before beginning their new journeys in life.

Sherrill Levitt, Suzie's mother, was in the audience that day to watch her only daughter graduate. She was both enthusiastic and a little melancholy about her daughter's rite of passage, according to a friend she spoke with that night. From all accounts, Sherrill and Suzie were very close. Raising her daughter had not been easy after her divorce, but she never complained. Suzie meant everything to her, especially after she and her twenty-eight-year-old son Bartt had a falling out years earlier. He had a drinking problem. He was volatile at times, and Sherrill and her son often got into loud arguments. That led her to finally throwing her son out of the house.

Graduation night would be an evening of celebration,

parties, and drinking. Suzie and Stacy had plans to attend one or two parties with their friend Janelle Kirby. They even talked about going to White Water in Branson, some 30 miles away, the next day. Perhaps they would drive to Branson later that night and get a motel room close to the water park, so they could be there as soon as it opened the next day. That was the plan all three had told their mothers, anyway.

Janis McCall remembered giving her daughter a goodbye kiss and telling Stacy to call her if her plans changed. She was apprehensive about her daughter driving to Branson late that night, particularly after attending a party or two. It wasn't so much that she was concerned about her daughter drinking. Stacy was a responsible person. She trusted her daughter would not drink and drive. But her fear was that Stacy would not be driving, and Suzie would.

Suzie wasn't a bad kid, but she reportedly hung out with a rowdier crowd and was prone to making bad choices - particularly boyfriends. One of those boyfriends and two of his friends had been accused of vandalizing mausoleums at a local cemetery. Suzie, it was said, had information about the crime and was considering testifying against the three boys, Dustin Recla, Michael Clay and Joseph Riedel.

Suzie and Stacy had been childhood friends who had drifted apart in high school. They appeared to have little in common and were going in different directions in life. But the end of high school had a way of reuniting old friends, and on the night of graduation, the two were hanging out again. They made plans together, and that included spending time with another friend, Janelle Kirby. Janelle and her boyfriend, Mike Henson, had planned to drive to Branson later that night along with Suzie and Stacie, rent a motel room and go to a water park early the next day.

But they decided against the drive later that evening, so

Stacy called her mother to tell her she'd most likely spend the night at Janelle's house. That made her mother happy. She wasn't in favor of driving to Branson that late at night. She told her daughter she loved her and to have fun. She would have never guessed that would be the last time she talked to Stacy.

Suzie also called her mother that night to tell her she planned to stay over at Janelle's house, too. The three girls left their last graduation party close to 2 a.m. and headed back to Janelle's, but with relatives from out of town staying overnight, there really wasn't room for her two friends. That's when the girls decided to spend the night at Suzie's house. Suzie had received a king-size waterbed as a graduation present from her mother, and the girls agreed they'd probably be more comfortable there. Janelle was invited too but declined. She thought it would be impolite to spend the night somewhere else when she had relatives at her house. No big deal, they all thought. They'd meet up with her in the morning.

Suzie and Stacy had driven separate cars to Janelle's house. Therefore, Stacy followed Suzie to her house when they left.

Suzie's mother, Sherrill, had spent the evening at home, watching television and talking to a good friend on the phone about varnishing furniture and hanging wallpaper. She and her daughter had moved into the house at 1717 E. Delmar Street only two months earlier. It was a modest home, just off the busy Glenstone Ave., on the edge of the old-money section of the Rountree Neighborhood. The home needed some upgrades, and Sherill was focused on the task. Her friend said Sherrill sounded normal, even upbeat and never indicated anything seemed amiss. Their conversation ended around 11:30 p.m.

It is unknown exactly when the girls arrived at Sherrill Levitt's house, but it is assumed they went straight there after leaving Janelle's. Whether they went right to bed or went out again is a matter of controversy.

A server at George's Steak House, a popular 24-hour diner on Glenstone about a mile north from Sherrill's home, told police the three women ate breakfast at the restaurant during the early morning hours of June 7. She claimed Suzie was intoxicated, slurring her words and walking erratically. She said Sherrill Levitt was trying to settle her daughter down. Sherrill, it was reported, was a regular customer at George's, and the server recognized her.

No one else at the restaurant collaborated the server's story. The server also said when the three women left, they were talking to three men outside the restaurant.

Later that morning, Janelle began calling Suzie's house around 8 a.m. She was up and ready to drive to Branson for their day at White Water. No one answered the phone.

They were sleeping in after a late night of partying, Janelle assumed. But when she hadn't heard from her friend by noon, she and her boyfriend, Mike Henson, decided to drive over to Suzie's.

It was a clear, sunny morning, temperatures hovering around 80 degrees, a perfect day for the water park. Janelle was a little upset that the girls were sleeping in so late. She even wondered if they had taken off without her.

But when she arrived at the Levitt home, all three cars were in the circle driveway. "That is odd," she said to Mike. "They must be home."

Janelle got out of the car barefoot and approached the house. Something shiny on the front porch caught her eye. It was broken glass. She walked carefully around it, not wanting to cut her bare feet. Mike spotted the light fixture to the right of the door. The glass cover had been broken. That was what was shattered on the porch.

Mike looked up at the light fixture and frowned. "That's odd," Mike said. "Babe, look, the bulb's not broken. Watch your feet."

"They better answer the door," Janelle said. "I'm ready to go."

Janelle knocked on the door. There was no response. She rang the doorbell. Again, nothing. She and Mike looked through a window on the porch with a view into the living room. The curtain was mostly closed, but a small opening gave the couple a tunneled view of the living room. They did not see anyone, although they could hear the television on in the background.

"Someone's gotta be home," Janelle said. "The TV's on."

"Try the door," Mike said.

Janelle tried the front door knob. The door was unlocked. This she found to be particularly strange since Suzie had mentioned on several occasions how concerned her mother was about security ever since the trouble with Bartt. "That's strange. She always locks all the doors and windows," Janelle told him. "She is constantly bugging me to do the same."

Janelle pushed the door open and stepped back. She and Mike both yelled Suzie and Stacy's names, hoping to wake them up if they were still asleep. There was no answer. After a few minutes, they decided to go inside. Janelle walked in first.

Sherrill's Yorkie Cinnamon lunged at her, barking and anxious. She petted him for a few seconds to calm him down. In the living room, the television set and a table light were on. The room was a bit cluttered but looked undisturbed.

They continued walking through the house, calling their friends. There was no response. The three women's purses were piled on the steps of Suzie's sunken bedroom. Car keys and a pack of cigarettes were out. That made Janelle uneasy. Suzie and Sherrill were both chain smokers. She could understand walking someplace or going with someone else and leaving their purses and car keys. However, neither Sherrill nor her daughter went anywhere without those cigarettes.

The door to Suzie's room was open. They walked inside. It appeared the two girls had gotten ready for bed. Sheets on the waterbed were messed up. Evidence of washed-off makeup was in the bathroom. Stacy had folded her shorts and placed them on her shoes beside Suzie's waterbed. The clothes Suzie had worn the night before were on her dresser, folded.

Janelle and Mike went into Sherrill's bedroom. The door was open. Cigarette butts were in an ashtray, reading glasses, and a half-empty pack of Pall Malls was on the nightstand. The covers on the bed were rolled down, and an open book was lying on the bed.

"It looked as if they had just been there." Janelle would say later. "There was nothing out of the ordinary, nothing that looked like it was out of place."

There was one small thing that Janelle found to be odd. The curtain in Suzie's bedroom was partially open. "It wasn't a big deal," she would later say, but all the other curtains in the house were closed."

Whatever Janelle and Mike saw did not bother them enough to contact the police. There was nothing in that house that made them think anything sinister had happened. They were concerned but figured there was a good explanation.

Mike went back to the porch and cleaned up the broken glass. He thought that he was doing his friend a favor.

Janelle decided to check the answering machine. The light was on, indicating there was at least one message. She figured the message might hold a clue to where her friends were, so she hit play. Instead, what sounded like an obscene message was heard on the answering machine. She deleted the message and walked out of the house.

Janelle and her boyfriend would make a couple calls, one going to Stacy's mother, who, until that point, had assumed her daughter was at the water park in Branson with her friends.

***

When Janis McCall was told that the girls' cars, car keys and purses were still in the unlocked house, she ran over to the Levitt's home.

She noted that her daughter's car was parked in the driveway, along with two other cars she assumed belonged to Suzie and her mother. Inside, she found the house undisturbed. Janelle and Mike had cleaned up some, and from accounts, several of Suzie and Stacy's friends had also been in the house looking for them or for clues as to where they were.

In Suzie's bedroom, Janis McCall found her daughter's shorts and shoes. The sight of both must have worried her because it meant wherever her daughter was, she was likely in her t-shirt and underwear

She immediately called her husband, Stu, to come to the Levitt house. Her motherly instincts had kicked in. She felt something was wrong. Her daughter would not leave the house without her shorts and shoes.

When she saw Stacy's purse on the floor, she looked inside. Perhaps, it held a clue to where was. Instead, she found her daughter's wallet, money and driver's license inside. Her car keys were there, too.

Suddenly the phone rang. "Oh, thank God," Janis said as she ran to it, anxious that it might be her daughter or someone who knew where they were. Instead, it was what she described as an obscene phone call. She ran out of the house and waited for her husband to arrive. Late that evening, Janis McCall would call the police and report her daughter missing.

***

Why did it take so long for anyone to call the police? It appeared no one thought anything sinister had happened to the three women. Why should anyone assume the worst? It was the day after graduation, and this was Springfield. Disappearances like this simply didn't happen here. There had to be a simple explanation for the whereabouts of the women. Their friends expected them to show up with some logical story to explain where they were all day.

But as the hours of that day piled up with no sign of them, a plausible explanation seemed more and more unlikely. From various accounts, at least ten people entered the Levitt house that day looking for the girls and disturbing potential evidence.

When the police were finally called, they found no clear signs of a struggle or a crime. It didn't appear to be a robbery. Nothing in the house appeared to have been taken. Sherrill Levitt's jewelry was on her dresser in plain sight. The television and stereo were not taken. Their purses were there, and Sherrill's even contained $900 in cash.

Investigators had few clues to go on, and those they did find were contaminated by so many people coming into the house that day. People had cleaned up. Some moved things around. Everyone left fingerprints. One of the potentially obvious clues, the broken light cover on the front porch, was swept up and thrown away. The obscene message left on the answering machine was deleted. The open curtain in Suzie's room had been touched and closed.

An uneaten graduation cake in the refrigerator with the words "Congrats, Suz!" was a reminder of the celebration just a day before. A reminder of how quickly things changed. It remained, but the women were gone.

No one wanted to believe a crime had been committed, not in this middle to upper-middle-class neighborhood. Three women disappearing from a home in the middle of the night – it couldn't be. No one heard anything. The family dog was loose in the house. The home was set back from the road a bit, but the neighbors were close. Someone would have heard something. Wouldn't they?

Panic swelled with friends and family, but everyone tried to remain optimistic. The girls had not been gone even a day. There was still a feeling the girls would come home, a singular hope to hold onto.

Police left a small blue note on the front door that read, "When you get in, please call 864-1810 and cancel the missing person report."

But Stacy, Suzie and Sherrill never came home. The missing persons' report was never canceled. Things changed that day in America's hometown.

CHAPTER 2

MEMORIES OF SPRINGFIELD

Brian had just finished his junior year at Parkview, and all was well in his world. He had been sports editor for his high school paper, which, among other perks such as covering key football and basketball games, had allowed him to write his own column: Brown's Bag. In his senior year, he would be Editor-In-Chief. He had finished a spring soccer league, and the Vikings' team looked like it would be good in the fall. "We might even beat Kickapoo this year," he told me after he arrived in early June for his summer visit in St. Charles.

For years, I'd been meeting his mother in Rolla when he and his younger brother Justin came to stay. They'd usually stay with me and Marcia and the girls over the Christmas holiday and then for two months over the summer break. This year was different. It was 1992, and Brian was turning seventeen. He had a car now and did not want to spend the whole summer with his dad. Brian was my oldest, and he was growing up. The plan was for him to stay for a couple of weeks and then return to his job at Ryan's Steakhouse. It would be years later before I'd know he'd already left Ryan's. That was just an excuse to return early. I was working a lot, my second marriage was strained, and Brian didn't want to be away from his friends for too long. I couldn't blame him.

For me, that summer was uneventful. For Brian, it was much different. He was coming of age. He was becoming a young man, and there was no turning back. Life was funny like that. It only goes in one direction.

What I didn't know at the time and would learn much later was that there was a big case developing then in the boys' hometown of Springfield. Three women had gone missing without a trace in the middle of the night from a house in a well-heeled part of town. Brian would tell me later, "Back then, everyone knew someone who had a theory or connection to the girls. The way I heard it was that this busser knew the server, and she was sure she'd waited on the mom and the two girls. Suzie – Sherrill's daughter – was drunk. This busser said he really doesn't remember, though. Everyone, he said, is drunk at George's, and that's pretty much true. Especially if we're talking about it being after one a.m."

According to Brian, the server had an interesting story all her own, but he said it's hard to know how much he heard was reliable.

"Look, memories are funny things. They are not to be trusted, especially if they are old. They change with time, particularly if you're not an active participant in what's going on. If someone tells you a story, you can imagine it and play it out in your mind, but the details aren't as fixed as if they happen to you personally – which is still flawed. The more you think about what you were told, the more you internalize the story and can make subtle changes to it without realizing it. I was told about this server almost 30 years ago, and I can't remember her name, but for simplicity's sake, we'll say she's Jane. Same with the busser – I'll call him Ben. And in my mind, right or wrong, they were possible keys to this whole case."

Brian said Jane was a young, single mother in her early

twenties. She fell in love with her high school sweetheart, married two months out of high school and divorced 15 months later. Her husband deserted her three months into her pregnancy. Jane was an attractive woman, tall, blond, with blue eyes, thin, with a bubbly smile and an outgoing personality. On the outside, she looked like someone that had the world in her hands. But, during the lonely hours of the night, Ben had seen a different side to her.

She was not as sure of herself as others thought. Her life was a struggle. The money she made from serving barely paid the bills. Her mother helped her in any way she could, but she had her own challenges. Jane's dad passed away three years earlier, and her mother's health had deteriorated since then. Unable to work and living on Social Security, her mother moved in with her six months earlier. Jane found herself taking care of her mother as well as her three-year-old daughter. There wasn't time to date. College was a fantasy now. Her friends had gone on to other places. She had never felt more alone at the time all this happened. In the middle of the night, when no one was around, and the weight of her loneliness was too much to bare, Ben could see the sadness in her eyes, and he could hear the shakiness of her voice as she fought back her tears.

She took the night shift six months earlier so she could be home to care for her daughter and mother during the days. At night, both were asleep and less likely to need her. Besides, her mother was not completely immobile. She was capable of taking care of her daughter's basic needs, particularly after bedtime.

George's Steakhouse was a 24-hour restaurant known by most locals of Springfield. They served breakfast all night, large portions, plenty of grease, and strong, black coffee, perfect for late-night partiers and early-morning risers. It was a popular hangout for students and long-time residents alike.

That night, Saturday, June 6, was particularly busy during the first half of Ben's shift. Kickapoo High School had their graduation ceremonies earlier that day. Graduation parties meant a lot of people were out late into the night, celebrating and drinking. George's had a staff of three cooks and four servers until around 2 a.m., when things slowed down.

"It's been reported that 'Jane' had seen Sherrill and the girls between 1 a.m. and 3 a.m., but if you look at the timeline and assume Sherrill wanted to sober her daughter up after she came home, they would have been at George's around 2:30 a.m.," Brian said. "What stuck with her were the three strange men who just came in before the missing women arrived."

Jane had a bad feeling. There was something off about them. Something that wasn't good. They looked rough, hardened, and scary, and they were relatively quiet. Most people who come into George's that late have been drinking. And if you don't like them, she said, it's because they're obnoxious.

"But these dudes gave me the chills. There was a coldness about them," Jane said later during an interview.

Ben never saw the guys. He thought he remembered hearing them, but he was in the back cleaning up. He remembered Jane's description of them later.

"They were dirty, nasty. They made rude, sexual comments to me. One of them grabbed my leg and started rubbing it up and down with his hand. I moved away, but they just stared at me. I thought they were going to do something to me," she said. "That's when the three women walked in. I was never so happy to see some customers. They pretty much left me alone after that. But I could see them looking at those women. It wasn't a glance, more like a stare. I don't think the women noticed those guys looking at them. They took a seat on the other side of the restaurant."

Jane had recognized Sherrill, and they were friendly. They ordered some breakfast but didn't stay long – maybe thirty minutes or so. Jane assumed she wanted to get some coffee in

Suzie. The men had left about ten minutes before the women.

"Strange thing was that while I was cleaning off the table, I saw the three women outside. They were talking to the men, the same creepy guys that I thought had just left."

Neither Jane nor Ben thought much about it at the time. Over the coming weeks, however, things would change. That was when news of the three women that disappeared from a middle-class home in Springfield spread all over town and beyond.

Eventually, Jane would see that the three women were missing and recall that night. Then she talked about it all with Ben after she'd spoken to investigators. Soon, those same investigators would come in to talk to Ben and ask him about the early morning hours of June 7.

"There wasn't much I could say, though. Yeah, I was working that night, but I didn't actually see the men. Or the three women. At least, I didn't remember seeing any of them. I was busy in the back catching up on dirty dishes."

The interview was short, and that was all Ben heard from the police. He couldn't corroborate her story. He later would see news reports that referenced a server from George's without using her name as being a possible witness. He always wished he would have paid more attention to everything that night, but what can you do? Even important days often look like all the others.

The buzz that was all over town would eventually die down. Brian would go to Southwest Missouri State in the fall of 1993, drop out and then return a decade later to get that degree in journalism he was pursuing. Life moved on as it always does.

"It still bugs me," Brian said. "I left for a couple of weeks, and Springfield was different. It didn't feel like a safe place anymore. Friends were unnerved. I was unnerved. Nearly twenty-eight years have passed, and the police don't appear to be any closer to solving it. It bothers me. I want to understand what happened."

My son and I have had numerous discussions about the Springfield Three over the years. Like most people in the area and region, we had seen the television shows when they aired stories about the Springfield Three. We've read the People Magazine story and checked out various blogs and websites dedicated to the case.

They all have good information, some more than others. I find the facts and recollections can vary quite a bit. Facts are blurred. Memories change and fade. Truth and fiction become blurred over time.

Brian became hooked on the story. And, I must admit, so did I. When he came to me and said that he wanted to investigate the Springfield Three himself, I cautioned him. "There's a reason it's never been solved," I told him. "The FBI has resources, manpower and technology you don't, and they've been involved since the very beginning. If they haven't found the women or arrested a single suspect by now, there just isn't enough evidence to do so."

"But, Dad," he said, "someone has got to know what happened to those women. Maybe the police have their minds made up, and they're wrong."

I knew then there was no stopping him. He had always been stubborn. It reminded me of the Lake Honor case I couldn't let go of. I guess, in that regard, the apple didn't fall far from the tree. I told him I knew a guy he should talk to.

"He's a colorful character," I said. "Booger is a straight shooter who will drive you mad and take you down every dark alley and dead-end road of a case."

"I'd like to interview him," Brian said.

That was mid-April 2020. We were under a worldwide pandemic. COVID-19 was running rampid. Businesses were closed, stay at home orders were in effect in Missouri. Social distancing had become a necessity. Brian was working for me, helping run our small family marketing business in St. Louis, and there wasn't much we could do.

"The timing is pretty bad right now," I said. "Most places are closed. It's been a lot of years since I even spoke to Booger. He might be out of the business now, maybe even dead for all I know. You know he's several years older than I a.m. Besides, he might not even want to talk to you. Like I said, he's an unusual character."

"Dad, you've always been a glass-half-empty type, and I'm more of a glass-half-full person. Maybe I got that from Mom."

There was nothing left to do but try to find Booger and wish Brian luck.

I figured that I was going to get the last laugh anyway. Booger McClain was going to be an interview that Brian would never forget.

"Why don't you phone him?" I suggested after a Google search found he had an office in Springfield still. "You can schedule a time and place to meet."

"Good idea, Pops," he said.

Brian always called me "Pops" when he felt he had gotten the best of me. He was feeling cocky. He was a former business reporter, and interviewing difficult sources was in his wheelhouse, I guess. I hated the term "Pops," and he knew it.

Brian called Booger, hopeful he could do some initial interviews over the phone or online.

"Good idea, son," I told him, trying to hold back my grin. I knew Booger wasn't the Zoom or Skype type. "Booger and I grew up in an age before computers, before cell phones, a time of typewriters and taking notes by hand. Booger hadn't changed, and neither had I. You just can't teach old dogs new tricks. He'll be lucky to get five minutes of Booger's time on the phone, I thought. Soon, Brian will figure out he's going to have to go to

Springfield.

He called, but there was no answer. An answering machine recording picked up. A loud, deep voice said, "Spit it out or keep it in your mouth. I don't give a damn. If you leave your name and number, I'll delete it when I get back."

"What kind of message is that?" Brian said. "Who is this guy?"

I just smiled. "Good luck, son."

I knew it would be at least a month before we'd get business back, so I gave him my blessing and told him to put his reporter's hat on. "Do what you can with all this, and just tell me all about it," I said.

I laughed, of course, when I learned Booger deleted what I'm sure was a carefully crafted interview request by answering machine.

Brian was stubborn, though. It's not such a bad quality to have. His stubbornness had helped my son be independent. He refused to ask for help, so he eventually figured almost anything out without help. The stubbornness forced him to learn things on his own. That could be an admirable quality. I'm sure he would have eventually gotten the interview on his own. A few hours later, I handed him a piece of paper. On it was written an address and directions and a time, 9 a.m. the next day.

"What's this?" he asked.

"You have an appointment with Booger McClain at 9 a.m. tomorrow morning," I said, knowing he could stay with family there or get a hotel. "The address is where you'll find his office. It is an abandoned warehouse on the north side of Springfield. You should probably pack and leave right away. Also, you should plan to stay for a few days at least. Knowing Booger, the interview is likely to last for a few days."

I smiled, and added, "I hope you like coffee." He just looked at me. We both knew that I had bested him this time.

He left for Springfield soon after. He called me from a Motel 6 on the north side of Springfield at about 10 p.m. that night.

"I'm here, Pops," he said.

"Good," I replied. "How was the drive?"

"Long and uneventful. Hardly anyone's on the roads except truckers."

"Did you eat something?" I asked.

"McDonald's," he replied. "Most places aren't open, just fast food restaurants, really. I stopped by George's on my way into town. The parking lot was empty. The lights were off. I guess they're closed down."

"Did you check out Joe's Diner?" I asked, "That's where Booger and I met over forty years ago."

"I hate to tell you this, Dad, but Joe's doesn't exist anymore. There's a strip center where it used to be."

"Did you say there's a strip club there now?"

"Umm, no," he said, unamused.

"Brian, good luck with the Booger interview tomorrow."

"Thanks."

Brian left his motel room early the next morning, drove to Division Street and followed it across the railroad tracks toward downtown. On both sides of the road were warehouses and offices, most boarded up and abandoned. He hoped to locate the building that housed Booger's office and then maybe grab a donut and some coffee at Casey's Convenience Store.

But finding Booger's office proved more challenging than he thought it would be. It was off an alleyway, apparently with no sign out front.

"I think I found it. It just looks like a warehouse," he said, not having seen the address, but he noticed Booger's candy-apple red '69 Chevy Corvette Convertible. The license plate said, "BOOG."

It was a plain, brick property that appeared to be three levels, but the first floor was lower. It had no elevator, only stairs and Booger's office was on the third floor.

A hand-written sign on the outside of a rear door read: "Booger McClain, Private Investigator, Suite 301."

Above the door was a camera, a surveillance device recording every movement.

"The place looked completely abandoned," Brian would say later. "It was dark inside, no artificial lighting, only light from outside beaming through the boarded up and broken windows."

It was three flights up, and the old wooden stairs had seen better times. On each floor, another camera was attached high on the wall, pointed downward to record any movement on the stairs.

He turned the knob on the door. It was locked. He knocked. A buzzer sounded, and the door unlocked. He walked in.

Inside, an elderly lady with gray hair, thinly built, and a kind smile greeted him with a hug, which alarmed Brian, who was wearing a mask and being very careful about germs. "Hello, you must be Brian," she said, unaware he was bothered. "My name is Rose. Mr. McClain is expecting you. Can I get you some coffee?"

"No thanks, Rose," he replied, stepping back.

"Ok, well, please have a seat. I'll let Mr. McClain know you are here," before motioning him across the room and immediately sitting back at her desk.

"She didn't go anywhere to get him or use the phone or anything. She sat down and went back to work. I didn't know what to think," Brian said.

The room was sparse. There were two wooden folding chairs against a gray wall with peeling paint. No decorations except for family pictures behind Rose's desk. Brian said he was glad at least he'd be able to keep some distance from these two without being rude about it, assuming wrongly the empty desk and oversized leather recliner were Booger's. He thought maybe the guy was in the bathroom. Next to Rose was a glass vase containing fresh flowers - you guessed it, red roses. He noticed a half-full coffee mug sat on the desk that read, "World's Best Aunt."

Also, on the other side of the room was a table with a coffee maker and pot containing what Brian said was a very strong pot of coffee. On a small shelf next to the table were an assortment of coffee mugs and what he called "a jug of Folger's coffee."

While Brian waited, Rose kept busy typing on a typewriter at her desk.

"Dad, she really had a typewriter. I couldn't believe it. Who is still using typewriters?"

After about five minutes, Rose left, as if by instinct, then came back after a minute, smiled at Brian and said, "Mr. McClain will see you now."

"Booger had his own office, just as big and even more empty and dark than Rose's," he said. "I was smacked in the face by the smell of coffee and cigar smoke when I walked in."

Behind a large oak desk sat Booger McClain, a large, intimidating figure with a bald head and dark, bulging eyes. He looked old, tired, and worn. His face was full, wrinkled. His eyebrows were bushy and gray. Behind him on a table sat a large, white Stetson hat. As he stood to shake hands, Brian noticed his thick, large hands, hairy, hardened. He wore a dress shirt, green, button down, long sleeves. The top two buttons were undone, a hairy chest showing through. He was wearing a thick gold chain around his neck. He wore jeans, worn and faded. He had cowboy boots on, freshly shined. The tips of the boots narrowed into a "V" shape, which made Brian wonder how his toes fit in them.

"They're rattlesnake skin," Booger replied when he saw Brian looking at his boots. "I got them in Enid, Oklahoma, a few years back at their annual rattlesnake round-up."

"What?" Brian asked.

"Annual rattlesnake round-up," Booger repeated as if he should have known. "Every spring, about the time the snakes are ready to come out of hibernation, hundreds of people show up to search under rocks and in holes for rattlesnakes. Afterwards, they have a big barbeque. You ever eaten barbequed Rattlesnake, son?"

"Umm, no. That doesn't sound great."

"You should take that fruity scarf off your face, son. If I'm sick, it won't save you," he said, continuing on without hesitation: "You don't know what you're missing. It tastes a lot like chicken, fresh, juicy, tender, and smoked just right. You'll never forget the taste."

Brian reluctantly took off his mask, knowing he'd probably be there a while.

"So, how'd you get the boots?"

"The roundup is like a state fair. Food, drinks, games for the kids and all kinds of craft and local art booths. One of the vendors was selling genuine rattlesnake boots. They wanted $300 for these. I got 'em for $150."

"Nice," Brian replied, beginning to fidget with his notebook full of questions.

"So, you're Alan's son, huh? I suppose I won't hold it against you. I figure you look a lot like your dad when he was younger. That's too bad," he added with a smile. "Did you have any trouble finding the place?" he asked.

"No, not much."

"Sure you did, son. Don't lie to me. I don't want it to be easy to find this place. Fact is, I don't want just anyone walking in on me. I've made a few people uncomfortable over the years. I'd rather them not show up here unexpected."

He looked Brian over. "Rose, grab this boy a cup of coffee," he shouted

"No, that's OK. I'm good."

"Nonsense, you'll hurt Rose's feelings if you don't have a cup. She's been making it for me for about 50 years now. Once you get used to her brew, you'll never want anything else. Isn't that right, Rose?" he shouted.

"I guess so, old man," she shouted back. "If the first cup doesn't kill 'em, they always come back for more."

"OK, I take mine with fresh cream and two raw sugars," Brian replied.

He could hear Rose laughing from the other room. Booger just stared at him.

A few seconds later, Rose entered Booger's office with two mugs of coffee. One mug was black with the words "Old Man" written on it. She sat that one down in front of Booger.

"Thanks, sweetie," Booger replied.

"Call me sweetie one more time. That cup of coffee is going to wind up in your lap," she said.

Then she sat a yellow mug down in front of Brian with the word, "Newbie" written on it.

"Here you go, sweetie. If he gives you any trouble, I'll be in the other room," she said with a sweet grin before walking away and shutting the door behind her.

"She's something," Booger replied when she was gone. "I've known that woman for a lot of years. She's a smartass with a heart of gold. Just don't get on her bad side. Three ex-husbands, and they haven't been seen since. I'm just kidding you, son," Booger said with a pause. "I think it was just two ex-husbands.

"She sure as hell makes a good cup of coffee, though. Take a sip," Booger said, raising his cup.

Brian took a drink and gagged. He said to me later, "Dad, it was the worst coffee ever. I couldn't hide that I hated it. I really don't even mind Folgers. I don't know what was going on there.

It was like extra concentrated and burned."

"Son, keep it down," Booger said. "Rose thinks that she makes the best coffee in town."

"There's no cream or sugar in it, and I guess it made me gag," Brian replied, still coughing.

"Rose serves nothing but black coffee, son. She says artificial flavorings destroy the integrity of her brew."

"It's okay. I am fine," Brian said, still recovering. "You know, my dad mentioned a server named Rose that worked at Joe's Diner back in the '70s, where he first interviewed you. I don't suppose...."

"Yes, she's the same woman," Booger replied. "A lot older, a bit more temperamental, but that's her. She worked at Joe's until it burned down in '81 or '82, I believe. Then she went to work at George's Steakhouse."

"Interesting. I used to go there a lot."

"Well, I'm surprised you didn't know her then. She worked the morning shift."

"I always went late at night."

"Well, I guess you wouldn't have known her then. Rose had quite a following, mainly truckers, ex-cons and dirty old men, but they all loved her. When Joe's burned down, her customers all followed her over to George's. She worked weekday mornings. I used to come in there almost every morning around 6 a.m. The day just didn't seem right unless it started off with a cup of her swamp coffee and her smart-ass personality."

"How'd she come to work for you?" I asked.

"She's only been working for me for a few weeks. All restaurants and most other businesses were ordered to shut down because of the corona stuff, and business was drying up before then. Rose needed money, and I had gotten used to her coffee, so I asked her to come to work for me for a time."

"Now, drink your coffee, son. She'll be back in here with

a refill shortly, and I don't want you to hurt her feelings. Besides, you'll learn to like that coffee before the day is out. This case you're interested in has more corners to round than any highway in the hills. We're going to be here a while."

Booger McClain stood from his chair in his office. He was tall, about 6'4". He was stout with a good size beer belly that rolled over his leather belt and oversized belt buckle. He wasn't fat. Other than his belly, Booger was solid, big-boned, and muscular. He was an intimidating figure.

"Follow me," he said.

Brian followed him to another room. The door was locked. He pulled out a key from his pants pocket and unlocked the door. He flipped on a light. Inside, all four walls were covered with a combination of whiteboards and cork board, 16 boards, eight of each. The whiteboards were completely filled with notes. Almost every space on the corkboards was filled with yellow Post-It notes with strings going from one note to another to tie different events together.

"Geez, I've never seen anything like this, Booger. What is this room?"

"It's my war room, son. It's where I solve cases. Everything written or posted on these boards is information about the Springfield Three. The answer to solving their disappearance is somewhere on this board."

"OK, but can you give me the condensed version of the case, you know, just tell me what happened to the women and who did it?" Brian asked.

"Damn, son. You're just like your Dad. Always wanting to cut to the chase. I thought you wanted to be an investigative reporter."

"Yeah, well, that's more my Dad's idea than mine."

"Well, hell, son, make your Dad happy and read all these notes. The answers are in there. I promise you. When you get done reading them, we'll talk again."

"There's thousands of notes in here. It will take me all night."

"Yeah, I figure you're right. I'll have Rose make you a cot and bring in a pot of coffee. When you get too tired to read anymore, just lay down and take a nap. Although if you drink that pot of coffee Rose is going to make for you, I doubt you'll need to sleep for a day or two anyway."

"Wait, Booger. Are you serious? You're just going to leave me in here until I read all of these notes?"

"Yeah, that's right. On one wall are the facts of the case, everything we know that occurred the night of June 6, 1992, and the morning of June 7. On another wall are all the known clues of the case, and on the third wall are the known suspects. Strings tied from one event to another tie the two events together. In some cases, there are groups of events that are tied together. You'll understand better once you get started."

"What if I get hungry or need to use the bathroom?" Brian asked.

"The door on the opposite side of the room is a bathroom. Inside a cabinet, there are some cookies and dried prunes. That should hold you over until morning."

"Great, thanks, Booger. I'm sure the combination of Rose's coffee and those dried prunes will keep me regular."

"They always have for me," Booger responded.

"One last thing, son. I need to lock the door with you inside. I can't take the chance of any of these notes leaving here. I trust you understand."

"Sure, what happens in case of a fire or emergency?"

"Well, there is a window."

"Thanks. What about my clothes?"

"They look OK to me."

"No, I mean my clothes are at the Motel 6. I thought that I

would be spending the night there."

"Well, son, unless you want to sleep in your clothes, you better make a quick drive over there and pick them up. While you're there, you may as well check out. There's no sense in wasting your money. You can bunk down here until you're ready to leave."

"Here? Where?"

"The floor. Rose will make you a cot."

"Thanks, Booger, but I think that I'd feel more comfortable in a motel room, you know, with a bed and a shower and some real food."

"No, you're staying here. Now man up, Nancy and go get your stuff. But hurry, I lock this place down in another hour."

Brian thought about objecting, but from the look on Booger's face, he wasn't in the mood for any sort of protest. Thirty minutes later, Brian packed his suitcase, checked out of the Motel 6 and was on his way back to the warehouse.

It was early evening, dinner time. The streets of Springfield were nearly empty. That struck Brian as odd. Normally this time of day, people would be coming home from work, going out to dinner, shopping. The streets would be busy. But the pandemic had changed everything. Businesses and restaurants were closed. People were staying home. It was quiet and peaceful.

A few minutes later, Brian pulled into a parking space in the parking lot of Booger's warehouse. He grabbed his suitcase from the trunk, locked his car and headed into the warehouse from the side entrance.

Booger looked amused when Brian walked into the office. "What's that you're carrying, Nancy?"

"It's my suitcase. What about it?"

"It's red, cherry red."

"So?"

"Well, I just don't see many men with bright red suitcases,"

Booger replied with a grin.

"Well, if you have to know, my wife picked it out. It was on sale. She got it when we went on vacation a few years ago. Besides, nobody cares what color a suitcase is."

"If you say so, son." Booger's grin left. "OK, son. It is time for you to get down to work. I need to lock you in the war room. But Rose will be here for a while, so if you need anything, just holler."

"Where are you going?"

"I'm going home to get my beauty sleep. But I'll be back first thing in the morning. Sleep tight, Cinderella."

With that, Booger left the room. Rose entered a few minutes later with a cot, a pillow and blanket and a pot of coffee that she plugged into a wall socket on a warming plate.

"Here, these should make you comfortable for the night," she said. "I'll be here for a couple of more hours. If you need anything, just yell."

"Can I ask you something, Rose?" Brian asked.

"Sure, what is it?"

"Is Booger crazy?"

"Of course he is," she said with a smile as she left the room.

CHAPTER 3

THE CLUES

Each wall was titled with a headline, "Clues," "Facts," and "Suspects." Colored strings were tied from one item to another, indicating they were grouped together and that they had a significance when tied together. Yellow sticky notes dotted all three walls to indicate a thought or idea that Booger had from time to time. Each wall was blanketed with details. It was like working a puzzle with several grouping of pieces but no discernable frame to put them all together.

Booger's system of presenting the case on his walls was organized chaos. Perhaps, Rose's response to Brian's question was right. Booger was crazy. Or was he a genius? Brian wasn't sure.

The door opened, and Rose walked in. "I brought you a fresh cup of coffee and an egg salad sandwich," she said. "I figured you'd be hungry. Cookies and dried prunes aren't exactly a meal."

"Thanks, Rose."

"I'm getting ready to leave now. Here's my phone number if there is any sort of emergency. I just live a few blocks away."

"Thanks, but I don't think I'll have any problems."

"You never know. Booger's had some attempted break-ins

before. That's why he's got those surveillance cameras all over the place."

"Thanks, Rose," Brian said as she left the room, locking the door behind her.

On a separate wall in the room, Booger had listed the clues of the case. Some were written as if Booger were writing a book. Others simply listed clues and tied them to various timelines and persons of interest.

As Brian read the information on the walls, his mind wandered from the memories he had of the weeks after the women's disappearance to the realities of Booger's evidence.

He remembered that within a week of the disappearance, Springfield was transformed. The News-Leader, KY3, KOLR-10, and KSPR-33 were abuzz with stories and updates on the search for the missing women. Southwest Missouri couldn't get enough. Soon, billboards were popping up all over town. Their three faces were around every corner. Within no time, if you walked into a Consumers Market, a Git N Go, or Boatman's Bank, you saw the three women's pictures on their front doors. In the days before Facebook and Twitter, this was how one could get the word out. And everyone, it seemed, was on the same page; somebody must have seen them. It was all so ironic and sad. They were everywhere and nowhere.

People living in the area at the time would be deeply disheartened to know that twenty-eight years later, their efforts were in vain. Sherrill, Suzie, and Stacy were known and loved by family, co-workers, and classmates from Kickapoo. They soon felt like family to the rest of the community and region. They still do for many.

All the questions people had back then remain unanswered. They still hang over the city like a morning fog over Hammons Tower. Why can't they be found? Who took them? Where did they go? How did they just disappear?

And after twenty-eight years now, still, no suspects have been arrested in the case of the Springfield Three. To all the world, it seemed they had vanished. No one was ever charged with kidnapping or murder. The women's fates may have been sealed before anyone even knew they were gone. For survivors like Janis and Stu McCall, there were two crosses to bear: the loss and the not knowing. How can one grieve like that?

So what happened?

Some believe the police made a lot of mistakes. And that might be fair, but it's easy to pass the blame. No one knew what they were dealing with at the time. How could they?

The two police officers who first responded to the Levitt home late on the evening of June 8 did a general search of the premises, took statements, wrote an incident report and left a note on the front door asking Sherrill to call when they returned. They found no visible evidence of foul play. Money was in the purses, jewelry was out in plain sight, and nothing appeared to have been taken. The house was in order, and there was no sign of a struggle. They did take the broken glass from the outside light fixture, but there really wasn't anything else to do.

Family members and friends had walked throughout the house. They had cleaned up inside. They had contaminated the crime scene if it were, in fact, a crime scene. No one was certain any crime had been committed.

Nothing the two police officers saw that night in the Levitt home resembled the scene of a struggle or fight. There had to be a good explanation for why the women were gone, right? One doesn't want to assume the worst. People close to them surely thought they'd hear from them soon. However, optimism fades quickly.

Those close to the Springfield Three weren't to blame, and neither were the police. When do three women ever just disappear from a house in the middle of the night? Nearby neighbors didn't hear or see anything out of the ordinary. The family dog was in the house. No one recalled hearing Cinnamon bark.

By most accounts, the gravity of the situation became clear on the morning of June 8 when the women still had not contacted anyone. Something must have gone wrong. And by then, there was no turning back the clock. The critical first forty-eight hours were gone. There was no way to press rewind on the unfolding nightmare, to keep people out of the home, to undelete an obscene message.

It is easy to forget when you're looking back, but in 1992, DNA evidence was in its infancy. Cell phones were rare – the girls weren't texting and leaving a digital footprint behind. There were no video surveillance cameras nearby. Police relied heavily on fingerprints and good old-fashioned investigation. They took evidence from the house where everyone had been. This was the foundation for a case, but if the evidence at the home told the story of their disappearance, it wasn't clear.

The FBI was contacted on June 9, and they quickly got involved. They, of course, weren't talking about what evidence they found. Much has been debated about what investigators knew and didn't know and when. To release all details would be reckless. Someone coming forward might have their story corroborated by things only someone involved or a key witness might know. But since no arrests were made, the public can only assume there simply hadn't been enough evidence to bring anyone responsible to justice.

So the police did what they could do. They asked the community for help. As it turned out, a lot of people wanted to help.

The case drew attention from far beyond Southwest Missouri. The Springfield Three was covered by America's Most Wanted, People Magazine, NBC's Dateline and others.

Hundreds, if not thousands, of tips poured in during the

early days of the investigation. Among them, one led authorities on June 14 to begin a sweep of wooded areas and streams near Springfield. Investigators also searched an apartment building not far from the Levitt home. Those searches were prompted by a note left in a newspaper rack at a local grocery store. It included a rough drawing of the apartment building with the phrase "use ruse of gas man checking for leak."

Was the note left by someone that was involved in the women's disappearance or by someone playing some sort of sick joke? The tip seemed to lead nowhere.

Another early development that many following the case remembered were reports taken that a potential witness spotted a silver-green 1964 to 1970 Dodge Panel Van at around 6:30 a.m. on the morning of June 7. The witness claimed Suzie Streeter was driving, looked distraught, and heard a man who had been giving commands at her from the back seat say, "Don't do anything stupid."

News of the van was everywhere. However, the tip came in July, nearly a month after the women went missing. While the police must have believed it was a credible lead, they were puzzled as to why the witness didn't come forward sooner with the information. The witness reportedly hadn't seen the missing persons' flyer for a few weeks.

The police did get the word out, though. They went to the trouble of parking a similar van outside the police department on Chestnut Expressway and asking anyone who might have seen the van or knew someone that owned a similar one to contact the police.

One online post made in 2014 by an unknown source may explain why police latched onto the theory that the silver-green van was involved. The potential witness, a man, came forward to report he was driving home from a friend's house around 3 a.m. on the morning of June 7 when he had an alarming encounter with a fast-moving van near the Leavitt home. The man shared his story in the comment section on the website Websleuths.com. He said he got a good view of the driver and even met with a detective just days after the disappearance. The Springfield police, according to the man's comment, took down his name and contact information but never followed up with him again.

Below is a summation of his comments on the Springfield Three case:

"Just found this page and decided to toss a little spice in the mix. Twenty-two years ago, as I was driving home from a friend's around 3 a.m.-ish, I was heading west on Grand St. As I approached the little side street a few houses down from the Streeter's home that crosses over Grand, a van came peeling out onto Grand (going left/west). The driver blew through his stop sign and ran me off the road. A few days later, I noticed the news broadcast of the 3MW and called the detective in charge, who asked me to come down to the station immediately."

He said he did and insisted he had a clear look at the driver. He asked if police had any pictures or sketches or suspects he could look at but said he was told no.

"When I paused - dumbfounded - the detective stood up and motioned towards the door and thanked me for coming in. This was approximately three days after the abduction. I left my contact info/name, etc., and never heard a peep back."

He said he moved across the country soon after and only had recently returned to find the case still unsolved. After noticing and responding to an ad on Craigslist asking for any information to help solve this case, he talked with a private investigator who offered to let him see a lineup of past possible suspects via email. One picture stopped him dead in his tracks. "For the first time in twenty-two years, I was looking into the face of the driver that ran me off the road that night."

The incident was so quick and violent that he said it caused his little girl to fly out of the back seat and slam into the driver's seat, and then throwing her to the floor. "I will NEVER forget the look on that man's face," he said. The picture he picked out was of Gary Hall. Gary Hall was the twin brother of convicted serial killer Larry Hall.

Originally from Wabash, Indiana, the brothers were Civil War buffs known to travel the Midwest, participating in reenactments. They may have done just that at Wilson's Creek Battlefield in the past, and Gary frequented the Springfield area because he drove a delivery truck.

"I told them it was an older model van with two front windshields (meaning it had a seam down the middle). Just seems strange that the VERY same description of the van I reported twenty-two years ago (3 days) after the crime, and still the detectives refuse to listen to me."

The man said he'd reached out to detectives again, telling them he could put a face with a name, but said he felt shut down and ignored. He said he remained certain Gary was the driver and believed someone else might have been in the back restraining the women, but there was a black curtain separating the front of the vehicle from the back, and he didn't see more.

Continued from the 2014 post: "Then I hear that Larry Hall (sitting in prison for life) makes it known that his brother (Gary) WAS INDEED involved in the crime along with a family member and friend. Authorities waited days before sending a detective to speak face to face with Larry to officially document what he had to say."

He said he believed investigators sent a woman detective to follow the lead, and Larry had a change of heart, implicating his brother after that. Larry would officially claim it had all been a dream, and he was mistaken. The man said Larry's recanting was suspect because he believes that when inmates lie about a case for attention, they tend to stick with that lie - and not later claim they were dreaming.

"Usually when they lie, they stick with their story as long as they can for the ongoing attention they crave."

He said he thought implicating his brother in the crime was Larry's way of trying to get back at him after they'd had a falling out and while Larry was trapped behind bars. Around that same time, Larry and Gary's mother had died, which could have led to a change of heart. Whatever the reasons, Larry said his brother wasn't involved, and the man who claimed to witness what may have been a quick getaway on June 7 never felt his story got the attention it deserved. Of course, the man's story was just one among many.

And, to be fair, any tip in the early days of the investigation was a needle in a haystack. The police and federal investigators were overwhelmed with leads in the summer of '92. It would be easy to lose some in the shuffle.

America's Most Wanted, which was highly popular in the early 90s, aired pictures and details about the Springfield Three on June 14, just a week after they disappeared. The enormous response the show generated was surely a blessing and a curse for authorities. It might have sent them down too many speculative roads all at the same time. However, that show had a history of helping solve seemingly unsolvable cases, so investigators had to take the leads coming in seriously.

One lead from a caller to the show's tip line seemed especially promising. According to reports, the caller had viable information that only someone with knowledge of specifics not realized to the general public would know. The person receiving the tip attempted to transfer the person to investigators but was disconnected. Pleas for the person with the unknown information related to the case to come forward went unanswered. Whatever that caller had to say was never made public.

On June 15, a tip came in about a transient who neighbors

reported seeing near the Levitt home in the days before the women disappeared. A sketch was released to the public showing a man with long hair and a full beard. Other neighbors confirmed seeing him walking through the area.

Nothing evidently materialized.

On June 24, a server at George's Steakhouse, one of Sherrill Levitt's favorite restaurants, reported she saw the three women at the diner sometime in the early morning hours of June 7.

"Suzie," she stated, "seemed to be very intoxicated, slurring her words and walking erratically."

"Sherrill was trying to settle her down," she added.

The server stated to police she saw the three women talking to three men as they left the restaurant. The sighting of the women at George's Restaurant was not corroborated by any other workers or customers.

Additional witnesses reported seeing the Dodge van in different areas of Springfield after the women's disappearances. A man told authorities that he saw the blonde female sitting in the driver's seat of a similar vehicle in the parking lot of a local grocery store. The individual said he wrote the van's license plate number on a newspaper, as the vehicle seemed suspicious.

The man allegedly threw the paper away before contacting investigators. Law enforcement officials agreed to hypnotize the man, but he was only able to provide the plate's first three digits. Authorities have been unable to determine the owner of the van based on the witness's memory.

"It could be another one of the many rabbit holes the police and other investigations went down in an attempt to solve the mystery," one investigator said.

Other witnesses reported hearing a woman's screams and the squeal of tires in eastern Greene County, Missouri, during the early hours of June 7. Officials searched the area, but no evidence related to the case was located.

Several detectives accused the former chief of police with impeding their investigation into the case in the late 1990s. Others disputed that contention and said that little evidence was available in the case from its onset.

The police chief, Terry Knowles, in an interview, after he retired several years later, admitted he micro-managed the case but didn't feel the investigation suffered as a result. "I don't recall anyone complaining during the early years of the investigation."

One of the original investigators theorized the women's assailant(s) took Cinnamon out of Sherrill's yard during the overnight hours of June 7 in an effort to gain access to the residence.

The officer speculated the attacker or attackers knocked on the door, pretending to have rescued the dog after it wandered away from the home. The investigator theorized that one of the women may have opened the door to retrieve Cinnamon and was overpowered by the assailant(s).

Workers and customers at the hair salon where Sherrill Levitt worked were interviewed, some more than once. Friends of Suzie Streeter and Stacy McCall were talked to, as well. Everyone who came into that house throughout the day of June 8 was interviewed. Neighbors were spoken to by investigators, and all indications were that most tips were followed up on. However, with such a wave of information coming from the public, who knows what might have been missed.

Police and the FBI seem to have considered every conceivable scenario of what happened to the missing women. What was generally agreed upon was the women went missing between 2:15 a.m. and 8:00 a.m. on the morning of June 7. Timelines support that Suzie and Stacy left Janelle's house at just about 2:00 a.m. Given a fifteen-minute drive from Janelle's house to the Leavitt home would have put the girls arriving at the house at approximately 2:15 a.m. Janelle and Mike arrived at the Levitt home at 8 a.m. the next morning. They had plans to drive to White Water in Branson with Suzie and Stacy.

After entering the unlocked front door and looking throughout the house for their friends, they left thinking the women must have been going to breakfast. After a few hours, they returned but again found no one home. They stated to police later that they thought the girls must have gone to Branson without them, so they decided to go to a local municipal pool to spend the day.

It seemed highly unlikely that the women would have been gone from the house at 8 a.m. only to disappear after that without being seen. So the accepted timeline is between 2 a.m. and 8 a.m.

It was important to note that neither Janelle, Mike, nor anyone else who entered the Levitt home that morning was suspected of foul play. They expressed concern, but it didn't rise to a level they thought the police should get involved. Again, early on, no one assumed the worst.

Of course, there were several curious things found or reported about the Levitt house on the morning of June 7. Whether they were clues to what may have happened to the women, only the police know.

First, a window in Sherrill Levitt's bedroom, one facing Delmar Street, was left open. Its screen was off. Police found it lying up against the house below the open window. Reports indicate the police tested for fingerprints on the screen and around the window. The open window and missing screen could have been innocent enough. It was a warm evening. Sherrill Levitt might have simply opened the window to get fresh air. But the missing screen was a little odd. Was it likely that she would have kept a window open with a missing screen? She was, after all, according to numerous reports, security conscious.

Another oddity was the Levitt's dog, Cinnamon. The

Yorkie was reported to have been loose in the home when Janelle and her boyfriend, Mike, entered the home that morning. Janelle remarked later that the dog ran barking at her as she came into the house. She added that Cinnamon seemed agitated, upset. Oh, if dogs could only talk, this case might have been solved that day.

The presence of the dog raised a few interesting questions. If the women were abducted from inside the house, did the dog know the person or persons? If not, the dog would have certainly barked. Would the barking have been noticed by any of the neighbors? Did the dog have some concern for Suzie and Sherrill, or was it blissfully unaware of anything and just irritated at being left alone?

A television was reported to have been left on in Suzie's room, although it didn't seem to be on a channel that got reception. The bed looked as if it had been slept in. Suzie and Stacy had removed their make-up from after the parties. We know this because residue was found in the sink. Jewelry had been removed and left near the sink to indicate the girls had readied themselves for bed. It was as if they were awoken suddenly and rushed out of the house.

Stacy's overnight bag was open, with her clothes neatly folded. The swimming suit she planned to wear to Branson the next day was in the bag along with her bra. Next to the waterbed, on a nightstand, sat an ashtray with cigarette butts in it and a partially full can of Coke. In Sherrill Levitt's room, an open book lay face down on the bed, reading glasses on a nightstand next to the bed.

Was Sherrill Levitt asleep when her daughter came home at approximately 2:15 a.m.? That, no one knows for sure. We could assume, however, she wasn't aware that Stacy would be spending the night. She wasn't even aware that her daughter would be home that night. In the last known conversation she had with Suzie, her daughter told her they would be spending the night at Janelle's house. That was the plan, and it was only changed around 2 a.m. that morning when the girls arrived at Janelle's house and discovered that the house was full with visiting family members. Janelle's mother had made a place for the girls to sleep on the living room floor, but that didn't appeal to them. Suzie suggested going to her house. She had a brand new waterbed in her room – the graduation gift from her mother. Janelle wanted to go, too. Her mom said "no," an incredibly fortunate decision in hindsight.

Sherrill Levitt was last heard from around 11:15 p.m. when she ended a phone conversation with a friend. Did she go to bed soon after the call ended? With the idea that her daughter would be spending the night elsewhere, she would be alone. A hot bath, a glass of wine, and a good book must have been appealing.

Being alone and known to be conscientious about security, she would have surely locked the front door. Yet, it was found unlocked the next morning. Various people reported Suzie carried a house key with her. Her mother insisted on the front door being locked. Did she use the key to enter the house that night? If her mother had been asleep, she wouldn't have wanted to wake her up. Was it possible she forgot to lock the door again after entering the house? Could someone or multiple other people have been in the house with Sherrill when the girls arrived at around 2:15? Other clues we know about from that night include the reported obscene phone call on the answering machine. It was evidently left the evening of June 5, which begs the question of why Sherrill or Suzie hadn't deleted the message already. It was reportedly deleted by Janelle when she entered the house on the morning of June 7. Was it possible Janelle was wrong, and the message was left later? What about other messages? It appeared all messages had been deleted by the time the first officers arrived late on the evening of June 7.

Another clue that Janelle and Mike reportedly discovered

was the broken light fixture on the porch of the Levitt home. They swept the broken glass up and threw it in the garbage. The police did recover it from the garbage and took it for examination. Only they know if any evidence was found on the broken glass. It was, I think, important to point out that the light bulb underneath the light fixture was not broken. In fact, it was reported to be on when Janelle and Mike arrived that morning.

Were the lights on in the house? There were conflicting reports about that. Some who were in the house on the 7th said some of the lights were on. Others said they hadn't noticed lights being on at all.

It seemed, at least, that few clues were leaked to the press or anyone outside of law enforcement. Was that because there simply weren't many, or were they held back so the police could determine if a suspect or witness knew information that only someone involved with the disappearances would know? Obviously, some details were held back. Only the police know what those were.

One potential clue could have been the cars parked outside the Levitt home. Police towed them away soon after the women disappeared. Did they search the cars? Did they take evidence from them? We can assume they did, but they didn't share whatever they found or didn't find with the public.

Janelle and other friends confirmed that Suzie always parked underneath the carport of the house. That was her space. But her mother's car was parked there instead on the morning of the 7th. That's not necessarily unusual. Perhaps her mom just wanted to park there for the night. Suzie's and Stacy's cars were parked in the circular driveway in front of the house, Suzie's in front and Stacy's behind, consistent with Janelle's recollection of Stacy following Suzie to the Levitt home.

Their cars were there, along with their cigarettes, clothes and evidence that they'd been in bed. All indications were they should have been home. To their friends, families, investigators, to the whole world, the only thing certain was they were gone. Poof. Just like that.

CHAPTER 4

THE SUSPECTS

Brian said it felt like he stared at the walls for hours as Detective Booger dragged the first day along, often veering widely from the topic of the three women. There were two walls he was looking at all day, coming together in a "V" dedicated to the persons of interest at Booger's warehouse office space. "The possibilities were overwhelming," Brian said. And yet, firm details - people and places - were known. "The answer has to be here, right in front of my face," Brian said, haunted by the host of suspicious eyes staring back at him from either side of the corner. "It felt like I was staring into the horizon, into the abyss." After a long first day with Booger, it was nearly midnight before Brian started reading through the enormous data contained on the walls of Booger's war room the detective had given him as "homework." "You know that man is exhausting, Dad. I know more about his dumb red sports car than any vehicle I've ever owned," Brian said.

"Yeah, I know," I said with a laugh.

The first suspect in the file was Bartt Streeter, Suzie's older brother and Sherrill's son. In the early 1980s, Bartt was kicked out of the home due to his drinking problem. Sherrill tried to rein him in with her son living under her roof, so he grabbed his stuff and took off. He reappeared in Springfield in the fall of 1991, trying to mend fences with his family after a rough breakup with his girlfriend, but it didn't seem Sherrill or Suzie knew about the falling out he had with her. Bartt and Suzie agreed to share an apartment together, reacquainting after roughly 10 years. It wasn't long until things went sideways. Bartt struggled to adjust to his new single life, still heartbroken and fighting his demons. When one argument between the long-estranged brother and sister got physical, Suzie moved back in with her mother. Police saw him as a person of interest from the very beginning. He was likely their first suspect. Bartt had a serious drinking problem. Rumors were he was involved in drugs, too. However, there was no strong evidence to back them up. He had a number of arrests, and all were drinking-related. He was known to have a temper. One charge against him was for resisting arrest. All indications were that neither Sherril nor Suzie talked to him again after the fight that prompted Suzie to move back home. It's uncertain, too, whether he ever came to the house at 1717 E. Delmar St., which was still new to the mother and daughter at the time of their disappearance. It would be 2018 before Bartt's legal troubles would extend beyond public intoxication.

A report of the incident in the Springfield News-Leader read:

Bartt Streeter, fifty-four, was arrested on Feb. 28 on suspicion of public intoxication, disorderly conduct and attempted false imprisonment, according to the Smyrna (Tennessee) Police Department. Sgt. Bobby Gibson with the Police Department said officers were dispatched to the VIP Nail Spa on Feb. 28 after witnesses said a man, later identified as Bartt Streeter, walked into the business and claimed he was there to pick up his granddaughter, a fifteen-year-old girl, at the nail salon. Gibson said the girl did not know Bartt Streeter, and she did not go with him. Bartt Streeter eventually left the nail salon, and the business owner locked the door before police were called to the scene, according to Gibson."

According to a follow-up article in the Springfield News-Leader:

"The family of Bartt Streeter issued a statement through its website Wednesday saying his actions that led to an arrest last month in Tennessee were exaggerated by witnesses and the media." Nothing ever came of the case. Family members were usually the first persons of interest for the police in any sort of disappearance, but Bartt Streeter seemed to have been eliminated early on as a suspect. He had an alibi during the time they went missing; there was no evidence tying him to the crime scene, and he passed a polygraph test. In the early days of the investigation, three individuals appeared to have gotten the most attention from the police and the FBI. Michael Clay, Dustin Recla and Joseph Riedel were three young men with reason to be upset with Suzie Streeter and her mother. Suzie had recently broken up with her boyfriend, Dustin. He and two friends, Michael and Joseph, had been in trouble with the law recently. According to police reports, they were accused of breaking into a local cemetery and vandalizing a mausoleum. They were said to have broken open several caskets, removed jewelry and gold teeth from a skull and attempted to sell the stolen goods at a local pawn shop. It takes a sick individual to desecrate a grave, disrespect a corpse, handle human remains and tear out their teeth. It was reported that Suzie Streeter had information about the crime, and that was what caused her to break up with Dustin. It was also said that she had planned to be a witness against the boys in an upcoming trial. This was motive. Dustin Recla and Michael Clay, in particular, were said to be extremely upset at Suzie and may have even threatened her.

Michael Clay was quoted as saying during a police interview that he wished they were all dead. That comment was made weeks after the women disappeared. Despite that comment and the inability to verify the boy's alibis for the evening of June 7, there wasn't any firm connection between the three missing women and the three boys unless you were to consider the server's story. The server at George's Steakhouse said the women left with three men. She also noted there was a pick-up truck in the parking lot at the same time. One of the boys - I believe it was Michael Clay - was known to drive a pick-up truck. That evidence in itself was flimsy. Even the server's story that the women were in the restaurant that night couldn't be verified by any other witness. It appeared all three men remained suspects in the case, but only because they couldn't be eliminated and nothing had been solved.

Another person of interest in the disappearance was businessman Gerald Carnahan. Carnahan lived in Springfield in June of 1992. He had been arrested and convicted of the attempted abduction of an eighteen-year-old Springfield woman from the side of Ingram Mill Road in 1993. In 1997, he was linked to the abduction and murder of Jackie Johns from a Nixa 7-Eleven store. A St. Louis jury found Carnahan guilty of first-degree murder and rape of Jackie Johns in 2010. It was a long, unsolved case.

Based on his legal history, one could say a man like Carnahan didn't need a motive. He needed an opportunity. Did he have one that night? Still, was it likely he abducted three women at once? There was no physical evidence tying him to the three women, even though he had long been suspected of additional crimes in the Ozarks. He had been questioned by authorities, and not surprisingly, he denied any involvement with their disappearance. On one wall was a photocopy of a story from the Springfield News-Leader dated September 24, 2010.

Timeline: Carnahan Case

June 18, 1985 – Jackie Johns' black Camaro is found in the parking lot of a 7-Eleven at U.S. 160 and Christian County CC. Large amounts of blood are found in the vehicle.

June 22, 1985 - Johns' nude body is found by two fishermen in Lake Springfield. An anonymous caller stated Gerald Carnahan was at the 7-Eleven at the same time as Johns.

June 24, 1985 – Carnahan was questioned about the homicide and provided an alibi.

March 1993 – Carnahan tried to kidnap an eighteen-year-old woman from the side of Ingram Mill Road. He was convicted of the crime in December and sentenced to two years in prison.

July 1993 – Police responded to an alarm at Carnahan's home. Carnahan, out on bond after the March arrest, kept officers at bay with a shotgun. He was later sentenced to 15 months for assaulting an officer and using a gun while drunk.

Sept. 17, 1993 – Carnahan broke into a Custom Aluminum Foundry in Aurora, stole $60,000 worth of equipment, and set the foundry ablaze. He later pleaded guilty to burglary, stealing and arson and received four years in prison.

Sept. 19, 1997 – Carnahan was released from jail after serving sentences for various crimes.

Aug. 8, 2007 – A Missouri Highway Patrol trooper assigned to the Johns' cold case allegedly linked Carnahan's DNA with evidence collected during an autopsy of Johns' body.

Aug. 9, 2007 – Carnahan was arrested and charged with raping and murdering Johns.

Aug. 10, 2007 – Carnahan was arraigned in Greene County Associate Circuit Court and pleaded not guilty.

Jan. 31, 2008 – A preliminary hearing was held, and Carnahan was bound over for trial.

March 6, 2008 – Carnahan was arraigned in circuit court, again pleaded not guilty. Prosecutors and Carnahan's defense began debating a change of venue to ensure a fair trial.

May 28, 2008 – Greene County Prosecuting Attorney Darrell Moore announced he will not seek the death penalty against Carnahan, in part because of Johns' father's desire for a speedier trial. Les Johns, then eighty, said he wanted to see Carnahan convicted before he died.

June 16, 2008 – The case was transferred to St. Louis County to be heard by Circuit Judge Michael Jamison. Oct. 2, 2008 -- Jamison set Carnahan's trial for July 27, 2009.

July 17, 2009 – The parties agreed to reschedule Carnahan's July 27 trial for Feb. 16, 2010.

Dec. 18, 2009 – A motion hearing was held. Attorneys and Jamison agreed to move the trial back two weeks, to March 1, to avoid the President's Day holiday.

Feb. 8, 2010 – Defense Attorney Dee Wampler filed a request to delay the trial, citing illness.

Feb. 19, 2010 – During a teleconference with defense attorneys Moore and Joe Passanise, Jamison agreed to delay the trial.

Sept. 13, 2010 - Carnahan's trial began.

Sept. 23, 2010 —Carnahan was found guilty of the first-degree murder and rape of Johns.

Steven Eugene Garrison was another suspect. Garrison was arrested on a weapons charge in August 1993. During his plea bargaining, Garrison told police a friend confessed to killing the three women during a drunken party. The information he provided, unknown to the public, led investigators to serve three search warrants at two sites in Webster County. Garrison said they would find the women's bodies and clues about their abduction and deaths. He also said a moss green van believed used to take the women would be found a short distance away, south of Fordland.

The property searched was the same site where in 1990, authorities arrested Francis Lee Robb, Sr., for second-degree murder in a case authorities said they believed involved a drug deal gone bad. Garrison was believed enough that a gag order concerning the three search warrants was issued by a judge. "Certain aspects of the information we received fit with other aspects of the case," Springfield Police Capt. Todd Whitson had said. Other items at the scene, which may have been tied to the Springfield Three, were found. What were they, and how, if at all, were they related to the missing women? That never was disclosed. The gag order prevented police from saying more even if they wanted to, according to Whitson.

Garrison was serving 40 years in a Missouri prison for raping, sodomizing and terrorizing a female Springfield college student in the summer of 1993. Curiously, according to police reports, he entered the apartment of the victim through an unlocked window. He raped and terrorized the woman over the next few hours. After tracking and investigating him and several of his associates for more than a year, police have since backed off Garrison, although, like so many others, he remained a person of interest.

Regarding others, Clark Perry Baldwin had long been on the radar of authorities. In 1997, Secret Service agents raided an apartment in Springfield belonging to Baldwin, a long-haul trucker from Springfield. As a result of the raid, Baldwin and two female associates were indicted on counterfeiting charges. Baldwin was sentenced to 18 months in prison and released in 1999.

Just weeks after Brian's "investigative retreat" with Booger, DNA evidence in May 2020 surfaced, which tied Baldwin to three women whose bodies were dumped in Wyoming and Tennessee. Court documents also allege he raped and choked a woman in Texas in 1991.

A Tennessee crime lab developed a DNA profile of the suspect in the 1991 death of a thirty-two-year-old pregnant from Topping, Virginia, and her fetus after a cold case investigator submitted evidence for analysis. A check in the national database linked the DNA profile of the killer of two Wyoming women in 1992.

Investigators zeroed in on Baldwin after finding DNA in a commercial genealogy database related to Baldwin's profile. In April 2020, the FBI began tracking Baldwin and secretly collected DNA from Baldwin's trash from a shopping cart he used at a Wyoming Walmart. Testing revealed it was a match.

Baldwin was suspected in at least two more murders, and one attempted murder. One case involved the 1992 death of Tammy Jo Zywicki, a twenty-one-year-old Iowa college student who was last seen after her car broke down on an Illinois highway. A man driving a semitrailer was seen near her vehicle. Her body was later discovered in rural Lawrence County, in Southwest Missouri. "Baldwin was definitely a creep who worked in the area in 1992," Brian said.

He was also suspected in the murder of a twenty-two-year-old truck stop convenience store clerk in Northern Iowa by the name of Rhonda Knutson. She was bludgeoned to death during an overnight shift in 1992. Baldwin lived in nearby Nashua, Iowa, at the time. Further, he also is thought to have possibly been involved in raping a hitchhiker from Kansas at gunpoint in his truck in 1991.

The twenty-one-year-old victim told police that her attacker struck her on the head, bound her hands and mouth and tried to choke her to death. He allegedly admitted to the assault but was released pending grand jury proceedings. Ultimately, he was prosecuted.

Baldwin lived in both Nashua and Springfield in the early 1990s. Springfield Three investigators were aware of his recent arrest and were looking into Baldwin to see if he could be connected to the missing women.

"Like Carnahan, the big question is, did this guy even cross paths with the women? Did he have an opportunity at all?" Brian said.

Then there was the person many considered to be the prime suspect in the case: Robert Craig Cox. His name first popped up when a tipster from Florida called a hotline after seeing the case of the Springfield Three on the national news.

"Cox is an unsettling character," Brian said. "I didn't know much about him before reading Booger's file. He was just a name I was familiar with. I understand now why he's gotten so much attention."

Cox was arrested and later convicted of first-degree murder in the death of Sharon Zellers, a nineteen-year-old woman who did not return home from her job at Disney World in 1978.

At the time, he was in the vicinity celebrating his recent graduation from Army Ranger basic training. He was staying with his parents in an Orlando hotel. It was late one night after his parents went to bed that Cox left the hotel room and headed out on his own, presumably to do more celebrating. When he returned to the room, Cox was covered in blood with his tongue partially bitten off. His parents rushed him to the nearest hospital emergency room, where he told the nursing staff that he had accidentally bitten it himself when he was in a fight at a nearby skating rink, but a surgical technician would later testify in the trial that someone else would have had to bite his tongue to cause the wound he had. Police would eventually find the body of Sharon Zellers only a hundred feet from Days Inn, where the Cox family was staying. At the time, Cox, who was nineteen and a U.S. Army Ranger at Fort Benning, was interrogated by police but not charged with the crime because the evidence was all circumstantial.

In 1985, he was convicted on two charges of abduction and assault of more women in California. After that incident, police felt they had enough to bring him back to Florida and indict him on murder charges in the death of Sharon Zeller. He would be found guilty of Zeller's murder and sentenced to life without parole, but the ruling was later overturned by the Florida Supreme Court for lack of evidence. Soon after, Cox was released and moved to Springfield, where his parents were living.

While back in the Ozarks, Cox had several jobs. He was employed as an underground utility worker, a job that was theorized could help him enter into unsuspecting homes. Note the clue left in the newspaper rack at a local grocery story days after the disappearance of the Springfield Three. "Use ruse of gas man looking for leak," the clue said.

He was questioned by police, but his girlfriend at the time said that he was with her the entire night of June 6 and that they attended church together the next morning. She would later recant that statement claiming Cox threatened her and told her what to say if questioned.

In 1995, Cox was arrested in Decatur, Texas, for holding an armed weapon on a twelve-year-old girl. Since then, he has been serving a life sentence in a Texas prison for aggravated robbery. "If there is a prime suspect, it's gotta be Cox," Brian said.

In 1994, a Springfield grand jury was convened to consider evidence tied to three suspects in the Springfield Three case, one of which is believed to be Robert Craig Cox. The grand jury determined that there was insufficient evidence to bring charges against anyone at that time.

In an interview with investigators, it had been widely reported Cox said, "I can tell you that I know the three women are dead, and the person that committed the crime has experience, and they were buried close to Springfield." Cox apparently refused to say anything else about the case as long as his mother was alive. "And then, there are the twins," Brian said.

Larry DeWayne Hall is suspected of murdering as many as forty-five women, mostly prostitutes, fourteen of which he either confessed to or the body had been found, and he was the main suspect. He and his twin brother, Gary Wayne Hall, were known in the early 1990s to have attended numerous civil war re-enactments. One they had been said to have attended was at Wilson's Creek Battlefield, which was just a few miles southwest of Springfield.

Hall was thought to have started his crime spree around 1987 at the age of twenty-four. He was accused of committing acts of necrophilia, torture, strangulation, stalking, rape, mutilation and murder. He was known to keep personal items of the victims after a crime. He was convicted of murder in 1994 and sentenced to life imprisonment without the possibility of parole.

In an interview conducted by investigators at a North Carolina prison, Hall claimed his twin brother and another man allegedly kidnapped and killed Sherrill, Suzie and Stacy and then dumped their bodies in the Mark Twain National Forest. Based on one report, authorities found evidence in Gary Hall's van that linked him to the women, although details of that evidence were never made public. Also, in the van, the word "Branson" was written on a piece of paper. Two women were brutally assaulted at a park in Branson about the same time the Springfield Three disappeared. Larry and Gary Hall were suspects in that crime but were never charged. Both were administered polygraph tests and passed. Springfield police investigated the Halls in 2009. According to them, Larry provided several conflicting statements that were inconsistent with the facts.

"Dad, there was a composite sketch done of a suspect at the time, and it looks a lot like Gary. Well, you know, either one of the brothers, I guess. But it's striking. And it backs up what that one father who was run off the road near Grand at 3 a.m. said, he'll never forget that face."

CHAPTER 5

THE AWAKENING

Everything could have easily been different. It made sense for Janelle to spend the night at Suzie's house. They were going together to White Water in the morning. What did it matter if she slept at her home or not? Janelle's mom wouldn't give in, though. Why? They had family in from out of town for Janelle's graduation; Kathy Kirby wanted her daughter to have a good breakfast, and maybe she was concerned that they had been drinking or about the crowd with which Suzie ran. Mrs. Kirby had her reasons. She didn't want Janelle to go. They could all stay there even if it was crowded, she thought.

Fate, if you believed in that sort of thing, had other plans. Suzie wanted to sleep in her own bed. That desire for home was universal. Wanting a good night's sleep was something anyone could understand. For Suzie and Stacy, too, it represents a thin, invisible line crossed. No one could have guessed that would be where these friends parted with lives so soon forever changed. Who would have known how big these little decisions were? Had Janelle gone too, it might have been four missing women the police searched for instead of three. Perhaps, however, Janelle would have made the difference somehow for the women and prevented whatever happened from happening. How cruel it must have been to not know. If only there were some answers.

Brian's head was racing as he read through Booger's notes. His eyes were heavy from the weight of possibilities. Why had he agreed to forego the motel? As a business reporter, no source ever demanded a sleepover. He could barely keep his eyes open. From his cot in the dimly lit warehouse office, he tried to press on entertaining scenarios, but it was useless. As he drifted off to sleep, he could see one in particular. It started when Suzie left Janelle's, heading toward her house while Stacy followed in her car. Neither girl noticed the moss-gray van stopped at a light on Glenstone. As the girls drove through that intersection, the van turned to follow, staying about fifty feet behind Stacy's red Toyota. Stacy had never been to Suzie's house before. She wasn't familiar with the neighborhood, so she stuck close to Suzie's car, not wanting to chance losing sight of her. She was completely unaware of the van behind her and the two male occupants inside.

The curious men – like hunters who had spotted stray game – decided quickly to track them, to see where these girls were going. As they turned off Glenstone and onto Delmar, the driver of the van turned off the lights and slowed in quiet pursuit. Suzie's home was close to the busy Glenstone Avenue, and the men could have seen right away the girls reach their destination. The driver watched with sharp eyes as both cars turned into the Levitt driveway. The other man was tuned in and alert.

When both girls got out of their cars, they watched them walk up to the front door. The porch light was on. The men, hidden by the cover of darkness, could see as Suzie struggled to find the right key, swaying in place with the weight of alcohol and a too-long day. Finally, she found it, unlocked the front door and walked inside, Stacy just a few steps behind her.

"Keep quiet," Suzie told Stacy. "I think Mom's asleep."

The lights were off inside, with Sherrill not expecting

anyone. Cinnamon, the family dog, must have heard the door but did not come running to greet the girls.

"Cinnamon must be asleep in Mom's room," Suzie said, as Stacy softly closed the door behind her. The door was left unlocked by accident. It was 2:30 a.m.

Sherrill had gone to bed nearly three hours earlier. She had talked to a friend on the phone until nearly 11:30 p.m. Then she turned out the lights, checked the front door to make sure it was locked, turned on the porch light, poured a glass of wine and headed to her bedroom with Cinnamon in tow. She got in her nightgown, propped the pillows up on the bed and laid down to read until her eyes got heavy. It wouldn't take long. Cinnamon jumped up and took her usual spot at the foot of the bed.

Sherrill loved her daughter. They were like friends. While many parents felt somewhat melancholy after their child's graduation with the knowledge that they would soon be moving out of the house to begin a new chapter in their life, Sherrill didn't need to worry about that. Her daughter would be staying home, taking cosmetology classes and very likely working at the same salon where Sherrill worked. She was proud of her daughter and happy that she would be staying in Springfield.

Sherrill's bedroom was just down the hall from her daughter's. Her door was closed. Suzie could see the lights were off in her mother's room. Sherrill was a light sleeper, but not that night. The combination of wine and a cool breeze blowing through the open bedroom window had put her into a deep sleep.

The girls put their purses down in the hallway just outside Suzie's sunken bedroom. Sherrill and her daughter had just moved into the house two weeks earlier. The sunken bedroom was something that Suzie found uniquely charming about their new house. Brian could see it all unfolding in his mind's eye as if he was a fly on the wall.

"This is really nice," Stacy said quietly when she first

entered the room.

"Well, it will be even nicer when we get all these boxes put away. Moving is such a hassle," Suzie said. "Check out the waterbed," she added. "My mom got it for my graduation present. Have you ever slept on a waterbed?"

"No," Stacy replied.

"Oh, you'll love it. You just kind of float on top of it. You get a great night's sleep," Suzie said. "I'm going to grab a Coke from the fridge. Do you want one?"

"No thanks, I'm fine," she said.

"OK. I think I'm going to check on my mom, too, to see if she's awake. Why don't you get comfortable?"

"Okay, thanks," Stacy said, smiling before she sighed in exhaustion as Suzie left the bedroom.

Suzie gingerly opened her mother's door, unsure if her mom would be awake. If her mom was up, she would tell her that Stacy was there too, spending the night. But the lights were off in her mother's room. She could hear her snoring underneath the covers, so she quickly turned her attention to the dog when she saw Cinnamon with her head and ears up.

"Come on, Cinnamon," she said softly, gesturing for the family pet to come with her. "Do you need to go outside?"

With a wag of the tail, Cinnamon jumped off the bed and ran out of the room to the back door so Suzie could let her out. A few minutes outside to do her business and the family Yorkie would be good for the night. Then Suzie went into the kitchen and grabbed the Coke from the refrigerator.

The men in the van had been watching, talking softly to themselves about whether or not they should check the front door or simply leave when they saw and heard Cinnamon. His barks stopped them cold. The men knew they were near a nice neighborhood and that their proximity to Glenstone could cover any noise they might make and provide a quick getaway. The house seemed well suited for them in that there were trees around to obscure views and no nosey neighbors watching at such an hour. Their hearts were racing. This was their thrill, the thrill of the hunt. They'd been quiet, invisible. The girls they'd followed didn't appear to know they were there, ready to pounce. They considered what to do next. This wasn't planned. This was an opportunity. They'd seen three cars in the driveway and knew two of them belonged to the teenagers, which meant there was likely a third person inside. Was it a roommate? Were these girls from SMS? Was it a parent? This was a potential problem, but the men had the element of surprise on their side. Surely they could handle two skinny girls and one more person if no one was expecting to defend themselves. And then, suddenly, there was this little Yorkie running around. The dog kept them still and in place. By the time Cinnamon barked to come inside, there was an unspoken agreement between them. The girls were still just right there within reach, and the men were now somehow invested in seeing where this could go, seeing if they could find quick entry into the house.

Suzie and Stacy spent the next few minutes in Suzie's bathroom, removing make-up together and talking in whispers, completely unaware of the danger they were in.

"Mind if I turn the TV on?" Suzie asked. "It helps me relax before falling asleep."

"No, I don't mind," Stacy replied.

She walked over to the television and turned it on. The screen was snowy. She flipped the channels. They were all snowy. "There must be something wrong with the antenna," she told Stacy. "We haven't got cable yet and that antenna is not very reliable. You mind if I leave it on? The noise and light will help me sleep."

"That's okay with me," Stacy replied.

The two girls got into bed and talked a bit about how crazy

it was that they were graduates now while Suzie drank her Coke. "It's the end of an era. We've made it," Suzie said.

"Yeah, it's crazy," Stacy said, quietly thinking for a moment before turning her attention back to sleep. "I like the feel of the waterbed. It's so cool and relaxing. It does feel like I'm floating." Suzie turned the lights off. The room was dark except for the light from that fuzzy television screen.

That's when the men in the van made their move. With their headlights off, they pulled the van up to the circular drive of the Levitt house just behind Stacy's car. From the back of the van, they grabbed a small bag containing masking tape, zip ties and one pair of handcuffs, for these were the tools of dangerous men.

They had been planning something like this for several hours while drinking in a bar two blocks from the SMS campus. The men had a sickness, greed and lust fueled by their drinking. They were in town for only a short time and thought they might find a victim in that bar, a young college girl. But the opportunity didn't come. The students were on summer break. Few people were in the bar that night, mostly couples, an older crowd.

So they drank until the bar closed and then drove the streets – one last attempt to find "the right dates" and had nearly given up when they saw the two cars go past them on Glenstone as they waited for the lights. It wasn't obvious at first that they were together. They saw Stacy's red car following Suzie closely with virtually no one on the road. They were young, attractive girls, by themselves, late at night when the roads were nearly empty, and the dark of night gave sick men a dark courage that they would never have during the day. Full of a lust for power and disappointed by their prospects, they were excited when they saw the young women both turn onto Delmar from Glenstone. "Look, one girl each?" the driver said. It was, for them, a lucky break – a chance to make something of their night after all.

They were out of the car, creeping in the dark towards

the house, when they saw the light in Suzie's bedroom go out. Now was the time to strike, to find a way in. The dog would be a problem one of them would need to handle quickly, but not because of its size. The Yorkie was small, but its bark could be loud. The other problem would be the third person. First, however, they'd search around the house for an easy entry. It wouldn't take long, either. The men soon found the partially open window in Sherrill's room. The screen was on. They used a pocket knife to loosen and remove the screen. It fell to the ground making a noise.

Suzie was nearly asleep when a sound from outside her mother's window woke her up. She went to her bedroom window to look out, ruffling the blinds as she did. Her view outside was limited. The only outside light was the porch light, and she saw nothing. The sound she had heard before stopped. Suzie climbed back into bed. Her friend, Stacy, was already falling asleep and didn't notice her friend get up, even with the movement of the bed.

Brian's attention turned back to Sherrill as if he was watching a movie in a theater he couldn't leave. With the screen removed, the men opened the window all the way. Sherrill didn't hear a sound. The room was completely dark. The men climbed through the open window slowly, quietly. They saw Sherrill lying in bed. They were fully committed now. Adrenaline took over. One man put his hand over her mouth, preventing her from screaming. The other held a gun to her head. She awoke disoriented and seemed to realize quickly that she had no control of the situation. Sherrill looked paralyzed with fear.

"Don't say a word. Don't make a sound," the man holding the gun whispered while the other man removed his hand and took the duct tape out of a small bag he was holding. He wrapped the duct tape around her mouth.

"Roll over on your stomach," he commanded. Sherrill did

as she was told. Once on her stomach, handcuffs were put on her wrists. She was immobilized except for her legs.

At this point, Brian wondered if Sherrill had any sense that her daughter and a friend were at the house. *"She must think it's just a robbery. She doesn't seem to recognize the men."*The house was dark and set back from the road. Her window was open. *"It had been too easy,"* Brian thought. He wanted to warn the girls in the next room to wake up and run, but all he could do was watch from above. Then, he could hear Sherrill try to talk through the duct tape. "Money," she said, muffled, "money," but the men didn't seem to care what she was saying. She had about $900 in her purse in the other room. They had other plans.

The men didn't tie her legs. This seemed like an opportunity. If they left her alone while they searched the house, then she could run, get outside, and get to a neighbor's house. However, they also didn't cover her eyes. They didn't seem to care if she saw them. This felt ominous. Without so much as a word, the intruders decided Sherrill wasn't going to leave their side.

With her under their control, the men forced her to her feet. They were moving her from the bedroom. Her body was trembling with fear. Her legs were shaking. It was nearly impossible for her to walk. She didn't appear to understand just what was happening or why. These were strangers in her home. Her eyes darted from one to the other, searching for some sign of recognition, of hope. She was looking into the endless void of their eyes, but the only thing to see was their excitement at her terror as a cool breeze blew in from the open window. One of the men helped her up, so they could leave the room. She kicked and cried as she went.

To Sherrill's shock, her daughter had come home that night, and she had brought a friend. Sherrill saw the girl's purses sitting just outside the door, along with her purse. They were open. She tried screaming through the hand on her face.

"Don't make a sound, ladies," one of the men said as the other held a gun to Sherrill's head. Cinnamon began barking. One man pulled three slices of beef jerky from his pocket and put it on the ground, and said softly, "It's okay," as if what was happening was all just a game. It was enough. Cinnamon stopped barking and went for the treat.

Confused, the girls put up no resistance. The man with the gun blocked the only exit while holding onto Sherrill. They had fought to quickly control the situation. The other man taped both the girls' mouths, forced them over on their stomachs and tied both their hands, one with handcuffs, the other with zip ties. Once the women were subdued, they were forced to their feet.

The girl's jewelry was in plain sight. The purses were open. "Money," Sherrill tried to say through muffled screams. "Money." Her mumbled cries and pleas were ignored. Instead, they forced all three women toward the front door. They never touched the purses. They didn't take any of the jewelry that was in plain sight. They weren't there to rob them, and Sherrill's stomach sunk as they were being hastily led out the front door.

***

Tears were now rolling down all three women's checks as they were forced outside. Two of the women, Suzie and her mother, were in the grasp of the two men. Stacy walked in between. She was the only one with an opportunity to move freely, to put up some sort of a fight, but she didn't have use of her hands. They were tied behind her back.

Stacy made her move the second she stepped foot outside the front door and onto the porch. She made a quick move to her left, toward the garage. She reasoned that they would not shoot her, that they would not want to alert the neighbors, and that she could run to the nearest neighbor's house for help. She was wrong.

The second she made her move, the man behind her, the man with the gun, swung to his left, tripping Stacy on the porch and simultaneously raising his hand fast, hitting the light fixture, which shattered, sending pieces onto the porch. The light, however, was not broken. Stacy's fall on the porch with the fixture breaking was the shock needed for the men to regain control. "Try that again, and I'll kill you," he scolded her, now holding her and lifting her up by one arm. "Do you understand?"

She nodded through the tears, resigned now to do whatever they said. The women were forced into the back of the van. The man with the gun got in the back with them. "Don't move. Stay still, and you ladies won't be hurt," he said.

The other man got in the driver's seat, started the engine and drove away. He was in a hurry to get out of the neighborhood before someone spotted the van. He blew through a stop sign turning onto Grand nearing, clipping a car. The driver of the car got a good look at him. "Damn," he said, hoping the driver didn't see him or the van or, if he did, the driver would not report the incident.

Not long after that, the three women began to struggle. Perhaps their intuition told them that they needed to resist, that they needed to try to escape. The gun their abductor held on them was not enough deterrent for them to sit peacefully while the two men raced to get out of town. They began moving around, kicking.

"Pull into the next parking lot," the man in the back ordered his partner. That parking lot was a 24-hour Wal-Mart grocery a few miles from the Levitt home. It was nearly 4 a.m. There were only a few cars in the parking lot. They pulled into a spot near the back, far away from any prying eyes that could be out and about. The lights of the lot were weakest in that area. That's where they would be assaulted – in a dark parking lot as most of the town slept. The assault would end any thoughts of resistance. It would defeat them morally and emotionally. There was no doubt about the men's intentions now. Now they each were just fighting to survive.

The assault lasted for nearly ninety minutes. The sun would be coming over the horizon shortly. One of the abductors removed the tape from Suzie's mouth. "Don't say a fuc'n word, or I'll kill you," he said. He ordered Suzie to get in the driver's seat and start the van. They could control the women more easily with only two women in the back. She turned on the engine reluctantly, wondering how she could find a way out of this for her mom and friend.

"Drive out of the parking lot and take a right. I'll give you directions as we go," the man with the gun said.

They had no idea that the noisy engine and its isolated location in the parking lot had gotten the attention of an elderly Wal-Mart customer. The man in the passenger seat was suspicious enough to write down the license plate number.

From the parking lot, the van traveled back through the north side of town, down several side streets and into a small subdivision filled with small, ranch-style homes, most with carports. "The house is on the left, two houses down. Pull into the driveway, underneath the carport," he said, still holding his gun low, pointing towards her. Suzie did as she was told. She was too frightened, too defeated to do otherwise. It wasn't just about her, anyway. Each of the women was worried about the others. Their concern for each other kept them from taking unnecessary risks.

The driver's side window was open just slightly. The men had forgotten that. It had been a warm evening. The van had no air conditioning. The man driving had cracked the window just a little to get some cool night air. He forgot to roll it back up all the way.

At first, the men didn't notice the elderly woman next door who was outside watering her plants as the sun was breaking.

She liked to do that sometimes just as the sun was coming up – plus, it was the coolest part of the day. Suzie noticed her, though. The woman got a good look at Suzie, distraught, crying uncontrollably in the driver's seat. The woman knew something was wrong. Then she heard a man's voice from the back of the van say to Suzie, "Don't do anything stupid." That's when she made a mental note of the van, grayish green, Chevy or Ford panel van, older model.

The van suddenly pulled out of the driveway and drove the opposite way, away from the woman. "Damn, it's almost daylight," the man holding the gun told his partner. "We need to get out of town."

They ordered Suzie to drive south. The roads were nearly empty, and the sun was rising over the Ozarks. Soon they'd be heading east, deep into the hills where the creeks meander through the low ground. As the dream faded, Brian could hear the water. It was all around him.

CHAPTER 6

BENEATH THE SURFACE

"Wake up, son. Wake up. Damn, why's the window open? It's pouring down rain outside. There's water all over the floor," Booger said as he shut the window.

Brian opened his eyes. Booger was standing over him.

"Son, didn't you feel the rain coming in? You're all wet. You're sound asleep in a puddle of rainwater. It stormed like crazy last night. Why did you open the window?" Booger asked, irritated and a bit shocked. "The rain could have destroyed some of the notes."

Brian rubbed the sleep from his eyes. That was when he noticed he was wet. He was trying to hold onto the dream, sure that he was close to knowing what had happened to the women. "I didn't open the window last night," he said, still not quite awake.

"You must have opened it, son."

"No, I'm sure that I didn't, Booger."

"Well, someone sure as hell opened that window. If you didn't, it had to be someone else. Did you hear or see anything unusual last night?"

"No, nothing. It was completely quiet. I stayed up late going over scenarios. I don't know when I fell asleep," Brian said, sitting up now and wiping water off his face.

"What time did you fall asleep, son?"

"I don't know. Maybe three in the morning. I was going over all your notes," feeling wet and flustered. This wasn't how he wanted to wake up. Brian thought of himself as being a composed person. He liked being even-keeled, and he didn't like being rattled. He didn't understand how he ended up on the floor, wet, and now he was being interrogated. He couldn't shake the thought that he wished he could have slept a few more minutes. Where had those men taken the women? They were east of town, in the middle of nowhere. It was a dream, and he was losing it now. Brian needed to wake up to remember what had happened. "I don't know exactly what time it was. I know it wasn't raining yet, and I'm certain the window was closed.

"Booger?" Brian asked with a concerned look, "Do you think someone tried to break in last night?"

"Well, either that or you walked in your sleep and opened the window without remembering." "Okay," Brian said politely but dismissed the notion. "How could someone have gotten up to the window? Your office is on the third floor."

"Well, it's possible if they used the fire escape."

"But why didn't they close it when they left?" Brian asked.

"Who knows, maybe you started to wake up from your beauty sleep, or maybe they just wanted to get you wet. Either way, I need to find out if someone was here."

"Do you think they came in the room, maybe took something?"

"We won't know the answer to that until we check the video feeds."

Just then, Rose walked into the room. "My goodness, what happened in here? Do we have a leak?"

"No, Brian just decided to get some fresh air in the middle of a rainstorm and forgot to close the window." Brian wanted to correct Booger but just let it go.

"Well, I'll get a mop and start cleaning up," she said.

"Thanks, Rose."

"Damn, there must be something wrong," Rose said, now looking at Booger with a bit of alarm. "You never call me Rose." Switching gears, she said, "I made a fresh pot of coffee and some homemade prune Danishes. Do you want me to set up a table for you before I clean up this mess?"

"Not right now. Listen, hun, can you pull up the feeds from our video cameras on your computer?"

"Which cameras? I can only get eight views on the monitor."

"Pull up the one on the other building, the one under the overhang. It probably wasn't affected by the rain last night. Then grab the five outside cameras with views of the parking lot. And, we'll need to check the two with a view of that window."

"Why? Do you think we had some unwelcomed guests?"

"Maybe. Just pull up the feeds and let me know when you've got 'em. Start at 3:00 in the morning. Also, do you know about when the rain started this morning?"

"Yeah, just about. It woke me up. I remember looking at the clock, and it was 4 a.m.," she said before darting out the door.

Brian turned to the detective, still a little shell-shocked to learn about all the video feeds and feeling like he needed to catch up to the reality of the situation. "Why did you want to know when the rain started?"

"The rain came down in buckets last night - or this morning, I guess. But there was fog, too. At least, I know there was fog when I got up this morning, so I'm assuming it must have followed the rain. If I was going to break in someplace with video surveillance, I would do it when visibility was weakest, during a rainstorm or fog. I've got a feeling whoever attempted to enter that window did so during the storm. The only thing that prevented them from coming in that window was probably you, son. They likely saw you inside the room and decided not to enter."

"But why did they leave the window open? They had to realize you would suspect someone of trying to enter when you saw the window open this morning," Brian said, now rummaging through his travel case for some fresh clothes.

"Maybe you started to wake up, son. They must have decided to leave in a hurry without closing the window for some reason," Booger replied.

"You don't think they came inside and took anything, do you?"

"I don't think so, but why don't you go in the other room and get a cup of coffee, and I'll take a look around to see if anything is missing."

Brian, now fumbling with his little red suitcase looking for something dry, grabbed a fresh shirt and jeans, then walked out and went into the restroom to change clothes. When he was finished, he walked into the reception room, where the coffee pot was.

"I've got the prune Danishes next to the coffee pot," Rose said when she saw Brian walking in. "Try one. It's an old family recipe. Booger loves them."

"I've never had a prune Danish before," Brian responded.

"You'll love them," Rose said with a smile.

Brian grabbed a cup of coffee and looked over the platter. They looked about as appetizing as they sounded, he thought. "Maybe in a bit," Brian said to Rose. "I'm not awake enough to be hungry yet."

The coffee seemed appropriate, though. He took a big sip and then nearly gagged. It was strong, really strong. "Um," he said with a nod, muffling his reactive cough.

Rose noticed the face with the coffee. "Booger likes the

first pot to be double-strength to get his motor running. I know it's a little strong, but you'll get used to it."

Booger came out of the war room and grabbed a cup and a Danish without seeming to look at either. "Damn, that's good," he said, anxious for what the video would show. "Take a Danish, son," he said with the tone of an order as if Brian had already insulted Rose by choking on her coffee.

"OK," Brian said reluctantly. He took one and placed it on a napkin. He didn't take a bite.

"I made them fresh this morning," Rose explained.

"Thanks," Brian said, nodding. "I'll just take it in Booger's office."

"Damn it, son. Take a bite. Rose makes the best prune Danish. Besides, it will clean out the old carburetor," Booger said.

Brian, now feeling forced, took a bite with them both watching and quickly added a big sip of the double-strong coffee to show his compliance. It was too much. He couldn't grin through it. He gagged.

"First prune Danish, huh?" Booger asked. Brian couldn't talk. He just nodded his head and coughed.

"How's the Danish?" Rose asked from across the room.

"Great," Brian replied, with tears in his eyes, trying hard not to offend.

"I hope you didn't fall asleep before you finished reading all my notes," Booger said. "Those are the key to everything. The answers to solving the mystery of the Springfield Three are on those boards. I spent months compiling every fact about the case I could. Some of the evidence, the clues, and the information about suspects are things that only me, the police, and the FBI know. But I believe the case can be solved based on everything I've put in my war room," he said, standing tall with his shoulders back.

"Can I ask you something, Booger?"

"You can always ask. I may not answer."

"Is that why you think someone might want to break into your office?"

"Son, you read the notes in there. Do you know, other than me and Rose, you're the only person that has ever been in that room? Those notes represent years of investigations into the case of the Springfield Three. There are people that suspect my notes hold the secrets of that case, secrets that some people don't want to be known.

"Everything about the case is in that room. I don't have a computer. Never trusted them. Other than my memory, paper copies and pics is all I got. You follow me? So, I don't let anyone in that room, and I don't ever leave the room unlocked."

"Well, you let me in there. Weren't you worried that I might have compromised your notes?" Brian asked.

"Son, did you happen to notice the two small cameras that were on the ceiling of that room?"

"No, were you watching me?"

"No, but the cameras feed directly back to Rose's computer. If anything was disturbed or went missing, I could check the video feeds. As you can see now, I've got this place covered like Pooh bear on honey," he said, with a dramatic pause at the end. "Besides, you were locked in there all night."

"Okay, I get the need for cameras, but why do you have so many all over the place?" Brian said, pointing outside and all around, making a lasso with his finger.

"I'm telling you we've had a couple of attempted break-ins. An old, nearly abandoned warehouse can be pretty tempting for someone wanting a place to party or spend the night or someone with darker motives."

"Come on, Booger. You must have twenty cameras around this place, not to mention the motion detectors. It looks like you're concerned about something a little more serious than a few kids breaking into the warehouse to party. What is it you know that you're not telling me? You wouldn't let me stay at the hotel."

"Well, let's just say that there are people that are interested in what I know about the Springfield Three case," Booger said in a calm and clear tone.

Brian noticed. "Are you in any danger?"

"No, hell no, I can take care of myself. But you better know, son, that the information I share with you, the details on those boards, is something other people want to get their hands on. There are people involved in the case, not just suspects but others too, that would just as soon never have this case solved. They're certainly not friends of mine, and once you start writing this article or book, whatever you and your dad plan to do, they are not going to be very happy about it. If you want to walk away now, I would understand."

Brian was trying to measure Booger now. *Was this an empty threat?* he wondered. *Is this guy just full of himself, or is he really concerned?* He didn't know.

"I'm not going to walk away, Booger," he said, reassuringly, trying to establish a more cooperative tone. Brian knew how to get more out of sources. This was where his years working as a journalist was paying off. "This case has haunted me since I was a teenager. I've got to get some resolution. I've got to get some answers. We want the same things. We both want this solved," he said, realizing he was feeling determined in this for the first time. "I just need to know what I don't know."

"OK then, let's take a look at the video feeds and see what happened last night."

Rose had programmed eight cameras into eight video feeds, all on one large screen. For not having faith in computers, Brian couldn't help but notice Booger had a lot of faith in his high-tech video system. He remembered his dad saying, "This was a man of contradictions." Booger hit play starting at 3 a.m. exactly. Two of the feeds were from cameras inside the war room.

The others were from outside the building.

"This is eight cameras, but you have others, too, right?" Brian asked.

"Yeah, but this is all we can pull up on the video monitor at one time. Rose has programmed the ones with the best view. We want to see what happened to this window. We can assume this would be the only breach of the building since none of the sensors at the front door or on the stairwell went off, so there's no need to check those cameras. Son, you concentrate on the four video feeds on the right side of the screen. Those are various angles of the parking lot outside the building. I'll keep my eyes on the four feeds on the left side of the screen, which include the angles from inside the war room. Hit the pause button if you see anything interesting."

"Will do," Brian said, now fully awake and excited.

At roughly 3:15 a.m., one video camera from inside the war room showed Brian turning out the light and lying down on the blanket that Rose had put in the room the night before. "Well, it looks like you fell asleep shortly after then," Booger said.

"It's a good thing you don't have any audio with those feeds. Otherwise, you'd hear me snoring right about now," Brian said.

"You boys ready for another cup of coffee?" Rose asked, walking into Booger's office.

"We sure are pudd'n," Booger replied.

"What did you call me, you old crow?" pleased to see the detective more in his element.

"I called you pudd'n. I would have called you shaky pudd'n, but I thought that might be a little sexist, and I'm trying to be a sensitive modern male in 2020, don't cha know."

"Sometimes, Booger, I just wonder what I ever did to deserve you," Rose said with a faintly sweet southern-belle voice. She then got back to the business of coffee.

"Brian, yours is only half empty. What's the matter? Don't you like it?"

"Oh yeah, it's great, Rose. I just don't drink a lot and was focused on the feeds."

"Well, I'll just warm it up for you. Nothing worse than a cold cup of coffee," Rose replied. "I notice you only took a bite of your Danish, too," she said, walking away.

"Sweetheart, if anyone calls or comes by, tell them I'm in a conference," Booger yelled as she headed out the door.

"If anyone calls or comes by, I'm liable to collapse from shock," Rose yelled back, now in the other room. "Other than Brian, you haven't had a visitor since I started working here." A minute later, she dropped off more coffee and Danishes before closing the door behind her.

"Tell me the truth, son," Booger said in a bit of a whisper once the door was shut. "What do you think of the prune Danish?"

"It was OK."

"Don't lie to me, son. Rose's Danish is as dry as the Sahara desert. There are some women that just don't belong anywhere near a kitchen, and by God, Rose is one of them. But don't you dare ever tell her that. That woman is remarkable in other ways, and I'll kick the shit out of anyone that dares to hurt her feelings. We must keep up appearances - and by that, I mean you. Leave some crumbs for her, and feel free to flush some of that down the toilet in a bit. You'll have to spend some time in there later, I guarantee."

After Brian laid down at 3:15, nothing unusual was seen for the next hour. Then at 4:10 a.m., raindrops began appearing on the video feeds from outside the building. A few sprinkles at first, and soon, a downpour. The camera picture blurred. It was impossible to see anything on the cameras outside the building except for one. That camera was positioned underneath an overhang on another vacant warehouse nearby and pointed toward Booger's building and kept a clear picture. "Watch that video feed only, son," Booger said. "It's the only good one now. Maybe we'll get lucky."

Booger focused his attention on the two cameras inside the war room. One of the two had a view of the window. It was impossible to see anything outside the window. The glass was fogged from the rain and falling temperatures outside. So, Booger mostly concentrated on the inside portion of the window, looking for any movement that indicated when the window began to open.

Suddenly, Brian hit the pause button on the video. It was 4:23 a.m. "There's a car, the headlights of a car anyway," he said, pointing at the far-right side of one of the video feeds.

"Yeah, I see it," Booger said, pleased the boy caught it. "Play the video in slow motion. Let's see if we can get any more detail."

The video camera set underneath the overhang of the other warehouse picked up the movement of a car on one side of Booger's building. But the camera had a limited view of the parking lot. The car only entered the frame of view for a brief second. Its lights could be seen for several more seconds. Then they went dark.

"Damn," Booger said, "The camera is positioned toward the other side of the building. There's only a split-second view of the rear end of the car as it moves outside the view."

"What about one of the other cameras?" Brian asked. "Maybe one of them has a better view."

"Rewind the video about two minutes and let's look at the other feeds," Booger said to Brian. He went back two minutes and re-started the videos. "There are four other outdoor video feeds. You take the two on the right. I'll take the two on the left. Hit the pause button if you see anything," Booger said.

One minute into the video, Brian hit the pause button.

"Headlights to a car are coming into view on camera 3," he announced. He hit slow motion, and they both watched.

"Damn, the rain is making it impossible to make out anything but the lights of the car," Brian said.

Thirty seconds later, the headlights were turned off. A few seconds later, two blurry figures could be seen walking toward the building. They couldn't make out any real details or even determine if they were male or female, young or old, tall or short. The view was just too skewed from the rain and fog. "There are no cameras on the side of the building where the office is," Booger said, "We'll have to wait to see if the camera inside the war room pointed in the direction of the window picks up anything."

For twelve minutes, they watched the video feed of the area around the window. "There it is," Booger exclaimed. "The window is being opened. See the glove at the bottom of the window pulling it up?"

"Yes, I see it!" Brian said excitedly.

A dark figure was at the window, but they couldn't make out much more. "Whoever it is must be wearing dark clothes. I can't see anything but their outline. It looks like they're wearing a dark mask, too," Brian said, frustrated.

When the window was opened all the way, the hand moved outside the window. For a few seconds, there was no distinguishable movement. Suddenly a light shined into the room. "Pause the tape," Booger ordered Brian.

It was a flashlight. The brightness of it mostly prohibited a good view of the figure, but some of the reflected light shown on the person who'd opened the window. There was some detail there. Booger studied the figure for several seconds. In the background, the second shadowy figure was now obviously present. "What do you see, Booger?" Brian asked.

"I'm not sure. Run the video in slow motion and stop it the second I tell you to."

Suddenly the door to Booger's office opened up. "Thought you boys might want a refill of coffee. I just made a fresh pot," Rose announced.

"Thanks, sweetie. We can use a refill," Booger said, smiling, turning all his attention to Rose, looking her up and down. This frustrated Brian. They were in the thick of it now, and this was an interruption.

"Booger, have you ever been sued for sexual harassment?" Brian asked.

"Nope. I guess it's the McClain charm. Women find me endearing."

"Sure, they do, old man," Rose countered.

"Rose, thanks for the prune Danish," Brian said, looking to say something nice after asking his question. He was feeling the need somehow to demonstrate how a gentleman behaves. Booger rolled his eyes in Brian's direction. In some unspoken way, he seemed to want to apologize to Rose for Brian not understanding their dynamic. Rose smiled at them equally.

"Oh, my goodness. You boys ate all those Danishes," she said, noticing the empty platter. "Nothing but a few crumbs left. I had no idea you were so hungry. You must've enjoyed those."

"Best prune Danish this side of the Pacific," Booger said.

"Well, I'll just have to make a double batch of them for you in the morning."

"No," Brian said before he could think. "No need. Please don't go to any trouble on my behalf."

"No trouble, Brian. It's reward enough just seeing the smiles on you boy's faces."

Brian was really hoping now he and Booger would return to the figures on the video feeds.

"Rose," Booger said, "Could you do me a favor?"

"Depends on the favor."

"Go downstairs and lock and deadbolt the door."

"Oh shit, what did you boys see on the video cameras?"

"Nothing to worry about, hun. I just don't want any unexpected visitors today."

"Okay," she said.

"Also, make sure the motion sensors are turned on in the parking lot."

"You boys did see something. What was it?" She was curious now.

"Don't worry your head. I just want to be careful. When you come back in, lock the office door too."

"Okay," she said again, this time slowly, with a look of concern.

When she left, Brian got his wish, and the boys returned to the videos. They ran the feed in slow motion and could see as the stranger pointing the flashlight moved the light around the room. When the light captured Brian sleeping on the floor, it stopped.

"Damn, son, you were sound asleep, didn't even see that light shining in your eyes. What did you take a sleeping pill last night?"

"No, don't need them. Sleep has always come easily for me, and I was tired," staring at the video, quietly shocked someone had been at the window and had seen him sleeping. He never knew, and it was unsettling.

"Well, you certainly slept right through," Booger said. "See the man behind the one in the window?"

"Yeah."

"Look at the left side of his chest, in the opening of his overcoat."

"I don't see anything," Brian said.

"Rewind just about three seconds. Then pause." Brian did.

"Now look at the side of his overcoat, just where it opens up on his chest."

"Okay, I'm looking, but the picture is really blurred. I can't make out anything."

"The edge of the shoulder holster, son. The leather strap and the edge of the gun handle. You don't see that?"

"No, I see something, but the picture is too blurry. I can't make out what it is."

"Okay, play the recording from there in slow motion," Booger said.

Seconds later, the person at the window began to turn. Just as he did, Booger yelled to pause the recording.

"See that?" he asked. "On the man's waist. The thing that is shining in the light from the flashlight."

"Yeah, I see it. What do you think that is?"

"Son, I believe that is a badge."

CHAPTER 7

A MOTIVE FOR MURDER

Brian could hardly believe his eyes. He had spent a day with Springfield Police Chief Paul Williams once on assignment. He had met most of the leadership. In his hometown, the police weren't nameless, faceless people. The idea of an officer or officers breaking into a private detective's facility was unbelievable. "Wow, do you think they are the police?" he said, not trusting his own eyes.

"Who said they are police?" Booger replied. "They could just be dressed as police. But one thing is certain. We haven't seen the last of them. They'll be back, maybe tonight."

"What are you going to do, Booger?"

"Don't you mean, what are we going to do, son?"

"I didn't think that I'd be sticking around. I planned to go back to St. Louis as soon as I finished my interview with you."

"Son, we haven't even started the interview, and besides, you're not going any place right now. They saw you last night. If it was the police that attempted to break in, they'd probably run the license plate number of your car by now. They know who you are and, most likely, what you are doing here. They may be watching for you to leave. You're safer staying here with me at least until whoever those men are get what they came looking for."

"What? You want them to break in and take the information you have about the case?"

"How else are we going to know who those men are?" Booger smiled. "Besides, I've got two friends here for our protection." Booger opened a desk drawer and pointed to two 45-caliber handguns.

"Yeah, I don't know about this. I've never fired a gun before," Brian said rather sheepishly, wondering just what he'd gotten himself into.

"Don't worry, Nancy," Booger replied. "The guns are for me and Rose. She's an excellent shot."

Rose came back into the office, locking the door behind her. "Okay, the doors are locked, and the motion sensors are working. Are you boys hungry? I made some egg salad sandwiches for you."

"All right. The only thing I like nearly as much as your prune Danish is your homemade egg salad sandwiches," Booger said with a smile reminiscent of a used car salesman greeting an unsuspecting customer. He quickly shot a dangerous eye at Brian without her seeing. "What is that secret ingredient you put in your egg salad, sweetie?"

"Egg," she said with a laugh. Booger immediately returned a bigger laugh and looked to Brian, who fainted a chuckle. With a sigh to bookend it all, she said, "Well, if you don't tell, I've got raisins in there and diced pieces of pickled beets."

"Umm, both! I love both of those!" Booger said with big eyes. "I like how they add such a flavor to the egg."

"Excuse me, I think I need to use the restroom," Brian said, ready to avoid a five-minute conversation about egg-salad sandwiches.

"What's the matter, son?" Booger asked. "Too much prune Danish?" Brian grinned as he walked away quickly, choosing not to respond. When he returned from the bathroom, Rose had left, and Booger was sitting at his desk reading a paper. "I don't know why I read this damn thing. It's not telling me anything I didn't get from watching last night's local news. I guess I just like the idea of reading something rather than have someone tell it to me."

Brian had a lot of thoughts about why it was important to read newspapers. "I gotta tell you, reading the paper in today's world is more important than ever." Before he could get started, though, Booger had moved on.

"Now, suppose we talk about what you read in my war room last night. Why don't you start with questions you have."

"Oh right," Brian said, "I'm not exactly sure where to start."

"Start at the beginning, the night of June 6, 1992," Booger said. He was direct and to the point. This was what Brian had been waiting for all along. He finally got to ask real questions and bounce ideas off this guy. "Okay, I was curious about why the girls decided to stay home that night instead of driving to Branson. Why do you think they changed plans?"

"I think the answer to that is the parties that the girls attended that night. They were having fun. They were drinking. Several people have said Suzie was intoxicated. I believe the girls decided to forego the late-night drive to Branson to be with their friends and enjoy the two parties they attended. They were teenagers celebrating the end of high school. After a few drinks, it just seemed like a better idea to make that trip the next morning," Booger said.

"What about Dustin, Suzie's boyfriend, and Michael Clay? Were they at either of the parties the girls went to?" Brian asked.

"I found no one to confirm that."

"Could they have met up at some time that evening?"

"Anything is possible, but nobody reported seeing them

together that night."

"What about the server at George's Steakhouse?" Brian asked. "She reported seeing the three women at the restaurant between 1a.m. and 3a.m. on the morning of June 7. She also stated she saw them with three men."

Booger folded up the newspaper and put it in his drawer as if he were taking some time to properly respond. "The police interviewed her, the other staff and customers that were reportedly in the restaurant that night. No one remembered seeing the three women. And if you consider the timeline of events that happened that evening, the story just doesn't seem likely at all. We know Suzie and Stacy left Janelle Kirby's house a little after 2 to drive to the Levitt home to spend the night. Traffic is light around that time, but conservatively, that still puts them at Suzie's house between 2:15 and 2:30. We also know Sherrill was not expecting the girls. Odds are, she was asleep when they got there. Let's assume, for the sake of argument, Sherrill wakes up and realizes Suzie's been drinking. Is she really going to want to get dressed and take her to George's to sober up? Why not just have her sleep it off? But, if they did decide to go, it would have been nearly 3 by the time they got there – at best. Isn't it easier to imagine the server was wrong? Maybe there were three women in the restaurant during the early morning hours, but I don't believe they were Suzie, Stacy and Sherrill. Or maybe she did see Suzie and her mother in the restaurant but had the date wrong."

This is a good point, Brian thought. Still, he wasn't ready to give up on the idea that the server was mistaken. *Maybe investigators had dismissed her too easily. She was familiar with Sherrill. Is it that easy for her memory to be wrong?* "Okay, but suppose the timeline is off," Brian said. "Suppose the women were at George's, and they encountered three guys there. Those guys could have been Michael Clay, Dustin Recla and Joseph Riedel. All three were upset about the prospect of Suzie testifying against them. Maybe they argued outside the restaurant. Maybe the three boys followed them back to the house."

"And maybe moonshine tastes like milk. Son, consider the facts," Booger said. "The police timeline is supported by Janelle and her mom and any number of people who could have heard or seen them leave. If the server's timeline is off, it means those ladies were there late when George's would have been slower. If it was slower, those three women and those three men would have stood out a lot more to anyone who was there, especially since those three women went missing just after that. No, the most logical explanation is that the server at George's just got it wrong. With any high-profile crime, there are a lot of people with good intentions that either remember things incorrectly or think they know something that might help police but instead send them down a rabbit hole. The police thoroughly investigated all three of those boys. Yes, it's true none had a credible alibi for that night, but there was no evidence to tie them to the disappearances, either. They were petty criminals, just teenagers out for a few kicks doing some stupid things. The break in at the cemetery, the crime that Suzie had knowledge of and may have discussed with police, was a juvenile crime, something kids do when they've had too much to drink and decide to do something stupid. It can be easy to overthink these things. Do you know what KISS is?"

"What? The band?" Brian asked, confused.

"No, it's one of those mammograms: Keep It Simple Stupid."

"Um, that's not what a mammogram is."

"The point is," Booger took the floor back, "that's not where the evidence leads. What do they say in journalism? 'Follow the money.' In crime, they say, 'follow the evidence.'"

Brian stopped for a minute. He knew he should let this go. It just seemed to him the server's account of events could have happened. Or, at least, it had. "How can you be so sure, Booger?

Michael Clay stated to police that he wished those women were dead."

"Yeah, well, that's one of the reasons that I'm sure those boys had nothing to do with it. If he had something to do with their death, he certainly wouldn't be making a statement like that to the police."

This was the first time anyone had broached the topic of death. Brian was a little surprised to hear the private investigator say it. It was, of course, the most likely outcome. In fact, Brian couldn't imagine a scenario in which those women had survived for long without being seen - let alone twenty-eight years. That would be impossible, right? Still, it felt indecent to assume. Disrespectful to their memories, somehow. "Maybe, maybe not. People say stupid things. I've read criminals often say stuff like that just so the police won't suspect them of actually doing the crime," Brian said.

"Look," Booger said, holding his hand vertically like he was doing a karate chop to make his point, "it's three decades later. If these boys were dumb kidnappers or murderers, how come nothing's happened? They haven't gone on to compile any long criminal records that I know of, and none of them ever snitched on each other. That doesn't happen. People that do stuff like what we imagine happened to those women always get in trouble with the police in the years that follow. Their lives fall apart. It's natural. The weight of it all is too much. The scrutiny, the guilt - unless they're total sociopaths, and there's no evidence of that. Have you ever known a secret that could be held for that many years between three different people? Those boys weren't master criminals."

The conversation suddenly stopped when the door opened, and Rose stepped inside carrying a pot of coffee and a plate of sandwiches. "You boys need a refill?" she asked.

"Yeah, fill us up, sweetie," Booger said with a smile.

Rose gave Booger a nasty stare but said nothing. Then her attention went to the desk. "Where do you want me to put the sandwiches."

"Just anywhere you can find space, darlin'."

She wrinkled her nose in disapproval. "How 'bout in your lap, you old geezer?"

"No, that's normally where you put the coffee," Booger said with a too-clever look. Noticing that Rose wasn't smiling back, he said reluctantly, "Here, I'll take them."

"You should really consider cleaning off your desk sometime." She said as she handed him the platter of sandwiches.

"I'll consider it," Booger said.

"If you eat all of them and want more, just let me know. I've got more egg salad left in a container."

"Thanks, Rose," Brian said as she turned to walk out the door shutting it behind her. Turning back to Booger, he said, "I didn't know you had a refrigerator in the office."

"We don't."

"Then how does Rose keep the egg salad cold so it doesn't spoil?" Brian asked.

"She doesn't."

"I assume her egg salad is mayonnaise based."

"What the hell are you talking about?" Booger said, frustrated. "How would I know what the hell she puts in her egg salad. The bigger question is, why would you be concerned, Nancy?"

"Please stop calling me Nancy. That's my stepmother's name."

"I thought your stepmother was named Marcia."

"No, that was Dad's second wife."

"Geez, how many wives has your dad had?"

"Just three. The third one is Nancy."

"Damn, and I thought I had trouble with women," he said.

"Anyway, Rose hasn't knocked off anyone yet with warm egg salad. Besides, she believes her coffee will kill off any bacteria on any of the food she makes."

"Booger, are you going to eat a sandwich?"

"Hell no. Do you think I'm crazy? Pickled beets and raisins? Doesn't that make you wonder about the other ingredients we don't know about, son?"

"You've got a good point. What should we do?"

"Wait about twenty minutes and then feed the toilet," he said. "Where were we?"

"We were talking about the three boys. Can I ask you if anyone mentioned if the boys were involved in drugs?"

"You can ask, but there is no evidence they were," Booger replied. "Why are you asking that?" "Well, a theory that was presented online in several blogs and stories about the case was that the kidnapping may have been drug-related."

"Did you see any reference to drugs on the boards?"

"No," Brian said. "That's because no drugs were found at the Levitt home. Nor were they found in the possession of any of the three boys or in the possession of Bartt Streeter, in case you were going to ask about him. If the police have evidence of drugs being a motivating factor in the disappearance of those women, they are not sharing that information with anyone."

"But drugs could have been involved?" Brian asked.

"And pumpkins may be purple, but if we are sticking to the facts, there was no evidence that drugs played a part in the disappearance of those three women. You seem stuck on the drug thing. Why do you insist on going down that dead-end road?"

Brian was a little flustered. In truth, he didn't know. "No particular reason, but I remember soon after the disappearances happened, there was a lot of suspicion that drugs may have been involved. I guess that made sense to me."

"Okay, son, tell me how you think that might be," Booger

said.

"Alright, I'll give you a scenario of what could have happened," Brian said. "Suzie was considering testifying against her former boyfriend, Dustin and his friends, Michael and Joseph. You said before that you never considered them serious suspects because these weren't master criminals."

"Uh-huh," Booger nodded.

"Well, suppose they were involved in drugs too, and Suzie was aware of it," Brian said, noticing he was talking faster than normal. "Maybe she had gone to the police about that, or maybe they were concerned she would. They would surely be upset about that. Now suppose they are no more than small-time drug peddlers or users, but Dustin had told Suzie more than he should have. Maybe he had told Suzie about his supplier. Then, not only the boys are pissed off at her, but now a dealer is involved. That dealer might do just about anything to shut up a person that was about to testify about his drug business.

"Now, I agree with you, Booger, that those boys aren't murderers, but they could have been involved with someone who was. In this scenario, the server at George's who reported the three women there between 1 a.m. and 3 a.m. on June 7 could be correct. She saw the women. Suzie was drunk, loud, and staggering. Perhaps Sherrill wanted to sober her daughter up some when the girls arrived at her house. She suggested they go to George's. They could have been there before 3 a.m. and just stayed enough to get some coffee in Suzie. The server said they were seen at the restaurant with three men. I think those three men could have been Dustin, Michael and Joseph. And maybe not, but you can't rule it out," Brian said, noticing Booger was growing impatient. "Maybe they were there to try to talk Suzie out of testifying, or maybe they were there to give someone else the opportunity to get into the Leavitt home while the women were gone. Anyway, I don't think they committed the abduction.

But maybe it was done by Garrison and someone else or people that were involved with the Robb Family. Francis Lee Robb was arrested in 1990 for murders related to drugs. His family farm in Webster County was one of the places that police searched based on information provided by Garrison. There was a gag order placed on the search warrant. I've got to believe that there was some viable information provided by Garrison to motivate a judge to issue a gag order on evidence found at that farm and the surrounding area. Even if Steven Garrison wasn't involved in the women's kidnapping, I think it's entirely possible he knows who was. Who knows, maybe two men came into the Levitt home, either through an unlocked door or through the open window into Sherrill's bedroom. They would have entered the house while the women were at George's and surprised them when they got back. They subdued Cinnamon and waited for the women to return. Then they could have tied and gagged them and then removed them from the home, breaking the light cover on the porch as they forced the women to a van." Brian was nearly out of breath. He wasn't used to drinking coffee. "What do you think, Booger?"

"I think your scenario has more holes than a slice of swiss cheese," he said. "Look, the George's sighting had to be wrong. I've said why; there were no other witnesses to the three women being there. Besides, there just wasn't enough time. More than likely, Sherrill Levitt was in bed asleep when the girls got home. Them going to George's just doesn't make sense; I don't care how much Sherrill loved coffee. And no three women at the diner means no three men at the diner. If the crime was drug-related, then Sherrill must have been the target. What do you suppose she would have known that would make someone want to kidnap her?"

Brian wasn't sure. "Perhaps they were looking for drugs. Maybe they were hidden in the home. Suppose the three boys weren't involved in drugs. Suppose it was Suzie," he said, realizing he was just reaching at this point. "She was known to hang around with a rough crowd. Maybe she was hiding the drugs for someone. Or suppose it was Bartt, Suzie's brother. He had substance abuse problems. Maybe he was into drugs or had stolen them or knew someone who had."

"But, if that were the case, son, don't you think the target would have been Suzie or Bartt? Besides, if the criminals were looking for drugs in the Levitt home, don't you think the place would have been a mess, that they would have rummaged all over that house looking for the drugs. Plus, Sherrill had all that money that was just left there. Since when do drug dealers not take the money?" He just looked at Brian, and Brian knew Booger was right. "Son, you are trying to fit a square peg in a round hole."

"Ugh. Yeah. I just remember being young, and the talk in my circles was that this must have been a drug deal gone bad, and maybe the girls weren't supposed to be there. Between that thought and the server seeing the guys at George's, I really thought there might be something there that investigators had overlooked." Brian realized that there were a ton of people who had followed this case more closely than he had. It was aggravating to feel like he was at a dead end. Booger somehow sensed what Brian was feeling and chimed in. "I keep going back to the fact that Suzie and Stacy were not supposed to be in the house that night. No one expected them to be there," Booger said. "If the crime was drug-related, then the target had to be Sherrill, and that just doesn't seem logical. By all accounts, Sherrill was a good person, never in any trouble. She really only had one vice: smoking. I'm not saying she was a saint; I just don't see how drugs were part of this. Suzie was a good person too. She had never been in serious trouble. She appeared to have a good heart and was well-liked by almost everyone who knew her. Like mother, like daughter. If Suzie had a weakness, it was in her choice of boys. Like many girls that age, she appeared to like bad boys. Dustin, certainly, was that type at the time, but he was never in serious trouble. He seemed to be more of a follower than a leader. Some described him as immature for his age, but a lot of teenage boys are like that. Girls tend to mature a little faster. It appears that was the case with Suzie. She already knew what she wanted to do after high school. She wanted to become a hairdresser like her mother. Based on friends' observations, she was good for Dustin. She seemed to make him a better person. It was Michael Clay who may have been the bad influence. He was more of a troublemaker. He took more chances. He appears to have been the catalyst behind the grave robbery that became the last straw for Suzie. Even so, Michael Clay was no more a murderer than Dustin. Police dismissed their involvement in the disappearances early in their investigation."

Booger reached for a cigar. He cut the tip and began to look for a lighter. Brian was just scratching the surface. There was so much to this case. Booger found some matches in a desk drawer and lit the stogie with three big puffs. "The police have only released a small portion of the evidence they have accumulated over the years," Booger said. "That's not uncommon. Law enforcement typically only releases certain details when necessary to facilitate new information from the public. Yes, it's possible investigators are holding back information about drugs, but that seems unlikely. The only thing that even loosely ties drugs to the women's disappearance is the statement made by Steven Garrison. You're right. He had said a friend told him that he was involved in the kidnapping and murder of the Springfield Three and that the women were buried on the Francis Lee Robb farm. And Robb was no Boy Scout; he did drugs and was a convicted murderer, yadda, yadda, but nothing points to drugs as a motive." He took another long puff before he continued.

"Granted, evidence was reportedly taken by investigators at or near that farm as a result of their search, but only the police know what that evidence was. A court order has sealed any information about their finding from the public."

"Okay, I hear everything your saying, Booger, but answer me one thing: didn't a grand jury convene to hear evidence on the case just a short time after the farm in Webster County was searched?"

"I believe it was nearly a year later, son. And the grand jury did not find enough evidence to bring charges against anyone."

"Weren't there three suspects the grand jury heard evidence about?"

"Honestly, I don't know. That was what was speculated, but there has been so much misinformation put out about this case that I'm not sure you can believe that."

"I have to agree with you," Brian said. "Forget the drug thing. But who could have done this? And why? And how did they manage to get away with it for so long?"

"First off, by saying 'they,' you are assuming there was more than one person involved in the abductions," Booger said. "That hasn't been proven, and, in fact, the police have considered the possibility that only one person was involved. As far as how the crime could go unsolved for so many years, you have to remember that there are no bodies. Without bodies, there's no case. Investigators could be certain they know what happened and just simply not have the evidence to prove it to a jury."

"So," Brian said, "you are certain the women are dead?"

"I think, after twenty-eight years, it's safe to say they are never coming back."

Brian appreciated Booger's careful phrasing. He stared for a second into the cigar smoke as it held the light coming in from the window. "Well then, where do you think their bodies are?"

CHAPTER 8

LISTENING EARS

"Booger, sorry to interrupt, but it's nearly 6 p.m. If we are all spending the night here, I need to run home and get an overnight bag," Rose said as she entered Booger's office.

"No, you can't go home, hun. It's not safe. You'll just need to stay here tonight."

"Booger, come on, I can't sleep in my clothes."

"Then, don't sleep," Booger shot back.

"Very funny, you old coot. I need to take my medicine. I need an overnight bag, and you boys are going to need something to eat. Just give me twenty minutes. I can drive home and be back right away."

Booger thought it over for a few seconds. "Okay, you can drive home, but I want you to take a gun with you, and I want you to go with Brian."

"I don't need a babysitter, old man."

"No, but he does. Do me a favor and take him with you. I need to check our security. Maybe you can show him how you make your special sardine and peanut butter sandwiches. A platter of those tonight sounds really good."

"Peanut Butter and sardine sandwiches it is! I just hope I've got some sardines left from the can I opened last week."

Brian showed a pained look on his face.

"Rose, I want you to leave your car at your house. Come back in Brian's car. Also, leave the lights on in a couple of the rooms."

"Why?" Rose asked.

"Because if anyone is watching your house tonight, they will think you are home," he said with a serious look on his face. "Brian, when you come back, drop Rose off at the side door. Then drive your car across the street and down the block a bit. Find a dark area to park. I don't want anyone passing by to be able to tell you're here because your car is right out front. Then walk back, understand?"

Brian felt pulled out of his comfort zone. None of this behavior was familiar territory for him. On the one hand, he wondered if Booger had lost his mind. *What kind of weird cat-and-mouse game was he playing, and with whom?* It had been unnerving, he thought, that some guys were looking to break into Booger's facility, but *that didn't mean he had the right to treat me like a hostage.* Still, he remembered what his dad had said before leaving St. Louis, "Booger is crazy. Just roll with it. We don't need you here right now, and you'll come back better for it." *He was right,* Brian thought. *I've got nowhere else to be.*

"Okay, Booger," he said, trying his best to not be sarcastic, "will do."

"Very good. I think you might have the makings of a detective," Booger said in a playful tone that let Brian know he was pleased not to have to fight over this.

"What about your car, Booger? You know the one anybody can spot from a mile away — the vintage Red Corvette convertible with a license plate that reads 'BOOG,'" Brian said, managing a bit of a dig on the private investigator but also sincerely wanting to know.

"Hey, don't worry about my ride. It'll be hidden by the

time you come back."

Booger handed Rose one of the handguns he had in the desk drawer. The 45-caliber handgun nearly swallowed her hand, but she seemed steady with the weight of it. Rose was a petite woman, barely 5 foot and skinny as a rail.

"Gray hair, tiny frame, even tinier hands, she sure doesn't look like someone who could handle a gun," Brian said.

Rose placed the .45 neatly in her purse, and she was ready. Brian followed her out the front door and across the parking lot to her car, a 1980 rusted blue Ford Pinto. It was a classic car that could easily pass for a demolition derby entry. When she started it up, Brian thought it sounded to him like a dying crane before the engine came to life.

Brian followed Rose south across Chestnut Expressway, a little northeast of the SMS campus, tucked into a quiet, older street north of the Rountree Neighborhood. "She wasn't much for paying attention to speed limit signs, stop lights or stop signs," Brian would say later. "Dad, I ran two stop lights and three stop signs trying to stay with her. The speed limit in these residential areas is twenty-five. She was going at least forty. I was certain one of us would get hit or stopped by the police, but we were lucky."

Rose pulled into the gravel alleyway that led to her tiny, one-bedroom frame house near the railroad tracks. The house was in bad need of a coat of paint. The concrete walkway to the front door was cracked and uneven. But the yard was immaculate. Dark green zoysia grass, freshly mowed, not one weed in sight. Brightly colored rose bushes along both sides and the front of the house. A large cherry blossom tree in the front yard.

"Watch your step," she said to Brian, pointing toward the uneven walkway.

Rose fiddled through her purse for several seconds, finally pulling out her house key. She unlocked the door, turned on the porch light and invited him in.

"You know that I have lived in this house for forty-seven years, ever since my first husband Earl died. He was a long-haul trucker, killed on an icy road in Pennsylvania two weeks shy of our fifth wedding anniversary. We had a small farm outside of Nixa, out in the country, a mile from any neighbors. It was Earl's dream to own a farm. It wasn't mine. Two weeks after I buried him, I put the farm up for sale and moved here. I needed to be around people. I like the city. There's people all around if you need 'em, but they'll mostly leave you alone."

"What about kids?" Brian asked.

"We didn't have any. I wanted them. He didn't. By the time I married someone that did want kids, I couldn't have them. Probably for the best; that marriage didn't work out," she said with a brief look of sadness. "Okay, enough of the reminiscing. Let me put together an overnight bag. Then, I'll make a stack of sandwiches to go. Make yourself comfortable."

Brian sat on the covered sofa and checked his phone. His son Chase had sent him a funny headline from The Onion. His son Mason had sent him the day's SnapChats. His father had sent him a selfie of him picking his nose. Before he knew it, Rose was in the kitchen making sandwiches. "You know Booger was only kidding about the peanut butter and sardine sandwiches. I think he wanted to see your reaction. Truth is, I've never even eaten a sardine."

"Oh, that's a relief."

"What do you say to some plain peanut butter and jelly sandwiches?" she said, smiling at Brian.

"Sounds good to me," Brian replied. "Thank you, by the way."

"I've got a bag of chips in the pantry. Why don't you grab those while I finish these up?"

"Sure, no problem."

A few minutes later, they walked out the front door, Brian carrying a brown grocery bag of sandwiches and chips along with some chocolate chip cookies that Rose grabbed from the pantry. She left lights on in the living room and kitchen, as well as the outside light next to the front door, just like Booger had asked.

They got into Brian's car and pulled out of the driveway. "I noticed you don't live too far away from George's," he said, adding, "or the Leavitt house, for that matter."

"Yes, they're not too far away. Sherrill and her daughter lived right off Glenstone, but just a few houses down from some really nice homes," she said with a pause at the end that made Brian think there was more she wanted to say. "You know, I knew Sherrill. Not well, or anything. But I knew who she was."

Brian was shocked. "Oh, really. That is interesting. How did you know her?"

"I saw Sherrill at her hairdressing salon several times. I only knew who she was by reputation."

"What do you mean?"

"Well, she was really quite popular. Her appointments were always booked up weeks in advance. I could never get in to see her anyway. She had a select clientele, a lot of well-heeled older women, if you know what I mean. They tipped pretty well, I heard. That's not a bad living if you get the right following," she said.

"What about the woman that spotted the van with Suzie driving? Did she live close to you?"

"Yes, she lived four houses down from me. Her name was Mary. She was an older lady who passed away in August of '92. I remember because it was just a couple of months after the women disappeared," she said, nonplussed. "I believe from a heart attack. I knew her fairly well. She was friendly, always outside gardening. She had the best-looking yard in the neighborhood. Her husband had passed away back in 1989, I believe. I guess gardening kept her busy."

"Did you talk to her after she spoke to the police?"

"Once, I took a casserole to her house. It was her anniversary. She and Harold had been married forty-five years before he passed away. I figured she needed company that day. I expected to see her outside because it was a nice summer day, but she wasn't. I knocked on the door. No answer. So, I rang the doorbell, and I saw her peeping her head out from behind the living room curtains. Finally, she opened the door. 'I don't feel very well,' I remember her telling me. It was out of character for her. Mary was always smiling, friendly, and outgoing, but not that day. She took the dish, thanked me and shut the door. I figured she was just depressed about her anniversary. But there was something else, Brian."

"What was that?"

"I could hear her lock and deadbolt the door as I started to leave. I took a few steps off the porch and turned around, and I could see her watching me from behind the living room curtain. I knew then that it wasn't depression that caused her odd behavior that day. That woman was afraid."

"Of what?"

"I don't know. That was the last I saw her, and it's always stuck with me. Like I said, she passed away not long after."

"Do you think her story about the van with Suzie Streeter driving was accurate? She was old after all, and as I remember, she waited several weeks before telling the police what she saw."

"Age had nothing to do with it. That woman was sharp. The Mary I knew wouldn't have lied about seeing that van. Besides, the police believed her story enough to find a similar van and stage it in front of the police department, hoping to receive additional tips. And it wasn't just the police that believed her story. The local and national news, Dateline and People magazine ran pictures of the van."

"Okay, well, suppose she got the van description right, but someone else other than Suzie was driving? Did she know Suzie?"

"I don't know if she knew her, but I doubt it. They lived several blocks away, but remember pictures of the three missing women were all over town. Mary must have thought that the woman driving the van looked a lot like Suzie's photo. She also reported that the woman driving was terribly upset and crying and that she looked directly at Mary just before a male voice inside that van warned her not to do anything 'stupid.' Rose looked directly at Brian. "If I were a betting person, I would bet that Mary's story was exactly what happened."

"I remember reading that the van pulled into a driveway next to Mary's house," Brian said. "Do you know whose house that was?"

"The house was vacant. It was for sale, and the people that owned it, a young married couple, had moved out a couple of weeks earlier."

"Did you know that couple?"

"No, not really. I saw them once in a while. They kept to themselves."

"Brian, you don't think that young couple was involved somehow, do you?"

"I doubt it, but it's worth looking into. Maybe Booger has some information about them. If he does, it's probably in his war room," he said.

"Brian, do you mind if I ask you a question?"

"No, I don't mind."

"Are you really going to write a book about the missing women?"

"Yes, I plan to with the help of my dad, anyway."

"But how do you reach a conclusion for your book? The crime is still unsolved."

"Yeah, I get it. We don't know what happened. It's arrogant to think me or dad could figure out something when a bunch of people smarter than us haven't. I suppose the only ones who really know the truth are the ones who were involved. Maybe this is silly, but I think there's something important about looking for answers, even if you doubt you can find them. Usually, I'm so busy working, and this whole COVID-19 thing has forced me to slow down a bit. It's got me wondering about a lot. My dad has always been into crime shows and the ID channel – stuff like that. He kind of dragged me into this, but I'm not exactly fighting it. This is keeping my mind off the real world, which sounds funny to say. Still, I don't know what we don't know, and Booger has a lot on this case. I have seen that war room now, and if we are ever going to sort out what's happened, I think this is the way, you know?"

Just then, Brian pulled up outside the side door to Booger's office. Rose got out and walked inside. Then he drove down the block and parked outside a closed business near Commercial Street, in a dark corner of its parking lot, shielded from the road. As he was getting out of the car, something caught his eye. It was a shiny piece of metal about the size of a pinhead sticking out from inside an air vent on the dashboard near the driver's side window. He would never have seen it, but the sun setting in the background was at just the right angle that it glinted in reflection. Brian used his fingers to pull a metal piece out about three inches. It was at the end of a long, black wire. *Damn,* he thought, *Is that a listening device?*

Brian held it out as much as he could and took a picture of it on his cell phone. Then he got out of his car and walked back to Booger's warehouse. He was a little rattled, looking around him as to see if anyone was following or watching before jumping a bit when the street lights flashed on. The sun was nearly down now. It was getting darker now. Clouds were gathering in the sky.

When he reached the side door to Booger's, it was locked. He pressed the buzzer and could sense someone watching him through the camera just above the door.

A long buzz in return told him it was unlocked. Brian walked in and started up the steps. He heard the door automatically lock behind him. Just as he reached Booger's office, Rose let him in. "Oh good, there you are. Booger is waiting for you," Rose said, closing and locking the door behind him.

"Damn, son. Did you park in the next county?"

"No, I was just being careful. Listen, Booger, I've got something that I need to show you." Brian said, pulling out his cell phone from his pocket. "I saw something sticking out of a vent in my car. I took a picture of it. What do you think it is?" Brian said, holding up the phone.

"Son, that metal head looks like a microphone. I can't quite see," he said, squinting at the picture.

"Here, let me enlarge the photo for you first," Brian responded.

"Yep, that's a microphone, alright. Son, I hope you didn't talk too much while you were in your car."

"I don't remember really saying anything on the way to Rose's house, but we did have a conversation on the way back," Brian said rather sheepishly.

"Oh, shit. That woman likes to talk," Booger said. "Rose, come in here for a minute."

After a few moments, she opened the door and said, "You know, old man, normally a request is followed by a courtesy response like, 'please!'"

"Okay, then come in here and sit the fuck down, PLEASE!"

"That's better, but you really need to work on your requests a little more."

"Rose, Brian found a listening device in his car after he

dropped you off tonight."

"No shit?" Rose responded.

"So, I take it, sweetie, that you may have said something in the car that you would rather someone else not hear?"

"Depends on who was listening, I suppose," she said.

"I think it's probably safe to say that whoever attempted to break in last night were the same ones that planted these tiny ears. So somebody needs to tell me what you two gals talked about in the car."

"I just told him about Mary. You know how I feel about that," she said.

Booger shook his head, pulled a stogie and a fifth of Jim Beam out of his desk drawer, lit the cigar, took a couple of puffs, poured a glass of whiskey and sat back in his chair without saying a word.

Brian and Rose just looked at him, waiting for some sort of response. He took two sips of whiskey and another drag from the cigar before he said, "Well, I thought that might come up. So, if I understand this right, you two, during a ten minute car ride from Rose's house to the office, managed to share with our friends on the other end of the microphone some of the most important details of all the information I have gathered. Did either of you mention the war room?"

"Yeah, I said I'd seen the war room now and thought it gave me and Dad the best chance to solve the case," Brian said, realizing as he spoke this might not be greeted warmly.

Booger looked straight at Brian before he continued. "Did you also announce that you and your paw are writing a book?"

"Yes, that did come up."

"So I send you out after a break in - with a gun for protection, mind you - and you two Chatty Cathies decide to let the whole world know we've got enough information here to solve this case and write a book about it?" His voice had raised to where he was nearly yelling by the end of the question.

"Well, we didn't actually say that, Booger," Brian responded defensively. "In all fairness, I think it would be a stretch for them to think that."

"A stretch, huh?" Booger asked with a cock-eyed look of disgust. "Let me tell you what a stretch would be. A stretch would be that the people listening to your conversation would chalk your little discussion up as pure bullshit and completely ignore what you said."

"Come on, Booger, it's not our fault," Brian said, "We had no idea there was a listening device in the car."

Booger took a deep draw off his cigar in what seemed like the equivalent of a deep breath to calm down.

"You're right," Booger said in a softer tone. "You had no way of knowing that anyone was listening to you. But you can sure as hell bet that we're going to have another break-in tonight. Guess we need to start planning for it." He was matter of fact, shooting a look to Rose that said, "This is why I didn't want you to leave."

"Booger," Rose said as calmly and clearly as she could before saying with a sweet smile, "I've got some peanut butter and jelly sandwiches and fresh coffee in the other room. Why don't we eat first?"

CHAPTER 9

THE HIDDEN ROOM

"Maybe he knew my car was bugged that night," Brian said later in St. Louis. "Maybe that was part of his plan to put me and Rose in that car, assuming all along we would talk about the case and someone on the other end of that microphone would be listening. He just seemed too prepared for it all." The private detective, it appeared, was ready for anything, Brian said. "From cameras to guns, he was obsessed. It all seemed ridiculous to me, but he clearly was right to be paranoid. Who cares about his notes, his war room? Why would someone want to bug me? Someone knew Booger was on their trail. And he must've known they knew because nothing shocked him."

***

There was a storm brewing in Springfield. The clouds turned thick and dark as the sun set on the high plateau of the Ozark Mountains. Thunder could be heard from a distance by the time Brian and Booger finished their sandwiches. Interstate 44, which runs from St. Louis to Oklahoma City through the northern edge of Springfield, is famous for its quick storms and changeable weather. Joplin, another popular I-44 and Route 66 hub, was home to one of the nation's worst tornadoes in 2011. The Joplin twister killed 158 people. Brian had talked about it at length before.

"It completely transformed the town. It tore a mile-wide path through its southside and wiped out whole neighborhoods. I worked at Springfield Business Journal at the time, and we had a sister business publication in Joplin then," he said. "I went there for an event about a month after the tornado, and it was the strangest feeling. The bulk of the clean-up was done, so there was just this ghost zone where you were in the city, but there were no businesses, no homes. The trees had been stripped bare and little tufts of leaves were beginning to sprout. It was eerie. I hate tornados."

With winds coming in from Oklahoma and cool air from the north often meeting warm air from the south in springtime, it wasn't uncommon for tornado sirens to go off in Springfield or to see evening funnel clouds dance in the skies overhead. "The air gets that familiar thick feeling. That night, after we found the bug in the car, it had that feeling," Brian said.

Just after dinner, Booger asked Rose to get three flashlights out of her desk drawer. While she did, he went into the war room for a few minutes by himself, shutting the door behind him. He emerged several minutes later carrying two folders.

"It was weird," Brian said. "I had spent the entire night in that room and looked at everything in there, but I didn't see those folders."

"Make sure everything is turned off and the lights are out," he told Rose. "Do you have the gun, sweetie?"

"Yes, it's in my purse," Rose responded.

"Good, now I want you and Brian to follow me."

"Why do we need the flashlights, Booger?" Brian asked.

"When we get down to the first floor, I'm going to turn the power off inside the building. It's going to get dark. You'll need those flashlights to make it the rest of the way from there."

"Rest of the way to where, Booger?" Brian asked. "Where are we going?"

"Someplace safe, you'll see."

The three walked down the flights of stairs to the ground floor. Booger stopped at the side door to the building to make sure it was both locked and deadbolted, which it was. Then he turned the corner to another door, which was locked. He pulled out a key from his pocket and unlocked the door. It opened to a large warehouse area, completely gutted now. It was a massive open area with a concrete floor, a tall ceiling, and large windows on one side.

"Have you ever eaten licorice?" Booger asked Brian.

"You mean the candy? Yeah, sure."

"You ever hear of Switzer licorice?"

"Yeah."

"They have a large plant in St. Louis. This used to be a distribution center for them. Sometimes, you can smell just a hint of licorice when you come in here," Booger said.

"All I smell is sweat, a hint of whiskey and the aroma of a cheap cigar," Rose said with a smile.

Brian waited for a quick dig back from Booger, but his attention was elsewhere. He was looking at a door on the nearside of the warehouse. He walked toward it without saying a word. It was locked. He used a key to unlock it. Inside was what looked like the electrical room for the building. Two large furnaces, a cable connection with a series of wires streaming into the wall and ceiling and two large electrical boxes. He opened the boxes.

"It's time to turn your flashlights on, boys and girls," he announced just before flipping the main power switches off on both boxes.

The building went completely dark. "Now, follow me."

The walls of the warehouse were made of red brick. Booger walked to the inner wall and followed it along its base. He slowed his pace when he got about two-thirds of the way through the warehouse. Suddenly, he stopped. He shined the flashlight down. Something on the floor caught his eye. One, two, three footsteps past that spot, he ran his hand against the brick wall until it came across a loose brick. He pulled it out, and suddenly a hidden door opened up from it. It was completely dark beyond the brick wall.

"After you," Booger said to Brian and Rose.

Brian went first, walking inside what appeared to be an empty room. He shined his flashlight directly in front of him and saw nothing. But as he stepped inside and moved his flashlight from side to side, he got glimpses of tables, shelves, and computers. Rose followed. They could hear the winds outside now.

"Did you know about this place, Rose?"

"No, I didn't. But it doesn't surprise me," she said.

Booger put the brick back in its spot in the wall, and the secret door began to shut. He then hurried to get in before it closed all the way.

Inside, Booger flipped a light switch on, and large fluorescent bulbs attached to the ceiling illuminated the room.

"Wait," Brian said curiously, "You turned off all the power to the building. How does this one room have lights?"

"This room has a separate generator that supplies it with electricity."

Inside the room were two tables, both with computers and large screens. On one side of the room were a refrigerator, sink, a stove and cabinets.

"I've got beer in the fridge, whiskey and coffee in the cabinets, Folgers just like you have upstairs, Rose, and there is a coffee maker on the table in the corner," he said like a boy showing off his new bicycle. "So, how do you guys like my bachelor pad?"

Rose stood there with her mouth slightly agape and said nothing.

"Yeah, it's great. I haven't even shown you the best part yet," he said.

At the far end of the room was a hallway. To the right was a full bathroom, shower, sink, and toilet. Past that was a bedroom and a small, single bed. It was a nice room, Brian thought, but nothing special. However, beyond the bedroom was a much larger living room, which had a big-screen television, a bar, a separate bathroom and two large, oversized lazy-boy recliners that were big enough to sleep in.

"Yep, this is my man cave," Booger said proudly.

"So, this is where you've been spending your nights lately?" Rose asked.

"Yeah, it's great. When I finish work, I just come downstairs."

"I remembered you had a house just off Glenstone," Rose said.

"I did. I sold it about three months ago."

Thunder clapped. It stopped them all for a moment. The room seemed to reanimate when she crossed her arms and shot Booger a stern look. "Don't you think that is something you might have shared with me?"

"Why? What does it matter where I live?"

"Well, because someone, a friend, might have brought a cake and birthday present over to your house a couple of months ago, and when you didn't answer, they might have sat them on the porch by the front door with a personal message that person wouldn't want a stranger to read. Then someone might have been hurt when you never said thank you for the cake and present. They might have thought you were an insensitive bastard, not knowing that you never received those birthday gifts."

"You did that for me, Rose?"

"No, you old coot. I'm just saying someone might have done that, not knowing that you moved," she said, not wanting to give him the satisfaction of thinking he'd received a present.

"Oh, okay. I see. I'm sorry," Booger said.

"Oh geez, aren't we so lucky? Please mark the calendar, the first time Booger McClain ever said he was sorry," Rose said, looking at Brian in frustration, who, in response, just kind of nodded his head as if she was being literal and he'd make the appropriate note.

Desperate for a friend in the room, Booger now turned to Brian and shook his head as if to say, "Don't mark the calendar." Then following an awkward chuckle, Booger said to Brian, "Women, right?"

Brian didn't respond back, nor did he show any outward sign of agreement or disagreement, both positioning himself out of the middle of whatever this was and giving a small victory to Rose, whom he feared more at the moment. Just then, the rain opened up from above, and Brian could hear it pouring now. It was a welcomed sound. What he knew he didn't want to hear with a bad storm approaching was silence. Brian moved to change the conservation. "Booger, why did you go to so much trouble to build what seems like a living quarters in a bunker, complete with a secret door that opens when you remove a brick in the wall? If you own this old warehouse, and I assume you must since you seem to have keys to every part of it, why not just build your apartment on the first floor like a normal person? What's with all the secrecy?" he said. "You must admit, Booger," Brian continued, not waiting for Booger to respond, "this place has the feel of a bomb shelter. What are you afraid of?" This was an old journalism trick in action. He was showing his source what he'd observed and drew a conclusion from it that challenged him to clear the record for the record.

"I'm not afraid of anything," Booger snapped. "This place, or something like it, is a dream I have had for most of my life. It's a place that no one knows about, where I can have complete privacy, where I don't need to deal with annoying visitors or phone calls."

"So, you have dreamed your entire life of becoming a hermit?" Rose said.

"No, Rose. I don't hate people. But after a hard day dealing with the stresses of life, I just want a place where I can decompress, where I can be alone with my thoughts to relax and do exactly what I want without anyone disturbing me. It's my treehouse."

"Your what?" Rose asked.

"My treehouse. You know, well, maybe not you, but I'm sure Brian does. All little boys, at some point, dream of having a treehouse in their backyard, a place they can go when they need to be alone, a place that's close enough to their house that they can go inside the house anytime they want to use the bathroom or get a bite to eat."

"So, this is your treehouse, and the office above is your home? Is that what you are saying, old man?" Rose said with a smile.

"Well, in a way, yes. I spend most of my time in that office, so I guess it kinda represents home to me."

"I don't think I'll ever understand men," Rose said, looking at Brian again. Brian didn't fight it and nodded. Then she was ready to move on. "Well, why don't I make a fresh pot of coffee? I got a feeling you boys are going to need it tonight."

"Sounds good, Rose," Booger said, glad to be out of the hot seat.

Brian wasn't satisfied with Booger's answer, but before he could press him on it, Booger motioned Brian toward the two large computer screens on a table next to the far wall.

"Sit down," Booger said when they reached the table. "I want to show you something."

He turned on both computers. The two large screens above them came alive as one monitor showed eight split views from outside the building while the other screen had eight views from inside the warehouse.

"Damn, I didn't know you had that many surveillance cameras around this place," Brian said before realizing the main power was off. "Wait. The video feeds."

"Yeah, they're on separate power, too," Booger said, anticipating Brian's question. "You could say I sorta planned for something like this to happen someday."

"You seem awfully worried about people coming after you here," Brian said, trying to continue what he wanted to know more about from before.

"No, they aren't after me. They're after the evidence that I have upstairs."

"So, you're just going to let them have it?"

"Yeah, I can't think of a better way to keep you and Rose safe."

"What about the evidence that you've gathered over all these years? You've put a lot of time and effort into collecting it all. You surely aren't just going to let that go," Brian said, letting Booger know that would be out of character. "If someone wants your evidence, they'd want to destroy it, so the case might never be solved."

"Son, they're not going to solve the case from whatever they take from the war room."

"What do you mean?"

"I've removed the key evidence. All that is in that room is a lot of loose, unconnected facts, nothing that can lead to any real conclusion," he said, seeming to relish holding the spotlight of attention. This was classic Booger. He relished any opportunity to show others how little they knew and how much he did. "It's the stuff everybody knows anyway. You've heard the story of the Trojan Horse, right?"

"Yes," Brian said flatly, hoping to take a bit of thrill out of Booger's big reveal.

"Well, that room is our Trojan Horse. Someone is going to break into that room tonight and steal what's inside. They'll take it directly back to the people who want that information. That's when I'll have them."

"What do you mean?"

"I've planted a couple of small GPS devices among the material in that room. When they take the evidence, I will be able to track them. I'll know exactly where they take it. It's my Trojan Horse."

"I get what you're saying, but it's the evidence that's the Trojan Horse, not the room," Brian said.

"Come again?" Booger was confused.

Brian was happy to demonstrate to Booger that the detective wasn't the only one who knew things. "The Trojan Horse was the trick the Greeks used against the city of Troy in the Trojan War when they hid soldiers inside the wooden horse and presented it as a gift. They were like, 'Well, we can't get in this city, so you guys win. Here's a horse. We're gonna sail away now.' The people of Troy brought the horse into the city and thought, 'This is cool. We're winners, and we got a big wooden horse.' Of course, they should have been thinking something was fishy because the Greeks hid some of their soldiers in it who snuck out in the middle of the night and opened the gates for their fellow Greeks who had turned their ships around and come back to Troy. They entered the city and won the war," Brian said with a brief pause for emphasis. "Your horse is the evidence, not the room."

Booger was irritated. "Damn it, son. Don't take everything I say literally."

"Boys, the coffee is ready," Rose announced from the kitchen.

"Sweetie, could you bring two cups into the man cave. The smart-ass college kid and I have some things to discuss."

"Oh, and you don't want a woman around in case she might actually have an idea, is that right?"

"No, I just don't want you around, darling. I don't want this boy here to try and show you how much he thinks he knows because it will wear you out."

"Uh-huh, okay," Rose said, sensing he'd had his ego bruised.

Inside the man cave, Booger went directly behind the bar. "Take a seat, son," he said, motioning for Brian to sit at one of the two stools parked at the bar. Booger pulled out a bottle of aged Knob Creek rye whiskey. "You ever had rye whiskey, son?"

"No, never have."

"It doesn't have quite the sweetness of regular whiskey. It has a stronger body to it and a smooth finish. This is true sipping whiskey. And, besides, it will cut right through Rose's coffee."

Booger poured from the bottle. "Here, take a shot now. It will cushion your stomach for Rose's coffee."

"Do you mean it cleanses the palette?" Brian said, thinking he was being funny.

"Yeah, that's right. Only instead of awakening your taste buds, it numbs them, so you won't taste her coffee."

Brian lifted the glass to his mouth and downed it in one large gulp. He began to cough and gag.

"Damn, son. I told you Rye whiskey should be sipped, not guzzled."

"Then why'd you put it in a shot glass. I thought everything that goes in a shot glass is supposed to be drunk in one quick gulp."

"Nah, you watch too many Westerns."

"Here, hand me your shot glass. I'll hide it before Rose comes in. I don't want her to think you need alcohol to prepare for her coffee. That's just insensitive," Booger said.

A few seconds later, the door opened, and Rose stepped in

carrying two cups of coffee. "I'm not sure about that pot of yours, Booger. When was the last time you cleaned it?" she asked.

"I don't think I have."

"Yeah, that's what I figured. It had some green mold inside it. I cleaned most of it out, but there was still some in there. It might affect the taste of the coffee a little," she said.

"Thanks, hun. Would you be a sweetheart and watch those two monitors in the main room. Tell me if you see anything." She nodded with a smile and then left.

"Geez, Booger. I don't know," Brian said. "It may not be safe to drink. You need to clean the coffee pot out every day. Mold can make you sick."

"Okay, Nancy, put your big girl pants on. I've been drinking coffee out of that pot for a long time, and it hasn't affected me any." Booger pulled back out the bottle of Knob Creek. He opened it and poured a shot full into Brian's coffee cup and a little more into his.

"Now, take a taste of Rose's coffee," he said.

Brian did. There was no gagging, no coughing, only what looked like the beginnings of a smile on his face. "You're right. I can't believe it," he said. "That coffee actually tastes good."

"Yeah, I know. I do that every morning," Booger said, now seeming pleased with himself. "See, son, you might know about books and all, but I know how to survive."

Brian couldn't argue. The coffee was good this way. Plus, he really wanted to know who might have bugged his car, and Booger's plan was better than anything he could offer. "Booger, why do you think the case of the Springfield Three has never been solved?"

"Well, it's hard to close a case and charge somebody with a crime when the bodies have never been found," he said. "How does the prosecutor tell a jury they know just what happened if the women were never found. I suspect it all comes back to that.

But I think they know — the investigators. They just can't prove it."

"So, you think those women were murdered?"

"Yes, I do."

"Why?"

"Why? There's a million reasons until you find the right one. And sometimes, there's no reason at all. It could've been random. It could've been revenge. It could've been a lot of things, but it was only what it was, and we don't know."

"What do you think, Booger?"

"I don't think anything. A good detective stays objective, considering only the facts. There are valid arguments for a lot of scenarios."

"Well, you've got to admit the police involvement scenario seems pretty far-fetched, although I guess it would explain why the men that attempted to break in last night appeared to be wearing badges."

"Son, those boys weren't police."

"How do you know?"

"Police don't need to sneak through open windows. If there is something inside they want to see, they simply find a friendly judge to give them a search warrant."

"Okay, then, who were they?"

"I don't know. I'm hoping we'll find out tonight."

"Look, I don't believe the police were involved. However, is it really out of the question that it could be a dirty cop?" Brian said, seeing doubt in Booger's eyes. "Hear me out. Something or someone was able to get those three women outside the house without causing a ruckus. A police officer could do that. Maybe an off-duty cop spotted the girls driving home after leaving Janelle's house. The girls had been drinking. Maybe they were driving erratically. He followed them, and when the girls pulled into the driveway, he decided to approach them."

"No, that doesn't seem likely based on witness testimony and the evidence," Booger said. "Evidence points to the fact that the girls went into the house, prepared to go to sleep and got into bed. Some time had to go by from when they arrived until they left again. Then, there is the broken light cover on the porch. If the women came willingly, how was the light fixture broken? And don't forget, there is the witness who said he saw the old, moss-green van leaving the neighborhood sometime between 3 and 3:30. The van was also spotted by others too, including the one woman who swore she saw Suzie driving it and a man's voice coming from inside. No, I don't believe a policeman followed those girls home, at least not in a patrol car."

"Yeah, that's all fair. I don't know. I'm just trying to make sense of who might be breaking into your office. If it's not police, then it's someone sporting badges. Do you think whoever abducted the women could have been someone dressed as a policeman?" Brian asked.

"That's more likely. It would explain why the women came out of the house without raising a fuss that might have been heard by neighbors," Booger said.

"Yeah, suppose someone in a van dressed as a policeman spotted the girls driving home," Brian said, now with a vision of what could have been. "He followed them. It was late at night. No one was on the roads. He saw them pull into the driveway. He watched them from the street and decided to abduct them. He waited until the lights went out until he assumed they were in bed. Then he rang the doorbell. When someone, probably Sherrill, came to the front door, he waved a badge. She opened the door, and he said that one of the girl's cars was involved in an accident and that he wanted to speak to them. Sherrill then calls the girls to the front door. They go outside on the porch, maybe he uses a ruse that there was damage to one of the girl's cars, and he wanted to show them. But something changed on the porch.

Maybe they saw the van, or maybe they became concerned because there wasn't a police car, or maybe it was just the way the man acted. Whatever it was, one or more of the women began to resist and, in the effort to get away, bumped against the light fixture, shattering the glass. That makes sense, right?"

"I've got to say you certainly have an active imagination," Booger said as he eyed the cigar in his hand, searching his pocket for a lighter.

"Okay, fine," Brian said, frustrated. "Couldn't it have happened that way, though?"

Booger took another sip of coffee before lighting the cigar in a small production of contemplation. "Look, it is possible the crime happened that way, but why didn't one or more of the women run or scream once they suspected something was wrong? One man subduing three of them without handcuffs, zip ties, tape over their mouths – it seems a daunting task."

"Not if he pulled a gun on them. You yourself have said before it could have been one person," Brian said, animated. "Suppose he was behind them on the porch, blocking an escape back into the house. Suppose he pulled a gun on one of them, held the gun to her head, threatening to shoot if the other women didn't cooperate," Brian said. "Or," he added, "suppose there was another man, two men dressed as officers. You know, I've thought before it was probably more than one guy. It would be easier for two men to control the situation."

"Yes, yes, that is possible too," Booger said, patting the air to suggest Brian calm down.

Brian was just talking it all through, and he felt buoyed somehow by it. He was on to something. "It would explain why there was no evidence of a crime found inside the home. It would explain the unlocked door and the broken light fixture, too, and it would explain why neighbors didn't hear any screams that night," he said. Brian hesitated for a second, expecting Booger to object. When he didn't, Brian continued. "Look, Booger, I can't believe cops were involved. Sure, I know there are bad ones out there, but there's no real evidence of that here beyond the shadows we saw outside a window. The thought I can't get away from, however, is that someone or someones took control of that house in an instant. Authority figures. The women left in an instant, without waking neighbors or grabbing purses and cigarettes."

"Son, what you say is plausible," Booger said, taking a long drag off his cigar. "The only thing I'd add is that the men weren't local."

This surprised Brian. He didn't expect Booger to agree somehow, and he certainly didn't expect Booger to make such a statement. "So you think whoever abducted those women weren't locals?" Brian asked, just trying to reaffirm what he'd heard.

"Look, son, what do I know? But I do think there is a strong possibility that those women were taken by someone not from the area, maybe visiting someone in town or there for some business or personal purpose. Or, perhaps, they were just traveling through town," Booger said before taking two big puffs back to back. A clap of thunder hit just before Booger said dramatically from behind a cloud of smoke, "I don't believe the abductions were done by someone from Springfield."

CHAPTER 10

THE NEW RESIDENT

"So, if you eliminate suspects that had lived in Springfield for at least a year, you cut the suspect list down significantly," Brian said.

"Yes, that would be true," Booger said, "if you could definitely eliminate those people. I'm pretty sure we're looking at a non-local or non-locals, but remember, the police haven't ruled out any of the suspects that we know of yet, and I don't think we can either. There were hundreds of clues in this case, some solid, others that led down dead ends. Don't think that the police haven't continued to work on this case. They have, and so has the FBI. They have kept silent about their best clues and the evidence they have."

"Can we agree?" Brian asked, "That there is a greater probability that the abductor of those women was someone that hadn't lived in Springfield for any period of time?" He was excited just to be narrowing the list down. If pressed, Brian couldn't say for sure why he was trying so hard to get Booger to commit to any particular person, persons or scenario for the record. Maybe it was a force of habit from his journalism days, or maybe he just wanted to feel like he was on solid ground. Something in him needed to press forward toward answers and away from indecision.

"Son, look at you putting your college education to some use. I suppose you're going to explain to me the mathematical equation for the law of probability now," Booger said, taking another sip of his coffee.

"No, but could you answer my question?"

"Well, if you want me to speculate, yes, I would say there is a greater probability that the abductor was not a long-time resident of Springfield. That is what I'm saying."

"Robert Craig Cox wasn't a long-time resident of Springfield at the time, was he?" Brian asked.

"Yes, that's true. So?" Booger replied.

"Well, he is the number one suspect, isn't he?

"I guess if you are reading blogs and amateur sleuth posts about the crime, many people speculate that he is the most likely suspect."

"I think it's more than that," Brian countered. The police seem to have narrowed their focus on him. Evidence points to him, and he doesn't have an alibi for the night of June 6. His girlfriend gave him an alibi early in the investigation, but she has since recanted it. The odds are decent that he's the person responsible for those women's disappearance – wouldn't you agree?"

Booger didn't say a word. He stood up, walked behind the bar and grabbed the bottle of rye whiskey, got two short glasses from the cabinet, put three ice cubes in both glasses and poured whiskey into both glasses, about two-thirds full. Then he handed one glass to Brian and sat the other one down in front of him. He sat back in his bar stool, pulled out a fresh stogie, lit it and took two long slow drags. Brian realized they were in back-to-back cigar territory. This must mean, he thought, things were getting serious. After several moments of silence, the detective spoke. "Okay, let's talk about Robert Craig Cox. Son, why don't you enlighten me why you think he is the most likely suspect?"

Brian rose to his feet, suddenly empowered and nervous like a prosecutor needing to make his closing argument to a judge and jury. He wasn't sure how much he really believed it was Cox, but it felt good to put him on trial. They were getting somewhere now, he thought. He walked to the other side of the bar and looked Booger squarely in the face to have his case fully heard. "First," he began, "let's consider his history. He was a sick man, a class-A psychopath. His crime spree began, as far as we know, in 1978, just after graduating basic training as an Army Ranger. He was staying at a hotel in Florida, celebrating with his family. It was late at night. His parents were ready for bed when he headed out on his own to continue the celebration. A few hours later, he barged into his parent's motel room covered in blood. His tongue had been partially bit off. His parents rushed him to an emergency room. Cox told the nursing staff that he had bitten off his own tongue, yet the medical examiner later concluded that the tongue was most likely bitten off by someone else, based on the angle of the bite. A few hours went by, and police located the nineteen-year-old body of Sharon Zellers. She had not returned home after a late night shift at Disney World. She was last seen walking home from work. Her body was found a hundred feet from the hotel where Cox and his family were staying."

Brian continued, "The Army transferred him to California from there. In 1985, he was charged and convicted on two separate cases of abduction and assault of two women. DNA collected from him then led to his arrest in the Sharon Zellers murder. A Florida jury later convicted him of the crime and sentenced him to life without parole. The ruling was later overturned because of a lack of DNA evidence. Upon his release in 1992, he moved to Springfield, where his parents were retired. That was just three months before the abductions of the Springfield Three. He was new to the area."

Brian paused for a minute to watch Booger's facial

expression. He hoped to see a smile or perhaps some look of agreement. He was, after all, stating the facts that Booger had listed in his war room. Instead, Booger sat there, stoic, smoking his cigar and occasionally sipping his drink.

Is he bored? Is he even listening to me? Brian thought. Booger was such a talker, such a showman. Brian was surprised that he hadn't been interrupted yet. He continued. "The interesting thing is that we can assume Robert Craig Cox knew one of the women, Stacy McCall. He may have never talked to her, but he had likely seen her before. One of the jobs Cox had while in Springfield was as a mechanic at the same used car dealership where Stacy McCall's father worked. Perhaps she visited her father there and was spotted by Cox. She was a very attractive girl, one who could have gotten the attention of a sicko like Cox without her or her father realizing anything at all."

Booger put down his cigar and spoke, "Wait, son, now you are speculating. There is no proof that Robert Cox ever saw or met Stacy McCall, and if there is evidence of that, only the police know."

"Okay, that's fair, but you got to admit that it is a strange coincidence," Brian said, now pressing on. "Then there is Cox's other job while he was in Springfield. Wasn't he employed as an underground utility worker, a position that could have given him indirect access to and knowledge of homes owned and lived in by unsuspecting residents like Sherrill Levitt? Consider the clue left in a newspaper rack inside a local grocery store. A handwritten note on a piece of paper with words, 'use ruse of gas man checking for leak.' That note, along with a rough drawing of an apartment building, seems to point a finger in Cox's direction. You know what I think, Booger?"

"No, son. What do you think?"

"I think Robert Cox's girlfriend or an acquaintance of hers at the time wrote that note and did the drawing. I think she knew that Cox abducted those women. I think she was afraid of him, of what he might do to her. He forced her to lie to the police to give him an alibi; she admitted that years later. I think the picture that was drawn on the note was either where Cox's parents lived or was where he took the women," Brian said. He realized he was speculating. He realized in saying it all out loud that this was no open and closed case for Cox. And still, he wanted it to be considered. "What do you think, Booger?"

"I think your theory has more gaps than a fifty-year-old pair of dentures. If Cox's girlfriend or an acquaintance of hers wrote that note, then she would have certainly told the police what she knew years later, when Cox was in prison, and she had no reason to fear him. She would have done that when she recanted the alibi she had provided Cox days after the disappearances.

"And the theory of the apartment building shown in the note being the one where Cox's parents lived has shakier legs than a newborn calf. They lived miles away from that apartment building at the time. Besides, police searched the area and surrounding woods a couple of days after the note was discovered. They even used search dogs. There was nothing found. If you want to speculate, it is more likely that whoever left that note knew nothing about the crime. Maybe they wanted attention. Maybe they had some other alternative motive, like throwing investigators off the trail. The truth is we don't know. All we know is someone left an anonymous note and drawing, which authorities investigated. Your finger comes from a nameless hand and doesn't clearly point to anything. Think about it. That person could have left an anonymous note saying, 'Robert Craig Cox did it.'"

He was right, and Brian knew it. He just stood there, deflated.

"Son, over the years, there has been a lot of speculation that the women's abductor used a ruse similar to someone warning of a gas leak to get the women out of the house. It's understandable why people would think that. There appeared to be little or no evidence of a crime inside the Levitt home. So, it makes sense why people would think the abductor must have gotten them to come outside without force. A person wearing a gas company shirt and saying that there was a suspected gas leak might be successful in getting the women to leave that house in a hurry without taking their purses or any of their possessions. But consider the timeline. The girls could not have gotten home before 2:15 a.m. After that, they changed and got ready for bed, so it would have been nearly 3 a.m. Ask yourself if it is likely that three women who were asleep or nearly asleep would have opened the door to anyone, even someone pretending to work for the gas company, at 3 in the morning. No. It just wouldn't happen. Even if that ruse was successful in getting the women to leave the house, don't you think they would put some clothes on or take some with them? Would they leave the house in their underwear or pajamas?"

Brian knew what Booger was saying was true, but he wasn't ready to dismiss Robert Craig Cox yet. "Okay, you make a good point. Still, if we were to single out one person, I think Cox has to be the most likely suspect. He liked young, attractive women. He was a sexual deviant that had murdered before. He had even been arrested in California for abducting and sexually assaulting two young women. He had told his girlfriend at the time of the disappearances that if the police asked any questions about him, she was to say he was with her the night of June 6 and that they went to church together the morning of the 7th. She was afraid of him. She did exactly what he told her and provided him an alibi for that night. Why would he insist she cover his butt unless he had something to hide?" Booger didn't answer. He sensed Brian wasn't really asking a question. He was just prefacing his argument.

"In 1995, Cox was arrested in Decatur, Texas, for holding a weapon on a twelve-year-old girl. He was sentenced to life for that crime. Then look at his statement to authorities while he was in a Texas prison in 1997. He said he knew the three women were dead and that the person who committed the crime had experience. He also said their bodies were buried near Springfield. It sounded almost like a confession, like he wanted to say exactly what happened to those women. But when pressed about it, he said that he would not talk anymore about the case while his mother was still alive. She is in her 80s now. Maybe he didn't want to hurt his mother any more than he already had. Don't you think he could have committed the crime and will confess to it once his mother has passed away?"

Booger started to answer, but Brian continued. "From everything I have read, it appears the police think he is the person most likely to have committed the crime, too. They just don't have enough evidence to charge him. I think they are hopeful he will confess after his mother passes away, and that's what they are waiting for."

Brian could tell Booger was interested but wasn't convinced. The truth was Brian wasn't convinced either, but it helped him to think if he could talk everything out. Plus, he knew the detective would be quick to shoot down any theory that was too far-fetched. "Booger, would you like to hear how I think it could have happened – how Cox could be the guy?"

"Sure, kid, let's hear it," Booger said, sitting up in his seat, seemingly energized by Brian asking to be judged on a subject he knew more about than almost anyone.

"Robert Cox had recently got out of prison and had moved to Springfield in the spring of '92. He was a sick man – mentally, I mean. Based on what I've seen, this guy had a perverted lust for women, particularly young women. To make things worse, he was a psychopath, or a sociopath, with no conscience. Prison didn't help sort out his mental issues. It only hardened him to ways not to get caught in the future. I think Cox was a predator with nothing to lose, searching the Springfield area for a victim from the very day he moved to town. He took a job as a gas line worker, which put him in neighborhoods where he was most likely to find the type of victim that fed his depravity.

"Where it gets interesting is that I have two theories on how Cox picked the three women. One is that he was doing work in the vicinity of the Levitt home sometime before the disappearances and spotted Suzie Streeter. She was his intended victim. He had been watching the home for a while. Neighbors reported seeing a stranger walking around the neighborhood. I think that stranger was Cox waiting for just the right time to strike.

"The other theory is that Cox saw Stacy McCall at the used car dealership where her father worked. Cox also had a job there as a part-time mechanic. She, too, was his type. It's plausible that he could have been interested in either girl. What I believe is that this guy was a hunter. But here's the thing: I don't think he would have been tracking those girls that night — at least not before they drove home to Suzie's. This was a crime of opportunity. Those girls were at the Kirby house, and no one expected them to leave, so even if he was stalking them, he would have assumed they were staying at the friend's house at 2 a.m. No - Cox, I believe, was out hunting for a girl late that night and came across Stacy and Suzie driving home — perhaps, a little erratically — around 2:15-2:30. Whatever he was up to, he switched on a dime and followed the girls to the Levitt home. Maybe he recognized Stacy, or maybe it was Suzie, but it doesn't matter, does it? The streets were nearly empty. He could drive a safe distance behind the two women and still see where they were going. When they pulled into the driveway, set back from the road, with plenty of trees to hide him, he watched, and he planned.

"He probably watched them enter the house. He would have seen the third car. He knew someone else was there. It didn't matter. His sickness is impulsive; it doesn't listen to reason. He had to come up with a plan right away to get those two girls out of that house and into his van where he could control them. He would wait until they were asleep until all the lights were out in the house. His odds were best if they were disoriented and groggy. He might have watched them move from one room to another. He may have gotten out of his vehicle and crept quietly around the premises. Maybe he took the screen off the window, or perhaps, he tried to take the porch light out and accidentally knocked the casing off, and it crashed on the porch. That could have woken them up. Sherrill could have checked on the noise and forced his hand, so to speak. If he had a gun, he could have held it on her and gone in and got the girls, taking them all out to the van," Brian said, seeing that Booger was following his line of thought closely. "Really, he had two options, right? The window or the front door. He could have gained access to the house and the women either way. He could have removed the screen, sat it on the ground and opened the window enough so he could climb inside. I believe he would have made some noise climbing into the window, maybe caused Cinnamon to bark. Remember the report that the people who entered the house the next day noticed Suzie's blinds were bent. Maybe Suzie heard a noise and was trying to look outside, and when she didn't see anything, she went back to bed.

"In this scenario, I think Sherrill was the unintended victim of this crime. She stood in the way of Cox's improvised plan. I believe he subdued her first, tied her up, and gagged her. Sherill might not have even known her daughter and a friend were in the house. Whatever he did to the three of them, he didn't do it there. He got them out of the house and fast. No time for purses or cigarettes – just go. He could sort the details out later. Cox needed them out of the house and in his control. That's why I think he took Sherill along. He could have subdued her and then threatened one or all of them if they didn't come with him quickly and now. 'Just do what I say, and nobody will get hurt,' he might have told them. And who knows about the light fixture? Maybe he hit it accidentally, raising his gun as they were rushing out the door. Cox then could have forced the women into the back of an old moss green or gray tone late 60s or early 70s model Ford cargo van. Perhaps he restrained them more once they were inside, but I don't think so. I bet he was in a rush to get out of that neighborhood. And, of course, that aligns with the witness who said the guy ran a stop sign and nearly crashed into the vehicle with him and his daughter.

"It all lines up, Booger," Brian said, taking a big sip of spiked coffee to wet his throat and catch his breath. Just before the detective could chime in, Brian continued. "From there, the van was spotted in a Walmart parking lot around 4 a.m. Then noticed in a neighborhood close to the Levitt home around 6 a.m. I believe the women were first assaulted in that Walmart parking lot. "Cox was looking for a place somewhat close by where he could take the women and not be seen. The Walmart parking lot was large and nearly empty that time of morning – it would have been good enough for someone sick and desperate and thinking on the fly. From there, I think Cox ordered Suzie to drive the van so he could maintain better control of the two women in the back. He ordered her to drive to a vacant house, maybe one he had scoped out previously. But that plan was foiled when an elderly lady sitting on her porch spotted the van and was suspicious of the crying woman at the wheel. "I know the woman driving was Suzie Streeter," she told police later.

"That woman provided the police the best description of the van. Her story was so believable that the Springfield police purchased a similar moss-green van and parked it outside the police headquarters. Pictures of that van have appeared on every television program and article that has covered the story of the Springfield Three over the years. If there is a piece of the puzzle that has remained unchallenged over the years, it is that van. I know Cox hasn't been tied to that vehicle, but I don't think it's a stretch to imagine a sicko could find an old, non-descript van to throw some girls in. From there, I believe the van drove out of town into the country, into the vast Ozark wilderness. And the girls would never return. Witnesses came forward in the days and weeks after the disappearances with reports of seeing that van in various locations throughout Springfield in the early morning hours of June 7, but the van was never spotted after that morning. I think those women ended up where that van ended up – perhaps, in a pile of ashes in the backwoods."

Brian could see Booger taking it all in.

"And maybe that's the connection to rural Webster County," Brian said. "That's where he went, disposed of the bodies and the van. Perhaps, the police went with search warrants years later based on a tip from another suspect in the case. They found some sort of evidence during their search. I believe one thing they found was burned remains from a similar van. A gag order was placed on the evidence the police found, so no one will know for sure what they found until that gag order is lifted."

Brian stopped talking. He waited for Booger's reaction.

"Rose, darlin', can you bring us another cup of coffee?" Booger yelled between puffs on his cigar.

"Keep your pants on, old man. I'll be right there," she hollered back.

The detective sat silently, arms folded, considering everything Brian had said. Then, suddenly, he seemed to get a twinkle in his eye, and he relaxed his arms. "How do you suppose Cox got back to Springfield after dumping the bodies in rural Webster County?" Booger asked Brian. "After all, your theory is that Cox burned the van and since that van was never spotted again in Springfield, so how would he have gotten back to town?"

"Maybe his girlfriend came out and drove him home?"

"Doubtful," Booger commented. "Remember, these were the days before cell phones were widely used. It's unlikely he had one. Also, his girlfriend attended church on the morning of the 7th. Besides, when she recounted the alibi she gave Cox years later when he was in prison for an unrelated crime, she would have likely told police about going to Webster County to pick Cox up. He would have been no threat to her then. Why wouldn't she have told them that?"

"Well," Brian countered, "I'm not sure. Maybe she was afraid of being charged as an accomplice. Maybe someone else was involved in the abductions. It would have been easier for two men to control those women than it would have been for one. Maybe he met someone in a bar, maybe a fellow ex-con, maybe someone just as perverted as he was."

Booger grinned, recognizing that Brian hadn't thought that through. "So you think those women are buried somewhere in the backwoods of the Ozarks? Maybe rural Webster County?"

"Yes, I do," Brian replied with a deep breath.

"You don't think there is a glimmer of hope that those women are still alive?"

"No, I don't. I suspect they were killed within hours of their abduction. I think Cox had planned that end from the very beginning. He had learned from his time in prison not to leave witnesses."

Brian continued. "And the fact is that without a body, it is extremely difficult to solve this case. He knew that. A body can tell investigators a lot about the crime and the person that committed it. With the development of DNA technology, many crimes that have previously gone unresolved can now be solved, but it requires some sort of DNA to do that. Maybe he used gloves in the Levitt home. Maybe there was some DNA evidence, but it was contaminated by the people that came and went through that house the day after they disappeared. But one thing was certain to him, those bodies couldn't be found. That was his key to getting away with this."

Booger put his cigar down and sat forward in his chair, looking directly at Brian. "Look, I'm not going to give you a hard time. Your theory is purely speculation, of course, but you have mixed in enough facts to make it interesting. I think the truth of what happened to those women will be known someday, and it may not be too far off from your theory."

Brian was relieved. This was a much better response than he had expected. Ultimately, Brian didn't know what had happened, but what he had laid out all seemed plausible. It all seemed likely. He had really only spent just a few days investigating the case, reading blogs and news reports and Booger, who had spent years analyzing the case, agreed the theory was probably close to the truth. It felt like a bit of validation to him.

"However," Booger added, "did you consider that the suspect who gave police the information about the farm in Webster County that eventually led to the gag order on the evidence they found had no known connection to Cox?"

Here it was, Brian thought. Booger was pulling the rug out from under him.

"Steven Garrison, now serving a forty-year prison sentence for an unrelated crime, told police that a friend of his admitted to killing the three women," Booger said. Now hands freed of the cigar, he was focused. "The friend, intoxicated at the time of his conversation with Garrison, was interrogated by police later and denied making the statement. Details that Garrison provided to the police about the abduction matched certain unpublicized details of the crime and were credible enough to convince a judge to issue three search warrants for the area and later to issue a gag order on evidence found at the scene. But I must stress, son, there was no known connection between Garrison and Cox."

Booger continued. "The property searched with those warrants had been owned by Francis Lee Robb, an individual that is currently in prison for a murder that was thought to be drug related. It is no surprise that people who cling to the belief that the abduction of the Springfield Three was drug-related point to this connection in rural Webster County. So, to get back to your theory that Cox was the murderer, consider one of the biggest clues in the case: the moss-green van. There has been absolutely no connection made between Cox and a similar van. I know you said it's no big deal for a guy like Cox to get an old van, but there's no record of him owning one at the time of the crime. He had not been seen driving one, and no one has come forth to tie Cox to a van of that type or anything close to that type."

"Maybe he stole it," Brian chimed in, realizing as soon as he said it how desperate it seemed.

"Maybe," Booger responded, "but a van of that type and color was not reported missing to the local police, or I'm sure they would have been all over it like pigs on fritters. It's a real stretch to try to tie Cox to that van."

"Alright, I hear you, but suppose that acquaintance of Steven Garrison was someone that Cox befriended, and maybe he involved that person in the crime. Maybe he had a connection with the Robb family and that farm in Webster County. Maybe the van belonged to someone that lived in Webster County. It may have been borrowed or stolen. If that van wasn't owned by anyone in the Springfield area, that would explain why it was never spotted after the morning of June 7. The van might not have even been destroyed. Police were looking for a moss-green van. A fresh coat of paint would have done the trick."

"Son, you're reaching. Plus, you have to think about the

kind of person Cox was. There is no evidence that he has ever worked with anyone else. This dude is a lone wolf – just like most sexual predators. Remember, police seriously considered Cox as their prime suspect. They even took a case to a Grand Jury. There just wasn't enough evidence to ever arrest him. I think there is a good chance that Cox didn't abduct those women."

"Then why did he say the girls were dead?" Brian asked, now feeling a bit deflated. "I know people sometimes talk from prison just hoping they might get a better deal or some attention, but why would he act like he had some connection to this, some inside knowledge on this, if he didn't?"

Booger thought for a moment and then responded. "Maybe he just enjoyed the thrill of knowing that his statement could torture the friends and families of the three missing women. He was a sicko, as you say. I don't hold a lot of credibility in anything he has said."

"Okay, but then why do you suppose Cox told his girlfriend to lie for him and provide him an alibi for June 6?" Brian asked.

"Whenever there is a serious crime, police talk to family members first. Most disappearances and most murders are committed by either a family member or someone who the victim knows. When those leads don't pan out, it is natural for the police to talk to parolees and ex-cons that live in the area, particularly ones that have a history of violent crimes against women. Cox probably suspected the police would eventually talk to him, and he would need an alibi. But you brought up a valid point, son. Where was Cox the night of June 6 and the morning of June 7? He wasn't with his girlfriend like, police were led to believe early in the investigation. His girlfriend years later stated that she didn't know where he was that night."

"Booger, are you saying that my theory that Robert Craig Cox abducted those women might be right?" Brian asked with a bit of a chuckle.

"Son, I'm saying that if you discount the van as a clue, then Cox would definitely be the prime suspect."

Brian couldn't help but smile.

"However, that would mean throwing out a clue that was validated by over a half-dozen witnesses. It is probably the strongest clue investigators have released to the public. To dismiss that clue was to dismiss most theories of what happened to those women that night."

Suddenly the door to the man cave opened up. "I brought you boys some fresh coffee," Rose said, walking into the room.

"Thanks, Rose," Brian said somberly before she left as quickly as she came. He knew everything Booger was saying was true. As far as it felt like they had come, they had gone in a big circle and gotten nowhere. He turned to the detective, "I'm going to need a shot for this."

CHAPTER 11

A STORMY NIGHT

A few minutes later, Rose returned with a plate of warm chocolate chip cookies. "I figured you boys could use a little snack to soak up some of that whiskey you've been drinking," Rose said, looking at the half-empty bottle of rye whiskey with a smile.

Brian, staring at the plate of what was obviously chip ahoy or some off-brand store cookies, just gave him a look that said you've got to be kidding."

"Thanks, darling. Did you make these from scratch?" Booger said in his salesman's voice.

"No, old man. Those are store-bought cookies. But I put them in the oven for a few minutes to warm them up."

"Sounds good, sweetie. Thanks."

"You know, Booger, your bomb shelter could use a good cleaning," Rose said. "It's more like a bachelor tomb, I'd say. And your stockpile of food could use another trip to the grocery store. You're down to two six packs of beer, three bottles of bourbon, a 5-lb can of Folgers and a half-empty box of malted milk balls."

"I forgot I had dessert in the cabinet. They'll go great with your cookies. Could you bring us the malted milk balls, sweetie?"

"I threw them out," Rose replied.

"Why?"

"They expired last year."

"Darlin', everyone knows there are two food groups that never have an expiration date: Twinkies and malted milk balls."

"Well, someone should tell that green fuzz that was growing inside the box. Did you get them wet? I don't even know how that's possible."

"Well damn, that's a shame. They would go perfect with a good, aged rye whiskey," Booger said.

"Yeah, I can see you boys have already started on one bottle," Rose said, looking at the two half-empty glasses on the bar counter. "You're not putting any of that in the coffee I made, are you?"

"I wouldn't dare," Booger said, not looking into her eyes.

"Hmph. I know you," Rose said, looking straight at him until he looked back. When he did, it startled him, so he quickly changed the subject.

"Anything show up on the monitors yet, Rose?"

"Just raindrops. It's coming down sideways outside, worse than last night, but I guess you wouldn't know since your bachelor tomb has no windows," she said. "Old man, what would ever possess you to build your home and not put some windows in?"

"Well, if I ever want to see what's on the other side of those walls, I can just go outside. Besides, not having windows helps me sleep. Hell, no matter what time of the day or night, I can just turn the lights out, and it's pitch dark in here. It's great for sleeping."

"Not too great for going to the bathroom, though. That room is disgusting. You should try turning the light switch on the next time you go in there. It takes a second."

"I'll keep that in mind if I can find it. It's impossible to see anything with the lights out," Booger said with a smile. "Rose, darling, why don't you move in here with me, and I'll promise to change my wicked ways."

"I might just do that," Rose said, holding back a grin, "just as soon as you get some windows."

"Ha!" Booger said, just before a loud crack of thunder shook through the room. The reminder of conditions outside refocused the detective. Even with the nasty weather, Booger sensed that tonight those men would return. "Please keep an eye on the video monitors, Rose."

"I will, but right now, you can't see anything. It's raining too hard," she said.

"Even if we can't see, I have motion sensors hooked up in the war room and in several spots inside the building. If one is activated, it will sound an alarm from the monitor. Come and get me if that goes off. Okay, Rose?"

"Good, so if I fall asleep, the alarm will wake me up," she said.

"I would prefer if you stayed awake and watched in case something goes wrong with the sensors. Why don't you just drink a couple of cups of your coffee? There's got to be enough caffeine in it to keep you up for a few hours."

She thought briefly about offering a smart-ass reply but decided against it. "Okay, boss," she said simply as she left the room, closing the door behind her.

"Booger, I've asked you before, but I don't think you gave me a truthful answer. What is going on here?" Brian asked. "You have some very elaborate and expensive video equipment to safeguard this warehouse, and you've gone to great lengths to set up your war room, to fill the boards and walls with facts about the Springfield Three, which are by your own admission earlier tonight not the real evidence. That evidence you brought with you down here to a place that seems a lot like a hidden bomb shelter. There is clearly more going on in this case than you want to tell me. What are you hiding? What are you afraid of?"

"First off, son, I'm not afraid of anything. I made a promise to the Streeter and McCall families that I would do everything that I could to solve this case and bring them some closure."

This was the first time he'd mentioned their families to Brian. "So, are you close to solving the case? It's been twenty-eight years, Booger. I have to admit, I'm not even sure what I'm doing. Yes, I've been interested in the case since 1992, but I don't have anything invested in this – not like you. I've never met with the families. I was a college drop-out who worked in restaurants, got married young and had kids; I went back to school in my late 20s. I was a business reporter, Booger. I never covered this case. I know less than the people with the blogs. What the hell is going on here?"

"I think I am close. Geez, you need a lot of hand holding. Maybe everything isn't about you. Maybe your being here just makes it look like I'm close. I have a few questions, too. I'm hoping to get some of the answers I need tonight."

This quieted Brian. Was the fact that he was meeting with Booger somehow setting off alarms with people who feared the detective could have cracked the case? When Brian worked at the business journal, he had been the one to cover any investigative or legal cases. When prominent financial adviser Nadia Cavner pleaded guilty to stalking her daughter's boyfriend, he dove into the court documents. When hotelier and Springfield icon John Q. Hammons died, Brian was talking with family friends and breaking the news of a private funeral outside of town. Someone could see Brian staying at Booger's as a threat – even though it had been four years since he'd worked as a reporter.

Booger continued, "Maybe not all the answers, but I think they will provide me some more puzzle pieces that will lead me closer to solving this. I need to know who these people are, Brian. They've been keeping tabs on me for a long time now. I've gotta figure out what happened to these women, and I think whoever was going to break in holds the key."

"Why are you so confident they will come tonight?" Brian's tone had softened.

"Because you're still here."

"What?" Brian asked meekly, though he now sensed the answer.

"You are the bait at the end of my hook. Those men are coming tonight because you're here and because they think that I'm going to give you the evidence that will help solve this case. They don't want an outsider to get a hold of it, and they sure as hell don't want a story published using that evidence which might embarrass a lot of people."

"Yeah, okay," Brian said, still a bit confused. "Wait, how did they know I was coming to meet with you?"

"Because they had a listening device on my phone. They heard every word of our conversation."

"So, you knew they were listening?"

"Of course, I found the device two weeks ago. I was just trying to figure out how to put that knowledge to good use. Then you called, and I got an idea. A little later, your dad called, and I agreed to meet with you. The whole thing felt like synchro-somethin'," Booger said, searching for a word.

"Synchro-something?"

"Yeah, what's that old Police song?"

"You mean Synchronicity?" Brian said with a smile. It had taken him a second to figure out because he thought Booger was referring to the actual police.

"That's it! Synchronicity!"

Brian laughed out loud now.

Booger blushed. "Laugh all you want. You're the bait, kid."

Both of them got quiet for a moment before Brian asked, "Seriously, do you think my life is in danger?"

"Hell no. Those men aren't after you. They're only after the evidence they think I was going to give you."

"Suppose they think you already provided me that evidence, that maybe I know enough to write the story already?"

Booger took another sip of whiskey before speaking. "Yeah, I really didn't think of that."

"Oh, come on, Booger. You're killing me." They both laughed.

"Stop worrying. Rose and I are packing heat, and she's a pretty good shot."

"How can I be worried? I'm in a bunker?"

"Bachelor pad," Booger corrected.

"Do you just want me to worry?" Brian asked, to which Booger just shrugged. The mood felt lighter now, so Brian changed the subject. "How many years have you been working this case?"

"Let's see now. I guess about twenty-eight years."

"What? You've been working this case since the women disappeared?"

"Well, not immediately after, and I've taken a few breaks over the years."

"So, who hired you?"

"The Streeter family got me involved when they thought the police were centering on Bartt as their prime suspect. I've only met informally with the McCalls; I wanted to let them know I was doing what I could."

"So, have you been paid to investigate for all these years?" Brian asked.

"No, son. I wasn't paid. I volunteered my services."

"For twenty-eight years?"

"Well, like I said, I've taken some time off."

"Wait, this just doesn't add up. How can you afford to work a case for twenty-eight years without taking any money? And look at the video surveillance equipment you have around here. You own this warehouse; you've built this massive bomb shelter – excuse me, bachelor pad – and that Corvette convertible you drive wasn't cheap. How can you afford everything?"

"Walmart, my boy. You can thank good, ol' Sam Walton for all of this," Booger said, grinning.

"What do you mean? Did you own stock?"

"I was a sheriff for a time in Branson back in the '60s. The job didn't pay much, so I did some moonlighting on weekends for a new retailer in Harrison, Arkansas. That store was a dump compared to any supercenter today, but I was impressed by the way they did things. Two things mattered: price and customer service. Plus, they'd take any return; it didn't matter who it was from. I got to know Sam pretty well because he traveled to all the stores, especially early on, so we saw a lot of him. He was a hell of a nice guy, a good old boy, down to earth, honest and damn smart. He and I used to go fishing together when he had free time, which was rare. He knew this great trout spot on the White River. Hell of a fisherman. I only worked for Walmart for a couple of years, but he told me when the company was about to go public – 1970, I think – so I got in on it in the very beginning. I figured betting on Sam was a good bet, and boy, was I right! I didn't have much money, but I used some savings initially and added here and there as I could. When my wife died in '71, I put the life insurance proceeds into their stock, which was a boost. Over time, well, you can imagine. It's allowed me a certain level of comfort and freedom to do what I want and when I want to do it."

"Wow," Brian said. "Yes, good bet."

"You know, I still think about Sam every so often. His wealth never seemed to change him. Here was a billionaire that drove a pick-up truck and visited his stores wearing blue jean overalls. He was just a regular guy."

"Just like Booger, right?"

"Ha! Maybe not. I like a little flash to keep 'em guessing," Booger said, smiling.

"Okay, so you're independently wealthy. Why stick with this for twenty-eight years?"

"It's a very interesting case. Plus, I haven't done much in years beyond buying and building all this. There hasn't been much to do. I just try to keep up with any news as it happens. I've worked on other cases, of course. Dozens," Booger said before striking a somber tone. "But I always come back to this one. I'd like to see it solved before I die."

The pair sat in silence for a minute. Rumbling thunder could be heard in the distance.

"You know that I've outlasted every Springfield police officer that was involved with this case from the beginning. They've all retired or left the force. I don't know about all the FBI folks. There's only one person that I can think of that has been involved with the Springfield Three as long as I have. Her name is Kathee Baird. Have you heard of her?"

"Yes, I ran across her name a few times in some of the blogs and articles I've read about the case."

"Yeah, I've never met her," Booger said, "but I've been an admirer of hers. She's a bit of an amateur sleuth, so I guess I'm partial. She provided investigators one of the best clues in recent years."

"You mean the parking garage at Cox Medical Center?"

"Yeah, that's the one. She said she was tipped that the bodies of the three women were buried underneath it. She brought in an expert in using ground penetrating radar to determine if it was possible that was the burial site," Booger said. "The expert, Rick Norland, had previously worked at the World Trade Center on the September 11th attacks using his GPR to search for people trapped beneath the rubble. It was 2006 when

Baird brought Norland to Springfield to use his scanner to search the car park. She supposedly stated that she never told Norland what the object of her search was. I don't know if that's true, but I like that."

He continued, "His GPR showed three anomalies, roughly three feet below the surface of the concrete. They were about two feet wide, and the soil changes were between five and seven feet long, which is to say they were consistent with a shallow grave for three bodies. The only way to conclusively know what was underneath that concrete was to conduct a core sample, drill down through the concrete and lower a camera to see exactly what was there. Baird took Norland's findings to the police. That went about how you might think. The cops weren't anxious to drill into the car park and with some good reason. First, it had been built a few years after the girls went missing. Second, excavation done to pour the foundation to build the garage should have unearthed the bodies if they were buried there. Third, the cost of digging up that area of the garage would be expensive. Besides, the lead that led Baird and Norland to that spot was said to have come from a psychic. The police passed on digging down even though I understand they've had a couple psychics come in for this case."

"So, do you think the women's bodies are buried there, Booger?"

"Oh, no, no. I think that the parking garage is another rabbit hole. But if I was willing to spare no expense to solve this case, I would work every lead that I had until it either panned out or fell apart. The parking garage is a lead – one that hasn't been disproven. I'd love to see them dig up the spot."

Brian was lost in thought with it all. He didn't blame the cops for not putting more stock in a psychic's vision. The anomaly, it seems to him, could be anything. He said nothing, though.

"Son, in my opinion, there are only two reasons why the

Springfield Police refuse to follow up on that lead. One, they think they know who was responsible for the crime, and the parking garage just doesn't fit into that scenario. Or, two, they or someone with a lot of pull with the police department might be embarrassed by what might be found underneath the concrete."

"What do you mean?"

"There is a possibility that evidence they recovered as a result of the search warrant in Webster County points to the bodies being disposed of elsewhere. I don't give a lot of credibility to rumors, but one that has floated around is that the women were driven to rural Webster County, assaulted, murdered, chopped up, burned or fed to farm animals. We've touched on Webster County, of course, and on the surface, that theory seems far-fetched. But as long as we're speculating, which I don't like to do, I think there may be some truth to it. Look, we know the women disappeared, and we know investigators have taken that property in Webster County seriously enough to search it. Maybe, as a result of their search, they found evidence that the women were in the area. There was speculation they may have found some articles of clothing and remnants of a burned-out van. If they believe the women's final resting place was in that area, there would be no need to search the ground underneath that parking garage."

"Ok, so what about the second reason? You think what the police find could be embarrassing somehow? To who?"

"Well, that's the interesting part. Kathee Baird gave what I've heard others describe as 'a bizarre interview' to a Crime Watch reporter investigating the disappearance, where she stated she was fairly certain she knew who was responsible for the missing women. She added she believes they were killed early on the morning of June 7. She feels that Sherrill Levitt and Suzie Streeter were the intended victims and that Stacy McCall was just in the wrong place at the wrong time. Baird claimed that she was fearful for her life and that she had received threats. She refused to talk about the case further. Through the Crime Watch report, she said, 'There is something very dark in this story. Something super-frightening, when you get down to it, of who you trust. Just be very careful. There's a reason this case hasn't been solved.'

"That caught my attention," Booger continued. "See here, you can either be of the mindset that Kathee Baird is some sort of a quack, a believer in psychics that has hung all her theories of what happened in the case to the bodies being buried below that parking garage – and maybe just wants some attention for herself – or you can be of the mindset that she has uncovered something that no one else has and that she has upset some people in that process. Look, I'm not saying the police did anything wrong, but there's a lot of pride involved here. If those women are under that parking garage, it might mean that certain clues or other directions to take the investigation were dismissed."

"Hmm, that's interesting," Brian said, remembering that just about every law enforcement agency there was involved with this case at one time or another. "Booger, I don't believe the cops were involved, but you've got me thinking."

"Go ahead, then."

"Suppose that Suzie's boyfriend Dustin and his friend Michael Clay were involved in drugs, maybe small-time peddlers that had knowledge of the drug trade in Springfield. Dustin shared that information with Suzie. She broke up with him, not because of the break-in at the mausoleum, but because of his involvement in drugs. When she threatened to go to the police to expose what she knew, she became the target of some pretty bad characters they knew."

"Son, we've already been down this dead-end road before. Those boys didn't have anything to do with the disappearance of those women. Besides, there was absolutely no evidence of drugs being involved in this case," Booger said.

"Just hear me out," Brian replied with a determined voice. "Maybe at one of the parties that night, Suzie was confronted by one of those bad guys, right? He warned her not to go to the police. She either dismissed him or didn't take him seriously. That's when the plan to take care of her was put into action. Someone followed her that night. Maybe they saw her leave Janelle Kirby's house with Stacy following in her car or saw her again from the road as they headed back to Suzie's and made a plan on the spot."

Brian continued, "I believe the vast majority of cops are good, but there's always one or two bad apples. Maybe there was a drug dealer connected with the boys who had a friend on the force – someone he could pay to get tips from or get rid of people. And maybe that's how they got the women out of the house – the bad cop shows up in his old, green van."

"No," Booger said flatly.

"Look, I realize that's not likely. And, trust me, I'm not a conspiracy theory guy. If I was a betting man, I would lay money down that there was no policeman involved. But Francis Lee Robb and Steven Garrison were some bad dudes and were involved with drugs, right? You just got done saying how every lead should be followed until it can be disproven? We know the initial investigation was botched because no one took the women's disappearance seriously at first, and everyone in the world contaminated the crime scene. Couldn't a bad apple steer things in the wrong direction? How can you be so certain no cops were connected to Robb or Garrison?"

"Son, I know what didn't happen, and I'm telling you, the police had nothing to do with this crime."

"How can you be so sure, Booger? Why couldn't the police be involved?"

"Because, son, I was hired to investigate them."

CHAPTER 12

THE BREAK-IN

Brian wondered if Booger said what he thought. "What do you mean? You investigated the police?"

"Yeah, between you and me, I wasn't exactly truthful when I said the Streeter family asked me to investigate the disappearances of the Springfield Three," Booger admitted.

"Okay, so how did you get involved in the case?" Brian asked. He was thinking to himself, this was the strangest trip to Springfield ever.

"There was suspicion during the early days of the case that someone on the Springfield police force might be interfering with the investigation, maybe several people. It was felt certain leads were not being worked properly, and some inaccurate information was being given by anonymous sources to the news media.

"I was approached by someone. I can't tell you who. That person asked me to take a closer look at certain officers. I wasn't sure I wanted to get into all of this with you, but I should be upfront."

"Doesn't the police department have an internal affairs department that normally does that type of thing?" Brian asked, knowing they did.

"Well, now, those aren't foolproof. The fact is that police departments don't always do a good job of shining the spotlight on their own people. There's a culture of loyalty with cops. Internal Affairs is often there for when it's obvious you have a problem. Here, there wasn't any clear evidence of wrongdoing, and no one wanted to suggest there was. This was more of a gut feeling that something was off. Sometimes, it was said to me, it's best to bring in an outsider."

"Hmm. Okay," Brian said, still wondering why Booger would've pretended to be working for the Streeter family.

"Early on, the investigation was micro-managed by the police chief. Everything went through him, all evidence, all assignments, everything - once it became obvious these women were actually missing, and the crime scene had been compromised. There was a lot of pressure on the detectives involved because it was becoming a big case in the media, and now the chief was watching over everyone, too. Pressure is a funny thing. It can bring out the best in people, or it can show you their worst. That pressure didn't let up when the FBI got involved, either. You'd think they'd all cooperate because they all have the same goal, but that's not how it works. These are competitive people. The dynamics are a little different everywhere, but some things never change. Springfield and Greene County actually have a long history of working well together - it's not like that in a lot of places - but they're both local. Everybody hates the feds. They're the big dogs on the block, whatever block you're on. They're the pros. And local cops are sensitive to the stereotype the feds have about local cops: that they're a bunch of bumbling idiots. To become a chief of police for a mid-size town like Springfield, you've got to be a prideful person. You have a bit of an ego. The Springfield Police Chief doesn't want to be shown up by the feds. None of the cops do. So there's pressure to make sure you're doing everything and doing it right."

"Yeah, I can see that," Brian said, thinking to himself that, of course, all the media attention on this would put added pressure on the investigators. "It's natural there'd be those dynamics. It's like how the armed forces are competing with each other."

"Right. The Army hates the Navy and whatnot," Booger said. "Well, anyway, I was asked to look at some local cops, check their backgrounds, take a peep at their bank accounts - and that was off-the-record, you understand? If you ever write about this, the official story is that I got involved because the McCall family asked me to."

"Don't you mean the Streeter family?"

"Exactly," Booger said. "The point is, if you're selling a book, make it a fiction. The real truth isn't believable anyway."

This was all beginning to make sense to Brian, finally. As a reporter, he learned the hard way all the best stuff - the things you really wanted to report - were always told off the record. That's when you knew you were near the truth.

"So what did you find, Booger?"

"Nothing, not a damn thing. As far as I could tell, the officers I looked at were just like all the others on the force: underpaid and overworked. So, I'm telling you, I just don't buy into any scenario that involves a Springfield police officer in the abductions. There were a million eyes on this thing - including my own. Everyone wanted to solve this case for a whole host of reasons."

"No, I get it. Trust me, I do," Brian said, taking a moment to let it all soak in before asking his follow-up question. "Do you think it's possible some perpetrator pretended to be a cop to get the women out of the house? You know the evidence better than I do. It seems an easy explanation, especially given that you were asked to check a couple of people out. Maybe the cops felt there was an impersonator."

"It's possible," Booger said, "but I haven't found any

evidence to support that."

"Yeah, I get it. I just can't get past this thought that there was somebody at that house who found a way - by entering or not - to get those women outside to leave quickly. Someone knocking on the door and flashing a badge could do that."

"Or anyone with a gun. Son, you're speculating," Booger said. "If a cop was asking Sherrill to come outside at 3 in the morning, don't you think that would be suspicious? Besides, even if that worked, one man trying to contain three women and get them inside a van would be highly unlikely."

"Yes, I know. Suppose it was two men, though. We haven't talked much about the two twin brothers, Larry DeWayne Hall and Gary Wayne Hall, who were suspected of pretending to be policemen in order to abduct and assault women. Police interviewed Larry Hall in 2008, and he stated his brother and someone else abducted and murdered the women in Springfield. He, by the way, is suspected of killing between 39 and 54 women, many prostitutes, dating back to the early '80s. Seems to me that those two characters could have abducted the women. I believe Gary Hall even owned a van."

"Yes, what you say is true. However, there are a few holes in the theory that the twins were responsible for the Springfield Three." Booger continued, "First, it's not clear that either brother was in town at the time the women disappeared. Second, there were inconsistencies in Larry Hall's story that didn't match the facts of the case. Third, Larry Hall denied any involvement in the crime, which makes the whole story about his brother less believable. Fourth, the van Gary owned was a different make, model and color than what a witness had described seeing that night."

"But didn't police find evidence in Gary Hall's van that indicated he was in or around Springfield the weekend of June 6, 1992?"

"There was some evidence found in his van that reportedly tied him to the Springfield Three. But specific details of what police took from the van have not been released to the public. One piece of information that did come out was a note with something about Branson and a receipt that indicated the van was in Branson during the time of a vicious assault on two women in a local park in the early '90s. We also know that Larry Hall had some familiarity with the Springfield area because he spent some time in the Federal Medical Center off Kansas Expressway. And, yes, we also know the twins were active in civil war re-enactments, which may have brought them to the Wilson Creek Battlefield. Still, there isn't anything we know of that ties them to Springfield on June 6th or 7th, 1992."

There was a pause, and Brian sighed. Before he could ask another question, though, Booger said, "One thing that is interesting, I have to admit, is that several of the women Larry Hall was accused of murdering were buried near the civil war re-enactment site. In a statement Hall made to investigators from his North Carolina prison in 2008, he said his brother and another man buried the Springfield Three women somewhere in Mark Twain National Park."

"Well, those two sound like prime suspects. Why haven't they been looked at in greater detail?" Brian asked.

"They've been taken seriously. Investigators gave both brothers polygraph tests. They both passed, and like I said, statements made by Larry Hall were not consistent with the crime. Then there was one other thing."

"What?"

"None of either brother's previous known crimes involved abducting three women, especially three women inside a home in a nice neighborhood. The twins seemed to prey on prostitutes, most from truck stops along highways. This crime just doesn't fit them. They went for the long-hanging fruit, so to speak, not anyone that was liable to put up much of a fight or gather attention. Why would they be in the middle of town, right next to an old-money neighborhood?"

"Damn, Booger. Every theory I seem to come up with, you shoot down. Why don't you just tell me who you think committed this crime?" Brian said, showing some frustration.

"I can't do that, son. I told you, in the beginning, there are no shortcuts. I'm not going to give you the answers, and you're going to need to go down a lot of rabbit holes before you find a tunnel," Booger replied.

"I don't even know what you're saying," Brian said, realizing in the moment his temper was shorter than it should be. He didn't like this arrangement, though. He didn't want to be just speculating about everything. He wanted the detective to tell him what he thought. Booger said he couldn't just give him the answers. But why not?

"Son, your dad didn't either forty-some years ago, but eventually, with my help, he arrived at an answer."

"No, he didn't, Booger. Those Lake Honor deaths were never solved. Dad didn't figure out anything."

"Oh, yeah. Well, he reached some closure, as I remember."

"Could you at least tell me the names of the three suspects who were objects of the grand jury investigation in 1994?" Brian asked.

"Son, that grand jury should have never convened. There was no solid evidence. Everything that was presented to them was circumstantial. The whole city wanted someone to be charged, and the police needed to show they were doing everything they could. I think they believed they knew what happened but couldn't really move forward, so they brought what they knew to the grand jury," Booger said, followed by a dramatic pause. "You can't capture a butterfly if you ain't got a net."

"What? Yes, you can, Booger," Brian insisted. "You can

catch one with just your hands. I've done it. That's not your best analogy."

"Well, they're not all winners, kid," Booger said with a laugh.

Booger had a way of aggravating Brian greatly and then easily disarming him.

"Anyway, there was no way that jury was going to have enough evidence to bring any of those three suspects to trial," Booger said. "It was a long shot."

"Okay, who were the three suspects?"

"Well, I think we can safely say that Robert Cox was one of them. Everything is sealed, officially, you know? The other two are a little iffy. Steven Garrison seemed a likely suspect in 1994. He had told authorities that an acquaintance had confessed to kidnapping and killing the three women. He had a connection with rural Webster County, where police searched based on information he provided, and this was the kind of guy who could've done it. So, if I was a betting man, I would say Garrison was the second of the three suspects."

Booger continued after lighting a new cigar. "The third suspect, though, is pure speculation. He could be the person that Steven Garrison said admitted to abducting and killing the three women. Or, it could even be Gerald Carnahan. He lived in the area at the time and was later convicted of abducting and killing an Ozark convenience store clerk, a young lady of eighteen years old. He was also convicted in 1993 of abducting a young college student in Springfield. The truth is there are always a few psychopaths around. I don't know who they brought in because no one told me."

"You know, Booger, I meant to ask you. There was one individual that wasn't listed as a suspect in your war room. His name is Clark Perry Baldwin. What do you know about him?"

"Yes, he's one of those psychopaths I was talking about,

and he had a Springfield connection," Booger said.

The two were talking about Baldwin just weeks before he was arrested in May on suspicion of three murders in Tennessee and Wyoming. In an odd twist of fate, a woman searching for her biological father, who discovered Baldwin was the guy, may have inadvertently given investigators exactly what they needed to solve their old cases. Investigators used what she found from the commercial genealogy database to pinpoint Baldwin as their prime suspect. Investigators trailed him, went through his trash for a DNA sample and discovered that he was the perpetrator.

"That's the trouble with a case like this," Booger said. "It could've been someone who knew the women, or it could've been any number of wackos one of them randomly came across."

"You know," Brian interrupted, "I was watching a television show about Ce Ce Moore. She has solved a lot of crimes by using commercial genealogy databases. Maybe she could solve the mystery of the Springfield Three."

"Possibly," Booger replied. "But she has to have DNA evidence to do her study. If there was any DNA evidence left at the Levitt house in 1992, the police haven't shared that information with the public."

"Yeah, and if DNA was left at the crime scene, the FBI would have certainly run it through their criminal database to see if there was a match."

"Yes, you're right, son. But maybe they ran it through and didn't come up with a match decades ago. That's the situation where someone like Ce Ce Moore can get results when the police can't. She can find ancestors with like DNA, use that to develop a family tree and eventually narrow the suspect pool down to a few or sometimes one person."

"But getting back to Clark Perry Baldwin, I read the authorities have or are still looking at him as a suspect in the murder of Gloria Jean Barnes in 1997. Her body was found near the Seven Gables, a restaurant and truck stop in north Springfield. Baldwin lived in Springfield at the time, as he did in 1992 when the three women disappeared. He was a cross-country truck driver for Marten Transport, right?"

"Yes. He could be involved in any number of disappearances. There are a lot of missing women out there. Look, the problem with Baldwin is we don't know what we don't know. Is he a possible suspect? Absolutely. But I'll say this, we know where the Levitt house is, and it's not near a highway. He doesn't seem likely to me."

"You know, Booger, you could give me a peak at the information you brought down from your office. I know you have your own thoughts about who's responsible. Why do you need me to draw it all out of you?"

"No, son. I'm leading you in the right direction. You just need to follow the evidence. Did you ever see the movie, 'All the President's Men?'"

"Of course, that is a great one. I was a reporter, you know. Our journalism teacher in high school made us watch it. It was good."

"Well then, you must remember Deep Throat?"

"Yes, he was the person in the parking garage that provided Bob Woodward clues to what Watergate was all about."

"That's right. But Deep Throat never provided Woodward the answers, even though he knew what they were. He always told him to follow the evidence.

"Wait a second, Booger. So you're trying to tell me you're Deep Throat?"

"No, I'm like Deep Throat. Son, I'm leading you toward the answers. You just don't realize it yet."

Suddenly a loud clamor of thunder shook the building. Lights flickered.

Rose came running into the man cave. "That was close,"

she yelled. "Are you sure that generator won't shut off? I can't imagine how dark this place would be without lights."

"Darker than a black cat in a mud pit," Booger replied.

"Damn, old man, it would be nice to have some windows in this dungeon."

"Bach-e-lor-pad, sweetie. Besides, I'm not a big fan of windows."

The storm, which was intensifying, prompted a break in the action. The boys decided to eat and refill their coffee. Thunder was booming more often now, and it seemed to be getting closer, occasionally shaking the building. The lights flickered on and off a dozen times during the height of the storm. Booger tried to assure Rose the generator would keep them on throughout the storm, but she didn't like not being able to see for herself what was happening outside.

"There's nothing like the feeling of being locked in a tomb hidden behind a secret wall that no one knows about, with the only thing keeping us from being buried alive are one hundred year old walls from a previously condemned building," Rose replied nervously.

"OK, negative, Nancy. Some of the walls are new," Booger said, smiling. "Do you really think that I would keep you in here if I didn't think it was safe?" Booger replied.

"I'm just honored you even told me about it," she said with a smirk.

Booger pressed on. "Sweetie, I really don't think there is anything to worry about unless we get hit by a tornado or unless there's an earthquake. Why don't I pour you a shot of rye whiskey, Rose?"

"You know that I don't drink, you old fool."

"Consider it medicine to calm your nerves. How about if I get you a cup of coffee and we'll put a little in your cup? You won't even taste it."

"Okay, but just a little," she said. "I'm not trying to fall asleep or throw my top off."

Brian couldn't help but wonder just how close these two were when he wasn't around.

Rose went and grabbed her coffee from the kitchen, which was half full, and handed it to Booger. She made sure to watch him closely with his pour. "That's enough!"

Booger stopped.

"You tried to sneak as much in as you could, didn't you?"

"No, just about a teaspoon full," he said.

She took a sip and began to choke. "Darn it, Booger, I can barely taste the coffee."

"Oh, that's nothing," he said with a laugh. "Trust me, hun. Two cups of Booger's special coffee, and you won't have any worries."

"Two cups of this, and I'll be passed out on the floor."

"Well, if you do, rest assured I won't let Brian take advantage of you when that happens."

"I'm not worried about Brian," Rose said, giving Booger a nasty look.

Two cups of coffee and 45 minutes later, Rose was sound asleep in the double-wide recliner. Booger got a blanket and a pillow from his bedroom and covered her. "She'll be out 'til morning. She's a lightweight, and I knew a couple of shots would calm her down," he said to Brian.

Afterward, Booger and Brian went into the main room to keep an eye on the video surveillance monitors.

There was nothing to see. The storm had rendered the cameras useless. Rain was regularly coming down sideways and in waves causing the cameras to fog up and limiting visibility, but they watched anyway, hoping to see the glimmer of approaching headlights like they had the night before.

"Booger, who do you think the men are that came last

night, the ones that bugged your phone? Are you certain they aren't police?"

"I'm not certain of anything. This case has turned me around a few times, and I'm a big boy who isn't easy to turn around, can't you tell," Booger said with a chuckle. "I've learned to just follow the facts and not to convince myself I know more than I do. Also, I'm at a disadvantage. The police and the FBI are holding a lot back. All for good reasons, of course, but they know details of the crime and have evidence about suspects I don't have access to. The line between truth and fiction - between what I know and what I've imagined - has been blurred over the years. The older I get, the less I know."

The two sat in silence for a moment, just listening to the storm above. It was a humbling reminder to Brian of how much was out of their control. He imagined they were two men at sea, sitting in the captain's quarters, clinging to their chairs as they rose and fell in thirty feet waves. The storm could wipe them out at any time, Brian thought, along with the little evidence they were guarding from who knows who.

"Brian, I don't believe cops were the ones that tried to break in last night. Men pretending to be cops seems more likely to me. I can understand why you were fixated on the cop idea with the women, you know?"

"Well, I wasn't fixated," Brian said.

Booger continued without listening. "If I wanted to get someone to do exactly what I wanted them to do without any resistance and no questions asked, I would pretend to be a cop. Hell, if you look at some of the most notorious serial killers over the years - Ted Bundy, Henry Lee Lucas and Gary Ridgeway, the Green River killer - they all used a ruse of being a cop to earn quick trust with some of their victims."

"Booger, you seem to be making a case for someone pretending to be a policeman abducting the Springfield Three,"

Brian said with a smile.

"Maybe I am, son. That would explain why nothing seemed to be disturbed in the Levitt home. It would explain why the women came outside without putting up a fight. Consider a couple of men dressed in police uniforms coming to your house in the early morning hours, just after your daughter and a friend have returned home. They bang on the door. They announce themselves as police officers. It's a ruse that would likely work even at that hour of the morning."

"That's what I'm saying," Brian said excitedly. "I mean, who knows, but."

Booger continued, again not seeming to hear Brian. "The police officer or officers say they spotted the girls driving home erratically. Maybe they said the girls ran a stop light. Maybe they say one of the girls hit something. It would certainly be believable. They would come outside to talk to the police. Maybe they wouldn't open the door for someone saying they were with the gas company, but they would surely open the door and come outside for a policeman."

"Yes, exactly," Brian said, considering it a small victory that he was seeing Booger thinking like he had earlier.

"But," Booger added, "it doesn't explain the van."

Brian felt a bit deflated.

"Wouldn't the women be suspicious if there was no police car in sight?" Booger asked, clearly not really wanting Brian to respond. "Maybe not, though, if the man or men pretended to be off-duty or undercover."

"Yes," Brian said.

"But then what about the open window in Sherrill's room and the screen found lying outside? What about the blinds that were disturbed in Suzie's room? What about the obscene phone calls left on the answering machine?" Booger said. "If the women came outside voluntarily, how do you explain those things?"

Now, Brian really felt he was at sea. "Well, maybe not all clues are good clues, Booger," Brian said, attempting to answer the questions. "Maybe the screen had come off that window before that night. Maybe the window was opened by Sherrill earlier in the evening to get fresh air flowing in her room. The blinds in Suzie's room might have been disturbed when Suzie rushed to the window to see who was knocking on the door at around 3 a.m. Not all clues have to be neatly tied to the crime."

"Exactly, son. Now you're thinking like a detective," Booger said. "I think I'm a little proud. You gotta see these things from all angles. You have to cast doubt on your own assumptions."

Brian didn't know whether to be pleased or irritated.

"Keep going," Booger said.

"Well," Brian said, unsure what Booger was looking for, "the police didn't seem to find any fingerprints, DNA or anything inside the house that may have been related to the abductions. That seems to indicate that the women left the house voluntarily."

"Right!" Booger said.

"What about the obscene phone calls on the family answering machine?" Brian asked.

"Well, friends erased those messages, so there was no way for the police to follow up on that clue. But consider why someone would leave an obscene message on an answering machine, a recorded message that, if it hadn't been erased, police could have likely tracked down the source of the call. Those calls could've been made by kids as some part of a childish prank, but who knows, right? It could have been someone involved or someone wanting to sidetrack investigators. The trick is sorting out real clues from things that appear to be clues. Maybe the porch-light cover being broken is nothing. It could've been loose and fell on its own hours after the women were gone. We don't know."

"True. So, if it was one or two men pretending to be police officers that knocked on the Levitt's door and got the three women outside, when do you suppose the women realized they were in trouble?" Brian asked.

"Almost immediately, I suspect," Booger said. "I believe it's more likely that two men were involved in the abduction and that those men moved quickly as soon as all three women were outside on the porch. One would have gotten between the women and the front door, preventing an exit back into the house. There could have been a brief struggle on the porch, which would explain the light fixture. That's what I think. It's not so different from you. I don't know about the uniforms because there were no witnesses of that, but it makes sense if there was a knock on the door. 'If' being the most important word there. Maybe one person climbed in through the window, and another waited on the porch."

Brian was pleased. This is what he'd wanted. He wanted to know he wasn't crazy. He wanted to know what Booger thought and to get some validation, too.

"You never know. The FBI could have a hair sample, and they're waiting for the right person to try and find their man through a database.

Suddenly, the conversation came to a stop. A loud siren blasted in the background. It was a nearby tornado siren. A couple of funnel clouds were spotted in the city.

The video surveillance monitors went dark about five minutes after the sirens started. The wind could be heard rattling the brick façade of the building. Brian and Booger sat still, trying to hear the tell-tale train sound a tornado makes or see something, anything, on the monitors.

Moments later, an alarm sounded on the wall above the video screens. Booger and Brian watched as one motion detector light went off, followed a few seconds later by another. The first alarm that sounded was a motion sensor outside the building. Not long after, a motion sensor from inside the building went off.

A few seconds later, the lights flickered twice, and then the room went dark. The generator had stopped working.

"They're here," Booger said softly.

CHAPTER 13

THE EYE OF THE STORM

The room was completely dark. The sound of the sensor alarms were ringing in Brian's head. He couldn't move, partly out of fear and partly because he was completely disoriented by the dark. To him, it was like waking in the middle of the night in his bedroom with no lights on. He thought that was disorienting, but this was much worse. His bedroom had windows. There was always some sort of light that came in from outside, even on the darkest of nights. In Booger's secret room, he suddenly felt like he was in a vault. He felt he was completely blind and was unsure how to maneuver in unfamiliar surroundings.

"Don't worry," Booger said quietly. "Your eyes will adjust shortly."

Brian didn't believe him. "Do you have a flashlight or maybe a few candles, Booger?"

"Sure, we have the flashlights we brought down from upstairs, but damn if I can find them in the dark."

"Can you at least turn off that blasted alarm?"

"Don't worry. It will go off any time now. Without power, the alarm will use up whatever backup battery power it has and stop."

Sure enough, a minute later and the alarm went silent.

Tornado sirens, however, could be heard in the background.

"Okay, son, I'm going to make my way over to the door. If I can get it open, we should get a little light from the outside windows in the warehouse. I may need your help, though. I normally just press a button, and the door opens automatically, similar to an automated garage door opener. But with no electricity, we're going to need to open it manually. I've never done that before, so I'm not exactly sure how difficult that is going to be. Why don't you hold on to my belt, and I'll guide you to the door."

"Okay, but where are you?"

"We're only a few feet apart. I'll back up to you, reach out when you feel me and grab onto the back of my belt." Booger moved backward in the direction of Brian's voice. When they touched, Brian reached out to grab Booger's belt. "That's not my belt, boy. Try a little higher."

When Brian had hold of the belt, Booger started moving slowly toward the door. After colliding with a table twice, he managed to get to the wall, following his hands to the door. With both pulling on the opening, they managed to pry it open enough to let in some light from the large windows in the warehouse.

It wasn't much, but it was enough to get the blinded men oriented to their surroundings. Booger moved slowly into his bedroom and emerged a few minutes later with his gun and a flashlight.

"Take the flashlight, son. Close the door after I leave and use it to find Rose's purse. Inside will be the other gun. It should be loaded. All you need to do is remove the safety, and it will be ready. If I'm not back by daybreak, grab the information that I brought down from the office. It's in my bedroom closet. Next to it will be a GPS tracking device. Grab it, too. Then, wake up, Rose, and both of you get out of the warehouse. Drive back to St. Louis. Don't stop for anything, and don't let anyone stop you.

I think you'll be safe when the sun comes up. But if someone is outside waiting, use the gun if you have to," Booger was straining to be quiet. Brian could tell the detective was being as direct and intentional with his words as possible.

Booger continued. "There's a special agent, Terrence Moffitt. He works in the FBI's St. Louis field office. Tell him I sent you and give him the information and the GPS device. If the men that broke in tonight take the information in the war room, and I suspect they will, that GPS device should lead the FBI to wherever they take that information. He'll know what to do with it."

"Wait," Brian said with a concerned look. "Where are you going?"

"I'm going to see who set off the alarms."

"I want to come with you, Booger."

"No, son. I need you to stay here and take care of Rose. If I don't come back by daybreak, you make sure she gets out of here safely. Take her back to St. Louis with you, at least until everything blows over."

Without saying another word, Booger stepped out into the warehouse closing the hidden door behind him.

Brian stood there at the door, not sure of what to do next. Booger instructed him to get the gun out of Rose's purse. He wasn't going to do that, not yet, anyway. He had never fired a gun before; besides, his hands were shaking so much now he wasn't even sure he could hold the gun. This was not a situation that he even considered being involved in when he left St. Louis two days earlier to do an interview. His mind was racing, but it was going in circles, unable to formulate any sort of coherent thought. Brian had never been this scared before. It was because of the way Booger looked at him. Booger was worried. The detective had always been cool, Brian thought and could shake off anything. *Booger was prepared for someone to try and break in, so what threw him off? Was it the storm?* Brian wondered. He imagined if someone managed to break in, they'd be able to see him or them on the video monitor. He never would've thought Booger would leave and want Brian to find and grab a gun in the dark. *What the hell is going on? Did Booger think they wanted to kill him? He wants me to take Rose to St. Louis?*

The storm was still raging all around him. Brian realized he needed to take a deep breath. He was the kind of guy who liked balance and needed to operate according to a larger plan. He sought harmony and good humor with others. He liked people who were fair-minded and situations that were predictable – and a quick exit when they weren't. He worked hard to always be the captain of a steady ship. In this moment, everything was turned upside down.

It was a lot for him to take in. *I want to see my family,* Brian thought.

Recent years had been unkind to him. His wife, Valerie, had gotten sick in 2016, and doctors couldn't figure out what was going on. She had contracted some sort of parasite from a family friend's rescued dog – of that, they were fairly certain – but, then, the medicine, which the whole family took as a precaution, had wrought its own damage. It completely stunted her immune system and left her with nerve damage and a host of other physical problems, not to mention anxiety and depression. For a couple of years, they went to see one doctor after another, never finding relief for her. It took a toll on their marriage, but not all at once.

Brian had left the high-stress world of journalism shortly after Valerie's health issues became serious. He had been burnt out, and it wouldn't have taken much for him to bolt. His rough plan was to eventually work for his dad's marketing company because his dad had expressed an interest in wanting to retire in a few years. In 2017, that's what Brian did; he started working for

Dad. But Brian's youngest son was just starting high school, and Valerie had a strong support network in Springfield, so moving everyone there was off the table. Their carefully crafted plan was to make due until Mason graduated in 2021 and then to sell the house and settle in St. Louis permanently. Brian would travel a lot in the meantime, staying in Dad's basement during the week and then going home on the weekends. By late 2019, however, the demands of work and travel were taking their toll on him, so Brian got an apartment in St. Louis. By this time, though, Valerie and Brian were fighting a lot. Truthfully, Brian blamed himself for much of their problems. He could never relieve his wife's pain. He wasn't there for her, too. Brian was focused on work. Their marriage suffered. After the holidays, they separated.

Their plan had fallen apart. Brian had hoped to sort some things out with his wife, to see his kids, to maybe get back what had been lost. The pandemic complicated all of that. Now, here he was, two miles away from his home, trying to understand a case from his childhood, needing to find a gun in the dark. God, it seemed, didn't care about Brian's plans.

He took a deep breath. In. Out. For a moment, time had stopped.

Suddenly, Brian could hear the storm again. He took this as a good sign. If the tornado was near, it might be silent. Brian then thought he should do what Booger said. He should find Rose's purse and get her gun. He needed to put one foot in front of the other. He had a flashlight. It wasn't much, but he had a flashlight.

Things felt clearer now. He had a purpose. He had direction. Brian had to let go of his expectations. He had to deal with the reality of the situation in front of him. "I need Rose's gun," he said quietly to himself.

Brian realized there was something interesting about the fact that in what seemed like a moment of panic for Booger, Rose was top of mind. Yes, Booger had wanted to get that evidence to the FBI in St. Louis, but where Brian had seen real panic in his eyes was when Booger mentioned Rose. There was something unique about that relationship. They argued back and forth at times, but it wasn't mean-spirited. It was a playful thing. They cared about each other, Brian thought. In a weird way, they were like an old, married couple. There must've been more to them than he'd seen on the surface. Brian knew Booger had been married once, a long time ago. His wife had died when she was young. They had no children. Had he ever fallen in love again?

Rose had been married before, too, but it hadn't seemed like a good marriage. Had she built walls up around herself? Did she love Booger? Did he love her? Brian's mind was racing now, but he wasn't panicked like before as he moved purposefully with the flashlight guiding his way. He would check on Rose first, he decided. When he got inside the room and to her bedside, he could hear her snoring from beneath the covers. She was sound asleep. He would head to the kitchen then and find her purse. The tornado sirens stopped.

***

Booger, meanwhile, moved slowly and quietly through the warehouse. The storm was still strong but seemed to be easing up a bit. The thunder was softer now as it moved farther away. The intense wind had shattered a couple of windows on the main floor. Water had come in from outside and was beginning to puddle near them on the floor. Booger moved on, gun drawn, quietly up the stairs.

As Booger reached the top floor, he saw that the door was open to the office that led to the war room. Booger turned off the flashlight. The open door provided enough light for him to see, and he felt he needed the element of surprise. There was no need to advertise to anyone that he was there. As Booger approached the door slowly, he raised his gun. Voices could be heard from inside. Whoever had broken into the building was still there. As he reached the entryway, he tried to peak around the corner. No one was in the main area where Rose had her desk. From the entrance, however, Booger could see two beams of light moving around in the war room.

The strangers had taken his bait. They had come for the information he had in the war room. Now, Booger had to make sure that they weren't going to get away.

As he moved through the office and neared the entrance to the war room, he could see two shadowy figures inside. They were kneeling down, looking through information they had removed from the corkboards on the walls. Their backs were to Booger, making it easier for him to sneak up behind them, to take them by surprise.

Six feet from the two men, he announced his presence. "Put your hands up, boys! Stand up!" That was when he heard someone behind him. Before he had a chance to turn around, he was struck on the back of the head. It just numbed him at first. He turned around. Then the second blow came before he could defend himself. That one knocked him out. He dropped the gun and fell to the floor.

The next thing he knew, the smell of smoke penetrated his nose and moved rapidly to his lungs, irritating his air passages, making it difficult to breathe. He coughed, then choked, gasping for air. He realized, too, that he could hear the fire alarm. That was how he woke him up. His head was spinning. The pain in his head was enormous. He struggled to get to his feet, to open his eyes. The smoke and heat were burning his eyes. That's when his survival instincts kicked in. He covered his mouth and moved toward the office door. Fire was all around him, but he had a path to the door. He stumbled forward through it.

The smoke had blanketed the hallway outside his office. That's when he first heard the approaching fire trucks, their sirens echoing through the night, the sounds getting louder and louder. Booger, barely able to see, moved in the direction of the stairwell, trying to hold his breath, still covering his mouth. Soon he reached the stairs and began moving down. The smoke was less intense now. He gasped for air as soon as he thought he was safe.

Booger was dizzy. His body swayed with every step he took. Sharp, intense pains were coming from the back of his head. His mind told him to move. His body demanded that he lay down. Just before he reached the second floor, his body won the argument. Booger fell to the ground, his mind unable to will his body any farther.

***

Back in the kitchen, Brian found Rose's purse and gun and was just sitting and listening in the dark. He had thought he'd heard Booger's voice at one point, then a brief commotion, but it was all hard to tell. He never heard a gunshot, which he was thankful for. Then he was pretty sure he'd heard footsteps on the stairwell. He told himself that no one should know about Booger's secret bunker. He'd stay put until he was sure things were safe. Then, he thought he heard the front door before things went silent. The storm had faded into the background now, and the threat of the tornado was clearly over.

Brian waited. "What should I do? Is it safe to check on Booger?" He was assuming the detective had confronted whoever had entered the warehouse, and they got away, but he couldn't be sure. Brian thought he should stay put for a bit and listen for more clues.

It wouldn't take long. After a few minutes of eerie silence, the fire alarm started blasting, and Brian hopped into action. He rushed into the room where Rose was sleeping. "Get up, Rose," he said. "We need to leave now."

She struggled to wake from a sound sleep. "What's going

on?" she asked, rubbing her eyes and yawning.

"I think the building is on fire," he said. "We need to get out of here now."

***

Fear shot through Rose's body as she awoke suddenly. She had always had a sick feeling about being trapped in a room without windows and no clear exits.

Still waking up, she asked Brian, "Where's Booger?"

"I'm not sure. Someone broke in. Before he went upstairs, he told me to get you out of here once it was safe. I think whoever was here might have left. Then I heard the alarm," Brian said. "C'mon, we've gotta go."

"We can't get trapped in here, Brian. I've seen "Towering Inferno." They try to run through the flames, and it doesn't work out. Don't panic. We will find a way. We have no other choice," Brian said.

***

Thankfully for Brian, he had never watched the movie "Towering Inferno." His mind had no thoughts of the flames that might be waiting for him on the other side of the door. He only knew that door was the way outside, and that's where he needed to take Rose. He had promised Booger that he would take care of her in the event that he didn't come back by sunrise. It wasn't morning yet, but Brian figured the fire alarm was a good enough signal that something had gone terribly wrong with Booger's plan, and there was a decent chance that he wasn't coming back.

When he reached the hidden door, it took all his strength to open it. When he did, smoke began pouring into the room. Rose closed her eyes. Her legs went limp. He pulled her into the warehouse, closing the secret door behind him.

"Come on, Rose. We've got to hurry," he said.

Brian put his arms under her shoulders and lifted her. She was a tiny woman, but her legs had gone limp in the confusion and smoke, making her difficult to carry.

As he moved through the empty warehouse, he saw the lights and heard the sounds of the fire engines outside. He heard the sounds of firefighters rushing into the building and up the stairs.

Where is Booger? he wondered. Thick smoke was pouring in from the stairwell, and he could hear the sounds of fire cracking from above.

"Help," he yelled as he got close to the side door.

Two firefighters heard his yell and rushed in to help, one taking Rose and carrying her outside while the other helped Brian to get out of the building.

Brian never saw the fire, only the smoke, until he got outside. That's when he saw the flames shooting from windows on the upper floor. Booger's office was engulfed in fire.

A firefighter rushed Brian to a paramedic waiting with an oxygen mask. Rose was already in the ambulance, lying down, taking oxygen.

"Wait," Brian yelled before they put the oxygen mask on him. "Did Booger McClain make it out of the building?" he asked desperately.

"We just got here a minute ago, but no one else has come out of the building," a firefighter said. "Where would he be?"

"On the upper floor, in his office," Brian responded. "Oh, God. Someone had broken in, and he went upstairs."

The firefighter got on his radio. "We've got someone on the upper floor. Look for him."

A minute or so later, two firefighters emerged from the building carrying a body.

"Oh my God, is that Booger?" Rose screamed, tears flowing down her face.

"He was on the second floor," one of the firefighters said to the guy who'd called out on the radio. The firefighters carried the man to a waiting ambulance, shut the rear door, and the ambulance raced out of the parking lot, lights and sirens blazing.

"That had to be Booger," Brian said to Rose, but they never got a good look at him.

The fire had destroyed the upper floor, including Booger's office and the war room. Much of the second floor was damaged too, and the stain of black smoke was around every window and crevice. Brian and Rose watched it all from a safe distance wearing oxygen masks and wrapped in blankets they'd been given. The main floor, it appeared, remained in tack. Remnants of the storm had kept most of the damage inside the building, and the firefighters must've gotten there quickly. Everything was contained within an hour.

The building was marked unsafe. Windows were boarded up, police tape was strung around the outer perimeter, and warning signs were posted.

After giving statements, Brian and Rose spent the rest of the night in the hospital as a precaution. Brian knew Fire Chief Dave Pennington from high school, and when he showed up on the scene, he had politely insisted on as much. They were fine, but Rose, in particular, had benefited from the oxygen mask, so they monitored them at the hospital for a couple of hours.

It was while Brian was lying in that hospital bed that he suddenly realized in his rush to get out of Booger's living quarters he had forgotten to take the evidence Booger brought down from upstairs, as well as the GPS tracking device.

Without them, he could not provide what was contained in the information to the FBI, to Special Agent Terrence Moffitt, even if he were able to get back to St. Louis. And, without the GPS tracking device, Booger would not be able to find the men that broke into the building. Brian would need to return to the warehouse and get those items as soon as he was released from the hospital.

Just before being released, two detectives entered Brian's hospital room. They had already talked to Rose. It was a basic police tactic to separate witnesses to see if they had consistent stories.

"Mr. Brown, could you tell us what brought you to Springfield," one detective asked.

"Why? Am I in some sort of trouble?"

"No, just routine questions, Mr. Brown."

"Okay, I came here to interview Booger McClain."

"Are you a reporter?"

"No. I used to be, but not anymore. I do some freelance writing."

"So why did you want to interview Mr. McClain?"

"He's an interesting character. I thought he might be a good conversation that he might have some colorful stories I could turn into an article or possibly use for a book. My dad knew him."

That's when the other detective spoke up. "He was a big man, tall and thick, but not fat, intimidating, with the serious look of a person that had probably never smiled his entire life. Am I right?"

"That's right."

"So, just a little interview, huh?" the first detective asked.

"Yes," Brian said, unsure where this was going or just how much he should say.

"Come on, Mr. Brown, aren't you leaving something out?" the first detective asked. "We know you're here to write a story about the Springfield Three. You thought Mr. McClain could provide you a perspective into the case that you might not get talking to investigators or family members. You decided to take a shortcut to get a story full of half-truths and innuendos just like all the other fake news people out there that draw conclusions before getting the facts."

Brian was shocked. He said nothing in response.

"Let me tell you something about Booger McClain. He's a blowhard, full of crap. He couldn't cut it as a policeman, so he became a private eye. Well, whatever information that man told you is pure horse manure and if you choose to print any of it, I'm afraid you're going to make a lot of people very upset."

"Okay, is that a threat?" Brian asked

The other detective spoke up. "No, son, no one is threatening you. We just don't want you to be embarrassed by writing things that aren't true."

It was obvious to Brian that the two detectives were playing some sort of game of good cop, bad cop. It might have been comical had Brian not just been through what he had. "Fine," Brian responded.

"Son," the good cop said, "What were you doing in that warehouse last night?"

"I was there interviewing Booger. He asked me to spend the night to keep him company, so he could stay awake to watch the feeds from the video cameras. There had been an attempted break-in at the office the night before. And he thought the people might come back last night."

"That's odd. There was no report of an attempted break-in two nights ago. Do you know if he called the police?"

"No, I don't think so. Nothing was taken."

It was the bad cop's turn. "So, Mr. McClain wanted you there to protect him in case of another break-in? I have a little trouble buying that."

"No, it wasn't like that. Someone had broken into my car. I found a listening device. Booger was afraid the men might be after me. He wanted me to stay and Rose too because he thought we would be safer there."

"Son, we found your car. We found Booger's and Rose's, too. There was no sign that any of the cars had been disturbed.

Are you sure there was a listening device inside, not just some loose wires and an active imagination?"

"I'm sure," Brian responded.

"Again, I'm concerned that you think someone has attempted to break into the warehouse and even gone to the trouble of planting a listening device in your car, yet none of you were concerned enough to call the police."

"Son, where exactly were you in the warehouse last night?"

"I was in an apartment, a place Booger had built to live in on the ground floor."

Bad cops turn again. "Oh, that's the icing on the cake. Boy, we've been through every inch of that warehouse. There is no apartment. Now tell us where in the hell you spent last night."

"Have you talked to Rose?"

"Yes, we talked to her."

"What did she tell you?"

"I'm not going to tell you that son. I want to hear what you have to say."

Brian thought for a bit. He didn't know if he could trust the police. He decided not to tell them about the hidden door and what was behind it. He took a chance that Rose had not said anything about it either.

"It wasn't really an apartment. It was a place he had in the back of the warehouse on the main floor. It was no more than a few blankets laid out on the floor, a place he could sleep if he didn't want to go home at night."

"That's the interesting thing, son. Mr. McClain sold his home a few months ago. From what we can determine, he left no forwarding address. Do you happen to know where he was living?"

"No, I don't. I only met with him at the office."

"Funny thing, Rose didn't know he had sold his house. She had no idea where he was living either."

"Son, were you the one that pulled the fire alarm?"

"No."

"That's weird. From what we can determine, there was only one fire alarm in the building. It was on the main floor near the side door. There were only a handful of smoke detectors in the building. None were operational. Someone flipped the fire alarm. Maybe it was Mr. McClain."

"One other question, Mr. Brown. Do you know why there were so many security cameras in and around the building?"

"Booger had told me that there were several break-ins, and he put up the cameras to get evidence of anyone that tried to break in again."

"Thirteen cameras, doesn't that seem a little excessive?"

"I don't know. Maybe he was worried about something else. I only met him two days ago. I don't know much about him."

"Can I ask you a question, detective?"

"Sure, what is it?"

"Did you catch the men that started the fire?"

"Son, I have no idea what you're talking about. We understand the fire was caused by a lightning strike," the bad cop said with a smile. "What makes you think otherwise, Mr. Brown?"

"I don't know, but I suggest you talk to Booger about that," Brian said. "He was sure someone broke into the warehouse last night. The motion sensors he had outside and inside both went off. That's why he went upstairs to confront whoever broke in."

"Son, we've seen no evidence of a break-in. Lightning struck the upper floor, the office where Mr. McClain worked. Fire investigators said the fire originated in one room of Mr. McClain's office; that it spread from there."

"No, that can't be," Brian replied. I think I would have known if lightning struck the building. Besides, I heard the motion sensors go off. Someone had to be in the building."

"Son, when a lightning strike happens, it fries every power source nearby. The lightning set off the motion sensors. We see things like that all the time. Hell, maybe it was the lightning strike that set off the fire alarm, too," the bad cop said with a laugh.

"Look, I just think you need to speak to Booger McClain. He has proof that someone broke in two nights ago and came back last night. They had to be the ones that started the fire. I don't pretend to know any more than that. You really need to talk to Booger."

"Son, that's going to be impossible," the good cop said in a somber tone. "Booger McClain is dead."

CHAPTER 14

A VOICE FROM THE GRAVE

Brian was in shock. He had just been with Booger a few hours earlier.

"No. No way. This can't be. What was his cause of death?" Brian asked.

"Smoke inhalation," the detective said.

"Can I see him?" Brian asked.

"No son. Only next of kin can see him."

"But he doesn't have any next of kin."

"He has a brother, well, half-brother, actually. Maybe you didn't know about him. He's a field agent for the FBI, a man named Terrence Moffitt. He's coming down from St. Louis today to claim the body."

"Are they going to perform an autopsy?" Brian asked.

"There's no need for that. The medical examiner already determined that he died from smoke inhalation."

"Does Rose know?"

"Yes, we talked to her before you. She took it pretty hard. The doctor gave her a sedative. I think she'll be sleeping for a while."

Brian just sat there with his mouth open for a moment. He just couldn't believe it. And yet, he knew how the smoke was billowing from the stairwell. It wasn't like what the detective said was impossible. Brian had been worried about Booger's condition.

"Mr. Brown, will you be going back home as soon as you're released?" the nicer cop asked.

"I don't know. I hadn't really thought of it," Brian said, still processing it all.

"Probably best if you did. You won't be talking to Mr. McClain anymore, so I doubt there's any need to stick around," the bad cop said.

This really irritated Brian. He wondered why it should matter where he went or what he did. "Well, the fact is, detective, that I have family here. I will probably spend some time with them before I go back," he said in a deliberate tone. "And furthermore...."

"We understand, Mr. Brown. Enjoy the rest of your stay," the good cop interrupted suddenly, directing his colleague with a hand at his back as both men walked out of the hospital room.

A few minutes later, a nurse walked in. "The doctor is releasing you, Mr. Brown. You can go home as soon as you sign the paperwork."

"I'd like to visit with Rose first, the woman who came in with me."

"I'm afraid you are too late. She was released about twenty minutes ago?"

"What?"

"She's already left the hospital."

"No, that can't be. The two detectives who were in here told me she was given a sedative and that she was sound asleep."

"Well, I think they must have been mistaken. She didn't receive any sedative that I'm aware of, and I saw her leave the hospital myself."

Brian was puzzled. He wasn't sure what to believe. "What

is going on?" he said in front of the nurse, but under his breath and not directed at her.

"Your clothes are here in the chair, sir. I'll be back in a minute with a wheelchair to release you." When she came back, Brian said, "Thank you, but that's not necessary. I can walk."

"Hospital policy, sir," she said. "Everyone needs to be wheeled out."

"Okay," Brian said, sitting down in the wheelchair, still spinning about how quickly things had changed. It was when he was near the front entrance to the hospital that he realized he didn't have his vehicle.

"Hey, I just realized that an ambulance brought me here. I don't have my car," he said to the nurse.

"No worries, sir. We can call a taxi, or you can request an Uber if you like, but you'll need to wait outside. That's hospital policy for discharged patients."

"Okay, yeah. I'll get an Uber."

She pulled the wheelchair outside near the curb, and Brian got out. After the nurse went inside, and while he searched through his app to find a ride, a black Chevy Malibu pulled up in front of Brian. A short, muscular man, about fifty years old, with a mustache and bald head, stepped out of the car. "Brian Brown?" he asked.

"Yes," Brian said, puzzled.

"I'm special agent Terrence Moffitt. Get in my car."

Brian couldn't believe it. This was Booger's brother – and an FBI agent? "Um, okay. What is going on? Where are you taking me?" Brian asked.

"A safe house. Rose is there, too."

"What? Why? Are we in danger?"

"No, it's just a precaution. I'll explain everything when we get there."

From the hospital, he drove to Battlefield Road, west to

Kansas Expressway, then north, west, and back east for a bit, zig-zagging through several residential neighborhoods before finally stopping in the driveway of a small ranch-style home on the west side of town. It was a quiet neighborhood. Special Agent Moffitt got out of the car, opened up the garage door, got back in the car and parked it inside.

"I'm afraid I've got another surprise for you too, Mr. Brown."

"What's that? And please call me Brian."

"Okay, Brian, I don't want this to come to too much of a shock to you, especially after Rose's reaction to the news, but Booger McClain is alive."

"What? Is this some kind of joke?"

"Yes, he's inside the house, and this is not a joke."

"But, I saw him carried out of the warehouse, and the two detectives that visited me said he was dead."

"Yes, I'm aware. I'm sorry to say you've been misled. Oh, Booger was hurt, all right. His head required a few stitches. But, as I'm sure you're aware, his head is pretty thick. Still, he suffered a concussion. He had some smoke in his lungs too, but not enough to do any real damage. He just needs a few days of rest, and he'll be just fine."

"But why pretend he's dead? I don't understand?"

"Let's go inside, and I'll explain everything to you."

They walked into the house. Rose, excited to see Brian, came running to him, reached out her arms and gave him a big hug.

"Did he tell you the good news, Brian? Booger's alive. He's doing just fine, resting in a bedroom. I know he wants to see you as soon as possible."

"Is it okay if I see him before we talk, Special Agent?"

"Yeah, go ahead, just don't be too long. He needs to rest. It's the bedroom on the left, the one with the door closed."

"Thanks."

The house was small, with a living room, kitchen, breakfast nook, small dining room and a narrow hallway with two bedrooms on the right and one bedroom on the left. There was a tiny, full bath on the left, also. Brian walked to the bedroom on the left and knocked on the door.

"Come in," Booger replied.

He was lying in bed, pajamas on, propped up by three pillows, reading a newspaper. A half-smoked cigar was sitting in an ashtray on a nightstand to the right of the bed. It was lit with small clouds of smoke gently rising from its embered tip. A cup of Rose's strong black coffee was next to it.

"Well, you look comfortable," Brian said, irritated but trying to smile.

"And you look confused," Booger replied.

"I am. What is going on?"

"Well, son, I guess I haven't been completely honest with you about my involvement in the Springfield Three case?"

"Yeah, I think we've covered that ground before, Booger. You weren't honest with me about the Streeter family getting you involved in the case. You weren't honest with me about why you agreed for me to come to Springfield and interview you. You weren't honest with me about the fortress of security that you had inside and around the warehouse, not to mention the hidden bomb shelter you had on the main floor."

"Bachelor pad, son."

"Okay, whatever you choose to call it, you weren't honest with me about it, and I doubt seriously you were honest about becoming wealthy from Walmart stock."

"As God is my witness, son, the Walmart story is completely true."

"Okay, so what's the story now? I've just been thinking you were dead, you know. I'm caught between being relieved and highly annoyed."

"Well, isn't that sweet?" he said with a smile, which relaxed Brian a bit. "Look, it was important that some people believed me dead. For that to happen, you had to be lied to, too. I didn't like that for you, but it was important for a variety of reasons."

"Okay, so catch me up," Brian said, thinking to himself this had already been a hell of a day, and it's just started.

"Son, I'm working for the FBI, have been for quite a few years now, undercover."

"Of course you are," Brian said with an eye roll he couldn't hold back. "You know I'm gun shy about believing you at this point."

"Well, if you don't believe that, then you're really going to have trouble believing this. I'm also working for the Springfield Police Department – undercover, naturally. We thought it would be better if at least a few officers thought I'd kicked the can. Maybe it'd give us time. "

"Oh sure," Brian said, looking at his wrist as if he was wearing a watch. "Speaking of time, I think I need to go. This is all crazy. You're crazy!"

"Look, I know you're upset, and you have every right to be. But we need you to stay. I may have got you a little too deeply involved in the case. I don't think it is safe for you to go home, not yet anyway."

"Booger, if I'm in danger, you owe me an explanation of who is after me and why?"

"Yeah, I guess I do, son. You remember when I told you that your theory of the police or someone dressed like a policeman being responsible for the disappearances of those three women may not be too far from the truth?"

"Yes, we've spent some time on that."

"Well, over the course of the last four years, the FBI and a special task force with the Springfield Police have been investigating a local drug trafficking ring. There was fear that some members of the force may have been influenced to look the other way and supply information beneficial to the drug traffickers. The head of the task force suggested an intermediary, someone local, someone familiar with drug activities in Springfield."

"Let me guess," Brian said.

Booger continued, "The FBI had an informant working within a local drug operation. The tips he supplied, though, were leaking out whenever the police got involved to issue a warrant or make a raid. The FBI was afraid their informant would be discovered. To ensure his safety, they decided to hire an intermediary. That intermediary would be the only one to have contact with the informant. He would pass information between their guy and the FBI and between the FBI and the task force. I had worked with Special Agent Moffitt a few years back on a child abduction case in Sikeston. So when my name was brought up, Special Agent Moffitt contacted me. The money was decent, and at the time, I thought all I would be doing was passing information along. I set up my office in that abandoned warehouse. When the informant had a tip, he would go to our designated diner, sit at a table where Rose was the server, order a cup of coffee and leave a silver dollar underneath his empty coffee cup when he left. Rose would contact me, and I knew the informant would come to the warehouse late that evening. The FBI set up all the security video surveillance cameras and sensors around the building. They wanted to make sure their informant wasn't followed. The hidden apartment on the main floor was built as a safe house. The FBI did that, too.

"When the diner closed because of Covid-19, the informant had no way to make contact with Rose and let me know when he had information. The FBI was just about to raid the farmhouse where the drug cartel managed their operations. They were concerned their undercover guy was either dead or unable to gather anything more. They decided to make arrests with the information they already had. The night before they planned the raid, the informant showed up at the warehouse. It was nearly midnight. A sensor picked up a car coming into the parking lot. Its lights were out. I watched the video cameras as the man parked the car in a dark corner of the lot. He got out and began walking toward the side door that led up to my office. The door was locked, so I knew he couldn't get in unless I buzzed him in, so I just watched, trying to figure out who he was. That was when I heard the sensor go off again, and I saw another car come into the parking lot. The man must have felt that something was wrong. He began to run back toward his car. That's when I heard the shots, at least eight of them. The man fell to the ground, and the car sped out of the area."

"Wow," Brian said, unable to hold back a reaction.

"I rushed downstairs and out the side door. When I got to the man lying on the ground, I recognized him. He was the informant. He was clinging to life. He was whispering something. I bent down with my ear to his mouth, trying desperately to hear what he was saying. He only said three words."

"Come on, Booger. What were they?" Brian asked, worried he was being teased.

"Sam, Springfield, Three," Booger said, followed by a dramatic pause.

"Woah. Sam?" Brian said.

"The FBI had investigated a man named Sam. He worked at Cox Medical Center as a security guard. He was an older gentleman in his sixties with an interesting background. He was an ex-Army Ranger, served on the same base with named Robert Craig Cox."

"No."

"Yes."

"Sam moved to Springfield after being discharged. He

had some family here. He went to work for the Springfield Police Department, although his time as an officer was short – less than two years. There is no record of why he left the department. Soon after, he took a position with Missouri State as a campus security guard. That job only lasted a short time, too. He's been working at Cox ever since. The FBI looked at him, not because of the Springfield Three case, but because of suspicion he was involved in the local drug trade. They considered him more of a small fish that might lead them to bigger fish. Naturally, Sam became a more serious person of interest based on those three words uttered by the informant on his death bed."

"Okay, wow. That's a lot to take in," Brian said with a bit of an exhale. "So, do you think Sam had something to do with the disappearances of the Springfield Three? And if that's the case, why don't the police or FBI haul him in for questioning? You know, put the squeeze on him, get him to talk."

"Son, you have watched too much television. Neither the FBI nor the local police has any real evidence that Sam was involved in the Springfield Three case. All they have is his name uttered by a dying informant, heard only by a private eye desperate for a break in a case he's been working for twenty-eight years. Hell, Sam could mean anything. It's not actionable unless there's more to go with it. However, that is when I came up with a plan. That's when my war room was developed. It had become clear to anyone on the inside paying attention that I might have sensitive information tying the Springfield Three case to drug distribution in the Springfield market. Police were asked to patrol the area around the warehouse and to report any suspicious activity. There was someone or some persons within the department who were leaking details of the investigation to certain high-up individuals in the local drug trade. So, the bait was set. A few days later, I discovered the listening device on my phone. Shortly after, I found two more listening devices in my office."

"Why didn't they just break into your war room and take everything you had?" Brian asked.

"I think they wanted to know exactly what information I had and who else knew about it. The listening devices would help them find that out."

"What about your video surveillance cameras? Didn't they pick up pictures of the men that broke into your office and planted the devices?"

"They were wearing masks and gloves and dark clothes. There were two of them. They didn't park in the lot outside. They walked onto the parking lot."

"I'm curious about the informant. What information did he provide to the FBI?"

"That, son, is confidential. I can say that he had a lot of detail about the people running drugs in and out of Springfield, but remember, the FBI was looking for bigger fish. Springfield had long been thought to be a rest stop of sorts for drug cartels moving product from along the I-44 corridor. If you're transporting drugs from El Paso to Chicago or anywhere from the border to the East Coast, you're probably going to come through Springfield. There was some speculation that Springfield might even be a distribution hub for points west and south coming through St. Louis because of the trucking companies headquartered here."

"What about the car that pulled into the parking lot that night, the one in which someone shot and killed the informant? Did your cameras pick up any detail of the car?"

"No, not really. It was as if the driver knew exactly where our video cameras were located. It was a black or dark-colored sedan, maybe a Ford. There was no license plate."

"Okay, so based on the three words that the informant said to you when he was dying, do you believe there is a connection between this Sam character and the disappearance of the three women?"

"Look, I don't know," Booger said, uncomfortable and adjusting himself in his bed. "But I do know that someone is very interested in the information I gathered about the Springfield Three, and this Sam is the first solid lead I've had in a long time."

"Yeah, okay," Brian said, trying to take it all in.

"What's important now is Special Agent Moffitt is going to need your help."

"You mean your half-brother?" Brian asked.

"What? Oh, right," Booger said with a chuckle before a deep breath that told Brian he was about to get serious. "There is something that needs to be done as soon as possible, something that can't wait for my head to heal enough to do it myself. I need you to talk to him, and I'm hoping you'll agree to do what he is going to ask you."

"All right," Brian said hesitantly. "What does he want me to do?"

"He's in there. Go ask him. I'm going to try and get some rest," Booger said. As Brian turned to leave, the detective added, "Thank you."

"For what? Getting out alive?"

"For what you're about to do."

Special Agent Moffitt was waiting for Brian in the living room.

"Hi, there. Please, take a seat," he said in a short quip. Brian could tell this was someone who didn't mince words. "Let's get right to it. There is something I would like you to do. If you decide not to, I will understand. I can't be part of it, and if something goes wrong, there's a good chance I won't be able to help you."

"Well, it sounds great so far," Brian said with a small laugh. "Have you worked in sales?"

"Brian," he said, ignoring the attempt at humor, "you

left some important information in the secret room in Booger's warehouse. Without it and the GPS tracker, we can't know who broke in and started the fire. Do you understand where I'm going with this?"

"Yes, but you're an FBI agent. Why don't you just go into the warehouse and get what you need?"

"In short, I have no legal reason for being there. It's a crime scene, and it's not one the FBI is investigating," Moffitt said. "It's also important you understand that I can't ask you to do this. Because it's a crime scene, even with Booger's permission, you're not allowed in there."

"Yeah, I get it. I'm actually glad I get a chance to go back. I feel really bad that I left everything there in the commotion," Brian said. "My only concern: is it safe for me to do this?"

"I'll be close by watching. I'll give you a throw-away phone. If someone comes, I'll call you. If everything goes right, you should be in and out of that warehouse within a few minutes. There'll be yellow police tape up, so you won't be able to go through the side door without breaking the bond, but there are numerous broken windows on the main level that are easy to get to. All you have to do is find a window that will give you access, crawl through and get the stuff you left behind. It should be relatively simple."

"A former editor once told me you're not a reporter unless you're willing to cross yellow tape without permission," Brian said with a grin.

"What?" the agent said with a look of concern. "That's really not advisable, generally."

"Oh yeah, sure," Brian said, with a sigh. "You must be fun at parties."

Agent Moffitt wasn't in the mood for jokes. "Great. In a few hours, it will be dark out. We'll go then."

Then Agent Moffitt's tone turned softer. "Did Booger

answer all your questions?"

"I guess, although I'm not sure what to believe. He hasn't exactly been honest with me before."

"Don't hold that against him, Brian. Booger is one of the most honest people I know. If he lied to you, it was to protect you."

When the conversation ended, Rose came over to Brian. "I'm sorry you got caught up in this mess. I know Booger is sorry about it too."

"Rose, it's fine. I am glad to see you're okay," Brian said. "I mean, I guess it has been a bit of a nightmare, but it could've been worse."

"If he had another idea to draw the men out, I know he would have used it. Booger's really like a big teddy bear."

"Can I ask you something personal, Rose?"

"Sure, I guess."

"Are you in love with Booger?"

"Well, my goodness, you weren't kidding. That is personal."

"I'm sorry. If you don't want to answer, I'll understand. It just seems like maybe...."

Rose interrupted, "Booger was in love with one woman in his life. I'm not sure they'll ever be room for another."

"You didn't answer my question, Rose," Brian said, looking directly at her.

"I think I did," she said with a subtle grin.

Brian smiled back, knowing that was as much as she would say about that. "So, do you think Booger knows who kidnapped the Springfield Three, Rose?"

"Brian, Booger McClain is a lot smarter than he looks, but he's working with a puzzle that is missing a lot of pieces. The Springfield Police, the Greene County Sheriff's Department, the Missouri Highway Patrol, and the FBI all know things that they haven't shared with the public. Booger is at a disadvantage, and I'm not sure they know."

They both sat quietly for a minute.

"I do think this Sam may be part of the big picture," Rose added. "Are you going to help?"

"Yes."

"Good. You're a good kid, Brian. You know that neither Booger nor I have ever had children. But if we did, we'd want them to be just like you."

"Thanks, Rose," Brian said, reaching out to give her a hug. He realized with the COVID-19 going around, it had been a while since he'd hugged anyone.

"Now, why don't you rest up a bit, and I'll make you and Special Agent Moffitt some egg salad sandwiches. You're going to need to eat before you break the law and risk your life, you know?"

"Yes, I think you're right," Brian said with a laugh.

Soon, Brian fell asleep, stretched out on the couch. He slept hard and dreamed that he was back in high school at Parkview, and the forked hallways were like a maze. He was fighting to get to homeroom on time and never made it. When he woke, Rose had a plateful of sandwiches on the coffee table about a foot away from his face. Rose saw him sit up and rub his eyes. "We didn't have any beets in the kitchen," she said, "so I substituted pieces of canned cherries and added a few walnuts that I found in the cabinet. Hope you like it."

"Oh, yeah. I am sure it'll be fine," Brian said, still groggy.

"Cherries, walnuts and raisins in an egg salad sandwich?" Agent Moffitt said to Brian. "What a delightful-sounding recipe!"

Brian raised his eyebrows. "Uh-huh."

Rose emerged from the kitchen a few minutes later, carrying a tray of sandwiches, chips, a steaming cup of black coffee, and a flower in a vase. "I'm going to see how Booger is doing," she responded. "He's bound to be hungry by now."

"Is there something going on between those two?" Agent Moffitt asked.

"Probably," Brian said.

The rest of the day passed in a blur for Brian. He caught Rose up on everything that led to him waking her and learned about what was going on with her at the hospital. Before they knew it, the time had come. It was a couple of hours after sunset when Agent Moffitt told Brian they needed to leave. He drove him to a vacant lot about two blocks away from the warehouse. "I'm going to let you out here. You'll need to walk to Booger's facility. I will be waiting for you right here when you get the materials."

Agent Moffitt handed Brian a burner phone. No one can know the FBI is involved in what you're about to do. If you run into trouble, hide and call 911. If I see anyone approaching the warehouse, I'll call you on that phone. Okay?"

"Yes. Got it," Brian said.

"Also, keep an eye out for anyone that may be watching. If you suspect that someone sees you, don't proceed. Come back here. Okay?"

"All right, I will."

And with that, Brian got out of Moffitt's car and began his walk toward the office, moving directly, sliding smoothly within the shadows, and trying to avoid the streetlights as much as possible. With each step, he scanned the area around him, attempting to look casual and not bring attention to himself while checking for parked cars with suspicious characters inside. With the warehouse in sight, he stopped to make sure he could approach it safely. He didn't want to make a bee-line for it if someone was watching. Once he felt he was in the clear, he moved swiftly toward the large glass windows of the warehouse, ducking under the stretched-out yellow police tape as he went.

It was dark all around him. The moon was hidden behind the clouds that night, and all the exterior and interior lights were off. The air was cool, and everything smelled of burned wood and plastic. Brian moved carefully toward the closest shattered window. Knowing he'd need to be careful climbing in, he took one last look around from the shadows. He didn't see anyone around, and everything was quiet except for one dog barking intermittently a few blocks away. *This is it,* he thought to himself. Then, he carefully lifted his leg up, over and through, straddling the window sill before he ducked his head under and through, bringing his arms and other leg around. He was thankful the ground outside the main floor was higher there, making the entry fairly easy. *I'm in,* he thought. That's when he realized everything was dark, and he had no flashlight.

"Crap," he said under his breath. Normally, if he needs a flashlight, he could just use his smartphone. Now, however, Agent Moffitt was holding it, and all Brian had was the burner phone. He pulled it out and flipped it open. It emitted a faint light. It wasn't much, but he didn't have a choice. He was in now, and he'd have to make it work.

His first steps were loud as he crunched glass beneath his feet and began moving slowly toward the hidden door. He followed the inner wall with one hand sliding across its bumps and grooves while his other held the phone in front of him. Once he figured he was about three-quarters of the way to the door, he slowed down and put the phone away, so he could begin feeling everything he could with both hands. "Loose brick, loose brick," he said over and over to himself, hoping somehow he could call it into his hands. After a few minutes, he started to panic. "Where is it?" He got the flip phone out one more time and could tell he was close. He then shut it away again and ran his hands along the wall. "There it is!" He'd found it. Brian removed the brick and pulled. It took a concerted effort, but the door opened wide enough for him to enter.

Just inside was the flashlight that he had left behind. *Thank God,* he thought. He picked it up, turned it on and could see smoke still lingering in the air. Booger's bunker didn't have windows, so the air was thicker and more suffocating than the hallway. He pulled his t-shirt over his mouth in a makeshift mask. With the aid of the flashlight, he was able to find the closet in Booger's bedroom and the folder inside it. Next to it was the GPS tracker. He sighed audibly once he knew he had what he needed. Now he just needed to get out of this bunker and warehouse and back to Agent Moffitt's car before anyone saw him.

Once out of the secret room and in the hall, he pointed the flashlight toward the window. He could see his way out. *I'm almost there,* he thought. That's when the flip phone rang. He picked it up.

"Hide, Brian. A police car is pulling into the parking lot." The phone went dead.

Panicked, Brian turned off the flashlight and started backing up towards the bunker when he could see the light of a parking car reflected on the wall across from the window. He had already closed the door and replaced the loose brick, so he knew he couldn't get back in easily in the dark, so he hid behind a nearby damaged filing cabinet. There he listened, trying not to move as he breathed through his slightly opened mouth to make as little noise as possible.

The patrol car seemed to be parked briefly, then Brian could hear it rounding the building. The spotlight was turned on, and the vehicle circled slowly, shining the light into the windows of the warehouse. Shadow and light reflected, including down the hall where Brian was hiding. *Can he see me?* he thought. His heart raced. His breathing became more rapid.

After a long minute, the patrol car turned out its spotlight and drove away. Brian waited long enough to make sure it was gone. Then, he quickly moved down the hall, and out the window he came in. His hands were shaking as they touched the window sill. Once out, he walked as fast as he could to the agent's car, not caring for shadows or looking for anyone. His heart was pounding.

"Did you get it, Brian?" he asked.

"Yeah, I got it. Let's get out of here."

"Check the GPS tracker," Agent Moffitt said. "Is it working?"

Brian looked it over, slightly out of breath. "Yes."

"Okay, great!" Agent Moffitt drove back to the safe house, watching as he drove to make sure no one was following him while Brian stammered through his replay of events. Brian felt like he'd drank five cups of coffee. He was jittering, and his mind was racing. He felt electric.

"I can't tell you how glad I am that's over," he said. Once they arrived at the safe house, he asked the agent, "What are you going to do with the tracker?"

"I'm going to find out where the war-room files went," Moffitt said. "Your part in this is over now. You accomplished your mission."

For the first time, Brian liked working with Moffitt. He suddenly felt he understood the draw of the job. "Thank you, agent," he said in stoic appreciation.

Booger was out of his bed and sitting in the living room when they came into the house through the garage.

"What are you doing up, Booger? You need to be in bed."

Booger ignored the question. "Did you get the tracker?"

"Yes."

"Good, let's go, boys."

"Excuse me? No way, Booger. Brian did his part. Plus, this is a criminal investigation now. I can handle it from here."

"Now listen, Terry," he said, using the agent's informal

name, which he knew irritated his friend. "I'm coming along, and so is the kid," looking at Brian with a smile.

Brian's expression was flat. He had no desire to go out again, and he hoped Booger could see it in his eyes. *Listen to the agent, Booger,* he thought.

Booger continued. "We've gone to too much trouble to not see this play through. Besides, you need a navigator for that tracker, and it will also be helpful to have a spotter in case someone's watching."

They went back and forth for a minute before Moffitt relented. "I guess we could use a backup on the way there."

"I'm happy to stay here," Brian said.

"Don't be ridiculous, son. You're a part of this now," Booger said, clearly not catching his clues.

"It looks like the files are a couple of miles away," the agent said. "I'm calling for actual backup, of course. We can have five guys at the location just minutes after we arrive."

Brian felt it was useless to fight the momentum. Like a tired agent himself, he followed them back to the car. "What do I need to do?"

"Just keep your eyes peeled for anyone following us," Booger said.

And just like that, Mission Two was underway. The agent drove as the detective barked out directions.

"Turn left here," Booger said, examining the GPS. "Keep going straight." Within about ten minutes, he said, "We're close now."

"What exactly are we going to do when we get there?" Brian asked.

"You two aren't doing anything," Agent Moffitt said forcefully. "We're going to sit and wait for backup. You both are going to stay in the car. Do you hear me?"

"Yes, sir," Booger said in a sarcastic tone, turning to wink at Brian, who had no intention of leaving the vehicle.

"Turn right at the next street," Booger said. "We're almost there."

Brian noticed they were near Missouri State, on the edge of the Rountree Neighborhood, when Booger said, "I don't have a good feeling about this." He was looking at the tracker in disbelief. "Here, Terry," he said, pointing ahead. "It's up here."

Agent Moffitt turned off his headlights and slowed the car. "This house, Booger?"

"No, the next one. The one with the gravel driveway," he said, barely believing the words coming out of his mouth. "The signal is coming from Rose's house."

CHAPTER 15

EDUCATED GUESSES

Agent Moffitt sat and waited for backup. Five minutes later, two FBI agents arrived, followed closely by an unmarked police car. A no-knock search warrant was issued for the house, and ten minutes later, another unmarked police car arrived with the warrant.

Authorities surrounded the house and forcibly entered the front door without notice. Booger and Brian followed orders and stayed in the car. They had to sit and wait for information.

No one, as it turned out, was in Rose's house. Nothing was disturbed. A rear door had been unlocked with what appeared to be a crowbar or a similar instrument. In Rose's living room, sitting on the couch, were two GPS devices. Booger would later confirm that they were the same devices that he had hidden inside material in his war room.

"Someone is toying with us," Booger told Brian later. "They purposely removed them and took them to Rose's house."

"Why?" Brian asked.

"I don't know. Maybe as a warning. Maybe they want me to know that they know more about us than we do about them. It seems to be an indirect threat against Rose or anyone that is working with me. It's just some kind of sick game."

The police took fingerprints from the back door and from the GPS device and other areas in the house, but the only ones they found belonged to Rose.

After Booger told her the next morning about the discovery in her house, Brian saw her break down. It was the first and last time Brian would see her cry. Months later, in St. Louis, he told his dad, "She was usually a rock, never getting too upset about anything, but that morning she felt violated. Her world no longer felt protected. She was afraid."

"Booger tried to comfort her," Brian said. "He tried to assure her that everything would be okay, that somebody was just sending a message, that it really didn't mean anything. But the fact was, Booger felt violated too. He felt like someone had played him for a fool, and he had no idea who that somebody was. All his planning and all his hope of finding a resolution to the case seemed further away than ever."

"Wow. I can't imagine," Alan said. "Those two have always been unflappable."

"So much happened there, Dad. We've been over most of it, but then I remember more I haven't said."

"Well, it's easy to see how with the warehouse burning down and Booger dying," Alan said, using his fingers as quotation marks when he said dying.

"I'm glad it's over," Brian said, realizing how that sounded. "Well, you know, I'm glad to be back."

Father and son had resumed work in April, alternating days at the office during the heart of the early coronavirus scare, to keep the family business alive. By May, business picked up briefly before settling into what Alan called "the new normal" by June.

Alan and Brian wrote in their downtime, recounting Brian's investigation with Booger in Springfield.

"Sometimes it feels like years ago, Dad," Brian said at the

office, preparing for an afternoon maildrop. "Other times, it feels like yesterday."

"Well, yeah, you went through a lot," Alan said. "I knew it was going to be an adventure. I just didn't know how much of one."

"It wasn't an adventure at all," Brian said in a cold and serious tone. "The Springfield Three is the type of case that plays tricks on the minds of those involved. I barely had anything to do with it, but I saw the toll it can leave on others. I saw what it did to Booger. Leads that seemed so promising one day turned into dead ends the next day. And think about the people closest to it. Police officers, detectives, FBI – all of them. They had the real pressure. I remember what it was like. The search for the three of them became part of the community's identity. The cops had to be acutely aware of the ever-present pressure to solve the case, especially those involved early on. Booger was no different. I know he believes he was so close to solving it. He was hoping that the men that took his work on the case and burned his warehouse would lead him to the answers he needed. At the very least, he was confident that they would provide him with more puzzle pieces which would give him a clear picture of what happened. And none of the original investigators from 1992 were still on the case. They had all resigned or retired. Twenty-eight years is a long time to go without any answers. But as hard as that was for law enforcement, for Booger, it was that much worse for the families and friends. The disappointment of not solving a case for loved ones is tough, but it doesn't compare to losing those you loved personally. Imagine the McCall and Streeter families, what their minds have been through."

In saying this to his father, Brian remembered he'd had a similar conversation with Booger back in March in Springfield. His mind went back to his hometown a lot these days, to the files he pulled from the smoky bunker to Booger and Rose and everything they'd been through together.

"I can't imagine losing a daughter or a sister or mother in a situation like that, taken from the safety of their home in the middle of the night and for twenty-eight years not having any sort of resolution," Booger told Brian back in the spring.

"Yeah, I can't imagine what it must be like for the McCall and Streeter families. Do you think we'll ever know what happened to those women?" Brian asked.

"Yeah, someday we'll know; hopefully, someday soon. I believe whoever is responsible for what happened that night is in prison now. A person's conscience is a powerful thing. Someday they will talk, or perhaps someone they confided in will talk. The truth will come out eventually. I have to believe that."

Brian had noticed the toll it took on Booger after the break-in at Rose's. For a few days after they found the trackers, he remained in Springfield. He went home and stayed with his family. He continued to check up on Booger, but he saw him sparingly. There was a feeling of defeat that hung over them, a feeling that no one knew quite what to do with the office now a burnt shell of itself waiting to be demolished. They had the files, which was great, but now what? They didn't know who was watching them or had any good ideas on how to find out. Brian, and the files, had been the bait, but the fish had gotten away. And just what did the files prove, Brian wondered.

Booger, still in recovery, rested and drank liberally at the safe house. Brian, who checked in on him once a day, had told him then he planned to return to St. Louis soon but that he wasn't in a huge rush. He was waiting to see what the detective's next move would be, and Booger didn't seem to know. To Brian, Booger was a beaten man. He looked depressed, numb. He didn't appear to have the same fire or sense of direction he had before.

On the third day after the GPS tracker was found at Rose's, Brian noticed a change in Booger's energy. He seemed finally ready to move on. That's when Brian began to learn what he had gone back to the bunker for three days earlier. That's when Booger gave him the files.

"Son, this is all the proof I have of what happened to those women. It's not a lot, but there should be enough information for a story," Booger said, handing Brian a case folder which was open now and had subfolders in it. Booger, ever the showman, pulled out a hand-written manuscript like a magician casting a spell with his wand as he handed it to Brian. "These folders have all of my thoughts on what happened and all of the supporting evidence. It's not enough to bring anyone to justice like I had hoped. But it may be enough to write your story. Who knows, maybe what you write will spark renewed interest in the case, and maybe it will result in additional leads. It might even lead to some answers. Son, I've had my time on this case. The rest is up to you."

Brian didn't know what to say, so he took it and said nothing.

"You need to realize, m'boy, my thoughts in here are pure speculation, and once you write it, there are going to be people that strongly disagree. There are going to be others that may be embarrassed or upset with what you write. You must also understand, if you choose to do this, to publish something, that I had an alternative motive for giving you this information. By you writing everything I know and have learned about this case, you will take the heat off of Rose and me. It is for a selfish reason that I am giving you this material. I'm not so concerned for myself. I've been involved in enough sensitive cases over the years to accept the fact that I'll always need to be looking over my shoulders. But Rose, she is an innocent. She doesn't deserve to live in fear of someone coming after her. If you and your dad do a book, you have to tell people we're fictional - that we don't exist. Whoever is watching us now will know differently, but it won't matter because the world will know everything we know. Do you understand?"

"Um, yeah. I understand," Brian said, suddenly feeling a big sense of responsibility.

"I only ask that you read everything here, and you read it all before you go back to St. Louis. After you read it and before you make a decision whether to write the story or not, I have one more place to take you. If, after that, you choose not to write the story, I will understand."

Brian agreed, shook Booger's now-extended hand and took the folders into the other room to begin reading. A few minutes later, Rose entered the room with a cup of coffee. "I thought you'd need this," she said.

"Yes, thanks, Rose. "Rose, can I ask you a question?"

"Sure, what's on your mind?"

"Do you think Booger is going to be okay? I've never seen him this down."

"Yeah, he'll be just fine. He just needs some time and space right now."

"What about you? How are you?"

"Don't worry about me. I'm a tough cookie. I'll be just fine."

Brian started to ask a question and then stopped. Having seen that Rose noticed, he said, "Look, it's really not my place, but I'm getting to know Booger, and for an outsider like me, it seems like he really cares about you. I think the fact that someone snuck something into your home has messed him up. Were you two ever, well, together?"

"Nah, we're just friends. Neither of us has anyone else, so we lean on each other kinda like an old married couple. I understand him, and he understands me, but that's as far as it goes. Maybe ten or fifteen years ago, there might have been a chance of us being together. Truth is that I think I've loved him for a long, long time. Maybe I should have told him that years ago. But I was always afraid he didn't feel the same way. I couldn't bear to lose what we had together, even if it was just friendship. Now drink your coffee before it gets cold."

When Rose left the room, Brian returned to the folders. The first one he grabbed was labeled "Overview" on the front. Peaking inside, there was one other main folder labeled "Booger's Story." Then, there were a few subfolders, all marked "Evidence." It was clear to Brian that he needed to read the two main folders, and the evidence was just supporting materials. He decided to set "Booger's Story" aside to read it last. Inside "Overview," this is what he found:

Victims:
Sherrill Elizabeth Levitt, 11/01/44
Sherrill was forty-seven (At the Time of Disappearance); she had bleached blonde hair, brown eyes, was 5'0," and weighed roughly 110 lbs. Sherrill was a heavy smoker. She moved to the Springfield area, where she had relatives, from Seattle, Washington, in 1980. Sherrill divorced her first husband, Brentt Streeter, shortly after her daughter Suzie was born in 1973. Once here, she studied cosmetology while working various part-time jobs to support Suzie and her son, Bartt. Eventually, Sherrill became a hairdresser, and a skilled one, by all accounts. She worked at New Attitudes Hair Salon on West Sunshine in 1992 and had amassed about two hundred and fifty clients at the time of her disappearance.

The mother and daughter moved into their home on East Delmar Street in April 1992. Sherrill had divorced her second husband, Don Levitt, in 1989. The divorce was said to have hurt her financially and prompted the move to the modest home on Delmar. It was reported that Don's creditors sought payments from Sherrill after their divorce, so she tried to locate him through an attorney but was unsuccessful. Sherrill told friends she left her first husband after he had suggested they get a divorce but remained living together so she could collect welfare assistance. Neither of her former husbands is considered a suspect.

According to family and friends, Sherrill was a private person who was close with her daughter.

Their relatives had them both declared legally deceased in 1997, and a bench was dedicated in their honor at the Victims Memorial Garden in Phelps Grove Park that same year.

Suzanne Elizabeth Streeter, 3/09/73

Goes by the name "Suzie" Streeter; was nineteen (ATOD); had bleached blonde hair; brown eyes; was around 5'3" (accounts vary) and weighed 102 lbs. Suzie had a scar on the upper right forearm and a small tumor on the left corner of her mouth. She was, by most accounts, easygoing, high-spirited and quite popular at Kickapoo. Suzie had a penchant for bad boys, such as her former boyfriend, Mike Kovacs. He had a reputation for a hot temper and a dark side and was accused of hitting Suzie several times. Suzie broke up with him in the fall of '91, but Mike didn't take it well. According to an Oct. 23 police report, Suzie and her mother filed a complaint that Mike and another unnamed woman for threatening Streeter and twice slashing her tires. She sought and received a restraining order against him that alleged physical and mental abuse - specifically, it claimed Mike "beat her up, slashed her car tires, threatened her by phone and harassed her at home, school and work." It is unclear to what degree investigators looked at him as a person of interest. He would have had a motive to seek revenge on both Suzie and Sherrill and should be considered a suspect.

After Kovacs, Suzie dated Dustin Recla. Dustin was charged with felony vandalism after breaking into a mausoleum with friends Michael Clay and Joseph Riedel at Maple Park

Cemetery in February 1992. The boys allegedly had pawned gold teeth they took from a skull, and Suzie was expected to appear as a witness at their trial. This had led to tensions between Dustin and Suzie and with Michael Clay as well, who reportedly said in an interview after the women disappeared that he hoped all three were dead. Investigators have looked at Dustin, as well as his two friends, as suspects. However, they have found no evidence tying the three men to the women's disappearance beyond the fact that the alibis for Dustin and Michael Clay were suspect.

Several classmates have said they felt Suzie Streeter was not herself at the graduation parties the night of June 6. They said she appeared to be stressed out and worried about something. Friends also stated Suzie didn't want to be alone that night and had made plans to be with Stacy McCall that evening, so she wouldn't need to be. Was she afraid of somebody that night?

Suzie was the daughter of Sherrill Leavitt and Brentt Streeter of Seattle, Washington. She never lived with her father and rarely spoke of him or her stepfather, Don Levitt. It was speculated that Suzie might have been dyslexic; she had difficulty reading and was placed in classes for students with learning disabilities. In 1992, she worked at a local movie theater and planned to enroll in cosmetology school in the fall of that year.

By all accounts, Suzie was close to her mother. Their relatives had them both declared legally deceased in 1997, and a bench was dedicated in their honor at the Victims Memorial Garden in Phelps Grove Park that same year.

Stacy Kathleen McCall, 4/23/1974

Stacy was eighteen (ATOD); she had dark blonde hair and blue eyes and was 5'3 and 120 lbs. Stacy had an off-center cleft on her chin, as well as birthmarks under her lip and on her right arm. A childhood friend of Suzie Streeter, she was a good student in high school and planned to attend Southwest Missouri State

University in the fall of 1992. She and Suzie had drifted apart through most of high school before becoming close again towards the end of their senior year. Stacy was popular and well-liked at Kickapoo and did not have any boyfriends who were considered suspects in the disappearance. She grew up in a strong and loving family and had a good relationship with both of her parents and with her elder sister, Lisa. Janis McCall, Stacy's mother, has long represented the family and is likely the most recognizable public figure associated with the case beyond the three women themselves. She has done countless interviews over the years with a variety of media in the hopes of finding her daughter.

Janis did not know at the time that Stacy had spent the night at the Levitt home because of the last-minute nature of that decision. The plan had been for Stacy to stay at Janelle Kirby's house on the night of June 6. Most people believe Stacy was not the target victim but was in the wrong place at the wrong time. However, her being an intended victim has not been entirely ruled out due largely to her possible connection to suspect Robert Craig Cox, who had worked at the same car dealership as Stacy's father. Ironically, Stacy and Suzie's friend, Janelle, had wanted to stay the night at Suzie's when the girls decided to leave around 2:15 a.m., but Janelle's mother refused to let her.

Stacy worked as a receptionist at Springfield Gymnastics and modeled wedding gowns for The Total Bride in the Brentwood Center at the time of her disappearance. Stacy's mother, Janis, continues to say that until there is conclusive proof that her daughter is dead, she will hold out hope that she is alive.

Victims/Conclusions:

The most likely intended victim was Suzie, given that she had two ex-boyfriends who were upset with her and one friend, Michael Clay, who had said he hoped she was dead. Further, she was said to be nervous the night of graduation, and it's believed the last known location for the three missing women was at her house. It may be that Dustin and Michael had nothing to do with the disappearance, but given that there are no obvious motives for abducting the other two women and that a witness places Suzie behind the vehicle of a van the morning of June 7, it's safe to say Suzie is the most likely intended victim.

The less likely intended victim was Stacy McCall. Though it's possible suspect, Robert Craig Cox might have known her, not even Janis McCall knew Stacy was staying at the Levitt/ Streeter home that night.

While all evidence points to the fact the three women went missing from Sherrill Leavitt's home, I don't believe Sherrill was the target. She had no known enemies, and no money was removed from her purse. Additionally, if she were the sole target, she would have been more vulnerable before the girls should've arrived at the house on Delmar around 2:30 a.m. It is possible, of course, that Sherrill and Suzie were both the targets.

Key Clues:

1. **Broken porch light cover**. The shattered glass was swept up on the morning of June 7, but it's important to note the light itself was said to be working, according to Janelle and her boyfriend, Mike, who were the first to come to the Levitt house the day after graduation.

2. **Sherrill's open window.** The window to Sherrill's bedroom was found open, and its screen was found leaning up against the base of the house outside. This could explain how a perpetrator or perpetrators gained access to the home.

3. **Suzie's blinds.** Several visitors to the home on June 7 described Suzie's blinds as disturbed. It's possible Suzie heard a noise

outside her mother's window or the dog barking and was trying to see what was going on.

4. **Cinnamon, the family dog.** According to Janelle Kirby, who was the first to enter the house the morning of June 7, Cinnamon came lunging toward her and was full of energy when she opened the front door. The dog was loose in the house, not shut in a room, which suggests the women left through the front door without time or thought to secure Cinnamon.

5. **The obscene phone calls.** One was reportedly left on an answering machine before it was deleted by people visiting the house on June 7. Janelle Kirby answered the phone with the second obscene call and described it as sick and perverted. The voice from both calls was said to be male. It is unclear if the calls were made by one person or more or exactly what was said. Suzie's ex-boyfriend Mike Kovacs had been accused of harassing Suzie by phone before, but there is no known evidence to suggest he was responsible for either of the calls. The clues may have been vitally important, or they might have been unrelated to the disappearance.

6. **Personal items left behind.** The women vanished in a hurry, leaving the house in the middle of the night without purses, cigarettes, makeup, jewelry, important medication and money. In fact, Sherrill had nearly $900 in her purse. The evidence in the home suggests Suzie and Stacy had readied themselves for sleep and had both gotten in bed before they left suddenly. Sherrill had been in her bed, too, where there was an open book, as well as reading glasses, on the nightstand next to her. Investigators have ruled out robbery as a motive.

7. **The three cars.** All three of the women's cars were parked in

the driveway the next morning. Sherrill's was under the carport. Suzie's was in the circular driveway, and Stacy's car was directly behind Suzie's. Friends said Suzie's normal parking spot was under the carport, but given that Sherrill didn't expect her daughter home that night, the order doesn't seem suspicious. The importance of the cars lies in the fact that they were all there, which supports a sudden abduction.

8. **The mysterious van.** The moss green or tan van remains a key clue from that night - one the police believed so strongly in that a replica van was positioned at the department headquarters on Chestnut Expressway. While descriptions of that van have varied over the years, it is believed to be a late '60s or early '70s Ford or Chevy cargo van, and a fairly distinct one at that. The most promising witness account came from the lady on the porch near Rose's house who saw a woman who looked like Suzie driving and heard a man say, "Don't do anything stupid." The other potentially critical witness put the van close to the Leavitt home, leaving the neighborhood in a hurry. Another witness saw the van with a male driver in a Walmart parking lot in the early morning hours of June 7.

9. **The message in the newspaper rack**. This clue alluded to a perpetrator using a ruse of a utility man warning of a gas leak to get the women outside. It also included a crude sketch of an apartment building. Investigators did bring search dogs to a wooded area near an apartment building not long after the note was discovered. What they found or didn't find was unclear. The note could have been an attention seeker or something to throw authorities off a particular trail. It also could have been something from someone who had some inside knowledge.

Key Clues/Conclusions: The women were at the house before some person or persons abducted them. The most likely getaway vehicle was the moss green or tan van reported by multiple witnesses.

Persons of Interest:
There is no shortage of potential suspects. Given the late hour, Suzie and Stacy drove to the Leavitt home. It's possible any number of people capable of kidnapping the women followed them home. However, I want to focus on the prime suspects - those who seem most likely to have been involved.

1. **Robert Craig Cox.** An ex-Army Ranger, Cox is a convicted murderer of women who was living in Springfield at the time of the disappearance. He had two jobs potentially connecting him to the missing women. He reportedly had done some work for the local utility company and was a mechanic at the used car dealership where Stacy's father worked. Law enforcement suspected that a ruse of some sort might have been used to get the women out of the house and had a specific clue that pointed to a gas man. His access to a gas-company uniform might have been able to get them out of the house. Cox also admitted to watching investigators comb through the Levitt home. He was considered a suspect early on, but his girlfriend at the time provided an alibi for him - one she would later recant. From prison, Cox said he knew the women were murdered and buried in the area. However, he has since refused to say anything more about the case while his mother is alive; she is eighty-two.

2. **Steven Garrison**. Garrison is a convicted murderer serving a life sentence in a North Carolina prison. In an effort to plea bargain with authorities, Garrison said an acquaintance of his had confessed to killing the three women. He provided police details of the crime, details that were reportedly things that

had not previously been released to the public. Investigators thought the information he had provided them was credible enough that local authorities and the FBI served search warrants on three properties in rural Webster County, near Marshfield. Some evidence was found, although a gag order was placed on it, so it's unknown to the public just exactly what investigators have. It is worth noting that speculation has surfaced that pieces of a burned-out older model van were discovered on one of the properties, as well as items of clothing possibly belonging to one or more of the victims. There is a possible drug connection with this suspect based on the properties searched in Webster County. One of the places searched was owned by the family of Francis Lee Robb, a convicted murderer suspected of being involved in the drug trade. It is also important to note that the acquaintance of Garrison, that supposedly confessed to murdering the three women, denied those allegations when he was interviewed by law enforcement, and there was no proof to tie that person to the crime.

3. **Larry DeWayne Hall**. Hall is a convicted murderer and suspected serial killer thought to have murdered between fourteen and fifty-four women. He is currently serving a life sentence without parole in a federal psychiatric prison in North Carolina. He has told investigators that his twin brother, Gary, along with an unknown accomplice, abducted and murdered Sherrill, Suzie and Stacy. He and his brother often visited Civil War battlefields and participated in re-enactments, and Springfield is close to both Wilson's Creek and Pea Ridge national battlefields. Investigators interviewed Gary Hall and searched a van he was driving, finding some evidence that may have connected a driver to being in the Springfield area. However, it's worth noting there have been inconsistencies in the details Larry Hall provided to authorities, and his other victims were typically prostitutes or

hitchhikers.

4. **Dustin Recla and Michael Clay.** These two friends of Suzie had the motive and opportunity related to the case where Suzie was planning to testify against them. The fact that Suzie was nervous and acting anxious on graduation night could be related to her disappearance. While they have weak alibis, there is no direct evidence tying them to the scene. Additionally, Suzie was not expected to be at her home the night of the disappearance and murdering three people seems like a shocking overreaction to vandalism charges.

Persons of interest/conclusions: I don't believe the Hall twins were involved. Larry's inconsistent details and the fact that the women were essentially in the middle of town run against the types of victims he was known to go after. Steve Garrison's story supports a lot of the evidence found and multiple theories about what happened to the women. However, until the gag order is lifted, we can't know what authorities have found. Regarding Suzie's friends, I can't get over the fact that nothing she had done or was planning to do justified murder - even to sick minds. Therefore, out of the most likely suspects, Robert Cox rises to the top. His history is well known, and, most importantly, he was smart enough and evil enough, in my opinion, to pull this off. The fact that the case hasn't been solved in twenty-eight years speaks to someone of his capabilities.

Where are the women now?

As much as some people might want to believe it's possible the women are still alive, I can't. And truthfully, the physical remains of the women could be anywhere in the Ozarks or beyond, including scattered to the winds. That said, there are two main theories of where the bodies could be:

1. **Rural Webster County**. Based on Steve Garrison's information, the potential burial spots are roughly a forty-five-minute drive away from the Levitt home. This area is remote enough and close enough to Springfield to easily be the final resting place for Sherill, Suzie and Stacy.

2. **The Cox South Hospital Parking Lot.** This is one I'd still like to dismiss, but I can't eliminate it. Authorities do not believe the site contains three bodies for several reasons, but until they dig it up, we'll never know. Had the expert's scan shown nothing, it would be a different story.

Motives: Below are the key possible motives for the abduction and murder of the Springfield Three.

1. **Revenge**. This is only a viable motive if you consider Mike Kovacs, Dustin Recla or Michael Clay to be the prime suspects.

2. **Drug related.** None of the women were known to have used drugs, and the fact that Sherrill's money stayed in her purse is a fact I can't get over. However, Garrison's potential involvement could point to more details that I simply am not aware of, so I thought I should list this here.

3. **Crime of opportunity**. This is what's most likely, in my opinion. Someone could have simply come across Suzie and Stacy driving to the Levitt house at 2 in the morning and followed them. They could have scouted the place and entered through the window. They also could have used a ruse to get the women out of the house in a hurry. What's clear to me is that there is virtually no possibility that robbery was a motive, which means sexual deviancy was. That's the cold truth.

Why hasn't the crime been solved?

1. **No bodies found**. Discovery of the bodies would provide investigators a ton of information they could use to solve the case. The bodies would likely tell investigators what happened to the women and how they died. There might be DNA or other evidence tying the murderer or murderers to the crime.

2. **Crime scene was disturbed**. This one is just an unfortunate reality. No one knew on June 7 where the women were or what had happened to them, which means nobody was thinking of 1717 E. Delmar as a potential crime scene. At least ten people had been in the home, which is far too many for investigators to know what evidence remained and what had been contaminated.

3. **Mistakes in the investigation**. This is always a possibility in any cold case, but given that the first forty-eight hours were largely lost, investigators were always behind the ball. Add to that the fact that this case received national attention, which would have ramped up pressure to solve the case quickly, as well as introduced an overwhelming amount of potential evidence, and you have a perfect storm for human error. For example, after the case was aired on America's Most Wanted, one important tip was believed to be dropped when a call was disconnected. But how many other mistakes were made that the public might never know about? I feel for investigators on all this. Everyone but the killer or killers wanted the case solved.

4. **Not enough evidence**. I believe this is a given and that there is every possibility that authorities are relatively certain who is responsible. But if there is no direct evidence or nothing that can compel a jury for a conviction, the case will sit. We know a Grand Jury was convened, and that didn't result in charges

being brought forward, so I think it's safe to say investigators are missing some key puzzle pieces.

How did the perpetrator(s) gain access to the Levitt home?

1. **Perpetrator(s) was a friend or acquaintance.** Sherrill or Suzie might have opened the door to someone they knew, but would they do that at 3 a.m.? This theory would explain why the family dog, Cinnamon, was loose in the house the following morning. It would also explain why there wasn't evidence of a struggle.

2. **A ruse was used.** This is one of the most common theories because it would explain how the perpetrator(s) either gained access to the home or got the women to come outside. But what sort of ruse could be effectively used at 3 a.m.? And what sort of ruse could get the women to leave the house without putting clothes on, grabbing cigarettes, or taking their purses? Robert Cox has been said to have been doing work for the gas company. Could he have knocked on the door wearing a uniform and warning of a gas leak? Or could a policeman or someone dressed as a policeman have gotten the women outside? Suzie and Stacy had driven to the Levitt house after leaving two parties. A policeman could have come to the Levitt home to investigate an accident or witnessed erratic driving. That may have been successful in gaining access to the home. Or, could a stranger have come to the door saying they were in an accident or had car trouble asking to use the phone. I doubt a man would have been successful using that ruse at that time of the morning, but perhaps a woman would.

3. **Entered through an unlocked front door.** Sherrill Levitt, based on what people that knew her said, was very security conscience. Since she thought her daughter would not be home that night, it

is very likely that she made a special effort to make sure the front door was locked before going to bed. However, Suzie would have used her key to open the front door when she and Stacy arrived home. It is certainly possible that she did not lock the front door after entering. That would have been the simplest way for the perpetrator(s) to enter. But what about the porch light? Janelle Kirby reported that it was on when they arrived later that morning. The glass cover protecting it was gone, shattered on the front porch, but the light wasn't disturbed. Would a perpetrator enter through the front door when the surrounding area was well-lighted?

4. **The open window in Sherrill's room**. If the perpetrator(s) broke into the Levitt home, this would be the most likely entrance. An open ground-floor window is an invitation to a sick individual. The screen was reportedly removed and lying next to the house. Did the perpetrator remove the screen and climb in through the window?

5. **Cinnamon found?** One rumor that cropped up back in the 90s was that someone could have stolen Cinnamon out of the yard before the night of June 6. Then that person could have showed up at 3 a.m. holding the family dog, and Sherill would have answered the door if someone would have claimed they had found Cinnamon. Once the door was open, if an abductor had a gun, he could have ordered the woman out to the van before they had time to grab anything or think about it. It's important to say there is no evidence that this happened, but the evidence doesn't dismiss this theory.

Conclusion: It's doubtful that a friend or acquaintance came knocking on the Levitt door at that hour of the morning. I also believe that a ruse was unlikely to be successful in getting inside the house or in getting the women to come outside. The women left that house without taking anything with them and without changing out of their night clothes. That seems to indicate that they were forced outside. So either the perpetrator gained entry through an unlocked front door or through an open window.

That was the end. Having finished reading the entire folder, Brian put it down and sighed deeply. *That's everything in a nutshell,* he thought, glad to have all the most important information in one place. *Well, everything except Booger's Story.*

He picked up the second folder, stretching himself into a better sitting position as he opened it.

CHAPTER 16

HOW THE CRIME UNFOLDED- BOOGER'S THEORY

It was nearly midnight when Brian finished reading the supporting evidence that Booger listed in the two folders. He pulled out the hand-written theory of the crime with great anticipation. Even in the short time he had known Booger, he knew that he was a man with a great deal of integrity. He was a person that focused on the facts of the case. Because there had never been a resolution to the case of the Springfield Three and because so many of the puzzle pieces needed to solve the mystery remained missing, Brian knew that Booger's theory had to rely on some speculation. But he also had confidence that much of Booger's theory would be well-grounded and likely very close to what happened in the case.

It was late. It was going to be a long night. Reading Booger's theory could have waited until morning, but Brian couldn't wait. He wasn't tired. He had been energized by what he had read so far. He had to know what conclusions Booger had reached. Waiting until the next morning was not an option. He had to read the story now. Another cup of Rose's extra leaded black coffee would help. Brian left the room. The house was dark. Everyone was asleep. He found his way to the kitchen, hoping Rose had left the coffee pot on. She had. The pot was nearly empty, but enough for one cupful remained. He poured himself a cup. The smell of strong, burned coffee, thickening at the bottom of the pot, stung his nose. One cup would keep him energized through the night.

Back in his bedroom, he took a seat at the desk, took a sip of the coffee and began to read.

"The crime was one of opportunity," Booger's theory of the crime began. This was a sex crime. It was the one and only motivator that resulted in this crime. The individual that committed the crime was a seasoned psychopath, a disturbed individual that had committed similar sex crimes in the past, an individual that had spent time in prison and had recently been released. In a way, the prison system was partially to blame for what happened last night. This person should never have been free to commit this crime. He was the type of sick, disturbed individual that should have never been released from prison. What happened to those women that night was tragic, and it was avoidable. Those women were not at fault for anything that happened to them that night. They were innocent victims that found themselves in the wrong place and at the wrong time.

Robert Cox was going to strike again. His sickness had never been treated in prison. The darkness inside him was fighting to get out from the very first day he was released from prison. He moved to Springfield because that was where his parents lived. Had they lived someplace else, had he chosen to move someplace else, then someone other than Sherrill, Suzie and Stacy would have been the victims, and Springfield's small-town innocence would never have been disturbed.

It's naïve to think that the three women were his first considerations in victims. He had lived in Springfield for a few months. His sickness was too deep inside him to assume he wasn't stalking someone else before the Springfield Three. He may have been looking for a victim from the first day he arrived in Springfield.

Stacy McCall had never met Robert Cox, but he had seen her at the used car dealership where her father worked. She was his type, young, attractive, full of life, with an innocence that Cox found addictive. She was exactly the type of victim he had sought out before. She was the type of woman that wouldn't give him the time of day. She was in a different class than him. He resented that. It made him want her that much more.

Cox had been with many women before, prostitutes, women he picked up in bars. They were good for immediate gratification, but they didn't excite him. They didn't feed his sickness, his darkness.

Cox had only been out of prison for a short time. He had a girlfriend, a young woman that he had met in one of the local bars. She had taken care of his needs, but she wasn't what he was looking for. In the beginning, their relationship was good, based on sex, but both thought it might grow to something more. Maybe Cox even hoped the relationship might have been enough to fight off his demons. Maybe he wanted to have a normal life and thought he could have it with this woman. His girlfriend certainly wanted that. She had a rough life. Cox was handsome, intelligent and good to her in the beginning. She fell in love with him.

Not long after they moved in together, Cox became more distant. The kindness that she had seen in him was replaced with a darkness. He became controlling, drinking too much, and striking her on occasion. He became verbally and physically abusive to her. The love she had for him was replaced with fear. He started staying out late at night, coming home drunk, and forcing sex when she didn't want it. She had to sense that something was wrong with him. She had to wonder what he was doing out in the middle of the night. She confronted him about it at first. She was jealous. Her first thoughts were that he had found someone else, that he was spending time with another woman.

But any accusations she made were met with anger, and verbal and physical altercations were the result. After a while, her love for him was replaced with fear. She learned not to ask questions.

His nights were often spent stalking the bars looking for the right victim. Cox had a sickness inside him that wouldn't go away and only intensified with time. The bars near the Missouri State campus became his hunting ground. But it was the end of the Spring semester. Most of the college girls that were his type were gone. The ones that remained were rarely alone. He most likely stalked some of them, but the opportunity to attack never presented itself. As much as he needed to feed the darkness inside him, he was still cautious, not wanting to return to prison because of a mistake.

His other job as a gas line installer put him into suburban neighborhoods, areas that had the type of victim he was looking for, young, attractive, and educated. That job fed his fantasy. But the opportunity to act never presented itself to him. Cox was smart. He had been in prison before and was determined not to go back. He had seen plenty of women that were his type. He had even stalked some of them. But the right opportunity never presented itself. They were married, had kids or lived with their parents. They weren't alone, particularly late at night when the streets were empty, and people were sound asleep. That was when he planned to attack. That was the time he would be least likely to be noticed.

Cox likely had several targets. The times he spent away from his girlfriend, he stalked them, waiting for the right opportunity, the time when they would be alone, in a place where no one would witness his crime.

Stacy McCall was one of the women he fantasized about, probably one of the least likely victims since he knew by attacking her, the police would tie him to the crime. He, after all, worked at the same used car dealership as her father.

I doubt he ever stalked Stacy before the night of June 6.

I theorize that Cox overheard her father talking about graduation, about his daughter's plan to go to Branson that night and rent a motel room with her friend to the water park the next day. Cox would have seen that as an opportunity for him. Maybe he planned to follow them to Branson and attack them in the motel. Maybe he planned on stopping them somewhere between Springfield and Branson. Either way, they would be alone at night, away from Springfield. Hell, the authorities might not even suspect a local was involved at all.

The van that was seen and assumed to have been used in the abductions is interesting. We know that Cox did not own a van, at least one that was registered in his name. I theorize that he either took the van from the used car lot or the garage where he worked, or most likely, he took it from a salvage yard. He was a capable mechanic, after all, so it is conceivable that he could have got the van in working order for the sole purpose of using it to abduct his next prey. A cargo van with no side windows would be a perfect way to hide his victim. The van would make it easier to control the woman. Besides, it would not tie back to him if it was spotted by someone.

I don't think he ever intended to attack more than one woman until the opportunity arose the night of June 6. He stalked Stacy that night. The first time he saw Suzie was that same evening. She was young, attractive and full of life. She fed his fantasy too. He fantasized about taking both of them. They fed a darkness inside of him that he could not control, so even when he realized that the women were not going to Branson that night, he couldn't stop.

I think that he spent that entire night watching Stacy and Suzie. He waited in the darkness outside the two parties and watched, waited. He was patient that night, determined only to strike if the right opportunity arose. He watched them leave one party and go to the next. He watched them leave the second party and go to Janelle Kirby's house. Had the girls stayed there that night, he likely would have abandoned his plan. There were too many people at the Kirby house, too big of a chance of getting caught. But when the girls left the Kirby house at around 2 a.m., Cox followed them.

Suzie was intoxicated. He saw her stagger out to her car. He saw her erratic driving. She would be easy to control, he reasoned. When the girls turned onto Delmar Street, Cox would have turned out his headlights and followed them. When they pulled into the Levitt driveway, it must have given Cox reason to pause, to consider if his plan was worth continuing. He had to see Sherrill Levitt's car underneath the carport. Now there were at least three people he would need to control. He had no idea whose car that was. Likely, he would have assumed it belonged to Suzie's parents.

Suzie pulled into the driveway first, and Stacy pulled in behind her. The lights were completely off inside the house. Sherrill didn't expect her daughter to come home that night. After hanging up with her girlfriend around 11:15 p.m., she readied herself for bed and got out a book she had been reading. She read until she fell asleep. Cox watched as the women walked onto the front porch. The porch light was on, so he had a good view of Suzie pulling the house key out of her purse and opening the door. The noise of the women coming home alerted Cinnamon, and the dog began barking. This woke up Sherrill, who came out of her bedroom to see her daughter and Stacy entering the house. That was a surprise to her, so she likely would have questioned her daughter about it in the living room. Cox would have seen the three women together through the living room window.

The location of the house was ideal for Cox, set back from the street, away from neighbors and away from anyone driving down Delmar. Plenty of trees. Good places to hide and watch. He likely pulled his van to the back of the house, along a fence line. It was dark back there, and unlikely that anyone would notice the van.

He got out and walked closer to the house. From that area along the side of the house, he would have a good view into both bedrooms. He would have seen Sherrill through the bedroom window. He would have also discovered that no one other than the three women were in that house. He made a decision at that time to carry out his plan.

It is purely speculation, but I believe all three women spent time in Suzie's room. Investigators found all three purses at the edge of Suzie's room to support this theory. It would be reasonable to think a chain smoker like Sherrill Levitt would take her purse, which contained her cigarettes, to Suzie's room if she intended on talking to the girls for very long. I believe that as Stacy and Suzie removed their make-up and jewelry and readied themselves for bed, Sherrill came into Suzie's room too, probably to ask about their evening and why their plans had changed, and they'd decided not to go to Branson that night.

That provided Cox the opportunity to enter the house unnoticed. The window in Sherrill's room was open. Cox removed the screen, lying it next to the base of the house, then opened the window all the way. Maybe Cinnamon heard it and began barking. But something got Sherrill and Suzie's attention. They went to the blinds to look outside and, in the process, bent several of them.

Anyway, Cox was successful in entering the house through Sherrill's open window. I reason that he hid in that bedroom for a period of time, waiting until Suzie and Stacy got into bed. He may have waited to strike until Sherrill returned to her bedroom, but I doubt it. I think all three women were in Suzie's room when he attacked them. He would have used a knife, gun or some other weapon to hold them at bay. It wouldn't have been that difficult since there was only one entrance and exit from that room, the bedroom door. He would have entered the room, blocking the only exit. The element of surprise would have worked in his favor. They were all three forced onto the bed. Sherrill was likely subdued first, probably with masking tape over her mouth and binding her hands. After the other two were bound, the three women were forced to their feet and led out of the house. Cinnamon would have been barking, but it's unlikely any of the neighbors would have heard him. Cox had decided in advance that the crime would not take place in the house. He knew that would mean leaving evidence and DNA and perhaps bodies. There was a much greater likelihood of the crime being solved and him getting caught if the assaults took place in the home. Plus, and most importantly, I believe Cox planned on killing the women from the very beginning. He knew that if the bodies were never found, it would be extremely difficult for police to solve the case.

The women had no idea what was happening. It's doubtful that any of them thought they were being abducted by a monster that had no intention of letting them live. He would have told them that everything would be alright as long as they cooperated. So, they did as they were told and walked out the front door. Maybe while on the front porch, one of them tried to get away, bumping into the light fixture, causing the cover to fall to the ground and shatter. It doesn't matter. I don't believe there was any evidence on the light fixture to aid the police anyway.

The women were forced to the van. In the cargo area, their feet were likely tied, making it impossible for them to escape. Cox drove the van out of the neighborhood, running a stop sign and nearly clipping a van coming from the other direction.

Cox, very likely not familiar with the area around the Levitt home, would have looked for a dark, quiet place to carry out his plans. I believe the Walmart parking lot provided his first opportunity. It was nearly 4 a.m. Few cars were around. He found a dark corner of the lot, one where lot lights were nowhere near. That's where he parked the van and began his sexual assault.

I believe that Sherrill Levitt was murdered then or soon after to keep the girls quiet. The women were terrorized for over an hour in the back of that van. At some point near the end of the assault, an elderly man walking by became suspicious of the van. He wrote down the license plate number but would later through the paper away. When the assaults were over, the sun was beginning to come over the horizon. Cox forced Suzie to drive the van, maybe so no one would see him in the van or maybe so he could continue the assault on Stacy. The big question is, why did Suzie drive the van into another suburban neighborhood? Why pull into the driveway of a house where a neighbor could be spotted watching on her front porch? Was Cox occupied with Stacy in the back of the van, and Suzie saw this as an opportunity to escape or alert someone that she was in trouble? There just doesn't seem to be any rationale for driving into a subdivision at 6 a. m. in the morning other than to bring attention to the van.

I must admit that after the sighting of the van by the lady on the porch, it is purely guesswork what happened after that.

Cox said in a statement to authorities years later, when he was in a Texas prison that he believed that the women were killed shortly after their abduction. I believe that was the case too. There were a couple of sightings of the van reported between 6 a.m. and 7 a.m. that morning heading east. If Cox had murdered the women somewhere in the Ozark wilderness east of town, they may have never been found, but could Cox take that chance?

It is curious that the van, a rather distinctive older model van, was never spotted after that morning. I believe that might be a clue to what happened to the Springfield Three.

Suppose Cox drove to a lake or large body of water. Suppose he murdered Suzie and Stacy there. Then drove the van into the body of water. If the water was deep enough, it would sink below the surface. With time, it would float away, likely to never be discovered.

Granted, this theory of what happened that night leaves a lot of unanswered questions like: How did Cox get back to his girlfriend's house after dumping the van? Maybe another car was waiting for him. That's doubtful, though, because this appeared to be a crime of opportunity. He didn't plan for the women to stay in Springfield, to spend the night at the Levitt home. He had no idea that he would need a ride back that night. So maybe he walked. Cox was an ex-Army Ranger. He was in good shape. It is conceivable that he walked back home. Or, possibly, he was close enough to a main artery back to Springfield that he could hitch a ride back. His girlfriend originally told police that Cox spent the night with her, and they attended church the next morning. But later, when she changed that story and admitted Cox was not with her that night, it would be good to know when exactly she saw him next. We know he didn't go to church with her the next morning, so it's entirely possible that there was enough time for Cox to dispose of the van and walk or hitchhike home.

Cox admitted later that he watched investigators at the Levitt home after the disappearances. He watched from across the street. It's a fact that many criminals have a fascination with the investigation of their crime. They watch the police, watch news reports, and read newspaper articles about the crime. Sometimes they even provide tips to police in an effort to involve themselves in the case. I find it telling that he would watch the investigation unfold at the Levitt home from across the street. I also wonder about the lead left in a newspaper rack at one of the local grocery stores a few days later. Would Cox have been so bold as to leave that clue himself in an effort to steer the investigation in a different direction? If so, it was a daring risk for him to take. The note implied a ruse of a gas man warning of a leak. He had to know that note would lead the police to him. He, after all, had worked for the gas company. Or maybe, the note was left by his girlfriend in an attempt to implicate Cox without exposing herself.

Many people believe this crime had to be carried out by two or more predators. That seems logical on the surface because of the abduction of three women. Logic would say that it would be much more difficult for one man to abduct three women than for two or three men to do so. But I believe the crime was carried out by one man, Robert Cox.

He was an ex-Ranger, a strong, smart man. His other crimes had all been done alone. Consider the fact that no one has come forward all these years with information about the person(s) responsible for this crime. Could Cox trust another man to stay quiet after all these years? Could he live out his sic fantasy with another man involved? If two people had been involved, it is likely that one of them would have talked to someone, a friend, an acquaintance, and someone would have gone to the police. How can anyone, even a psychopath, live with what he had done to those women. At some point, they would talk to someone. And I can argue that even Robert Cox has battled with his conscience on at least two occasions. He has made statements which would lead investigators to think that he was the person responsible for what happened to the Springfield Three. I believe that is why we haven't seen any real movement toward the resolution of this case by investigators. I believe they know who is responsible, and that person is Robert Cox.

The problem is there just isn't enough evidence to bring him to trial. Buried in the files of evidence found in the Springfield Three case was a shoe box found in the back of a closet in a small house in Springfield. That shoebox contained personal items, two rings thought to have belonged to the women. Cox had been known to take souvenirs from previous victims. The rings had been handled by several people, so getting DNA or any viable information from them was impossible. The curious thing is that I couldn't find any information about the house where this shoebox was found. It would be interesting if that house turned out to be Cox's mother's house.

Even if it was, though, there just isn't enough evidence to charge Cox. He stated while in a Texas prison that he was certain the women were dead, that they were murdered shortly after their abduction, and that their bodies were disposed of close to Springfield. Could those have been the statements of a man fighting with his conscience, wanting desperately to get what happened that night off his chest?

Later he would state that he refused to say anything else about the crime as long as his mother was still alive. She is 82 years old now. Did he want to spare her any more grief? He loved his mother. She was a good woman, a Christian woman. If he was the person responsible for what happened to the Springfield Three, that news would have been devastating to the one person that still loved him.

It would also be interesting to know what evidence was presented to the Grand Jury back in 1994. Robert Cox was a person of interest that was a focal point for that grand jury. Did the alibi his girlfriend gave him for that evening play a part in the Grand Jury's refusal to indict Cox? Would things have gone differently if she had not lied to the police that interviewed her in the days following the disappearances?

Will we ever know what exactly happened to the Springfield Three? I think investigators already do. They are just waiting for Robert Cox to connect all the dots. I believe he will talk someday, someday when his words can no longer hurt his mother.

CHAPTER 17

GREEN DAY

Brian could hardly wait until morning to talk to Booger about his theory. If the detective had suspected that sitting down with a former journalist for a few days might prompt him to write a story about the cold case that had haunted his hometown for twenty-eight years, he was right. Brian knew if there was ever any doubt that nothing he could do would solve the case. However, he was primed to shine a light on it, to bring attention back to this tragedy, and to start new conversations about it. He was filled with something like a religious zeal to spread the word. Maybe nothing he could write would bring closure to the victims' families, but it could prompt new leads if the right person read what he'd publish. There was hope for an ending for the police, for neighbors and friends of the women, and for people like Janis McCall, who had shouldered the personal and public weight of it all.

It was exciting to think Booger was right. Brian definitely thought the detective must be close. Everything Booger said about Robert Craig Cox rang true. For some time now, Brian was certain in his own mind someone followed those girls to the Levitt home, and a lot pointed to Cox as a prime suspect. Still, he had questions just like Booger did. Namely, what did investigators know that the public didn't? Brian would definitely have to conduct some interviews with agents who had worked the case directly, he thought.

One thing that troubled him was why the case stalled. *Were investigators simply waiting for Cox to confess to the crime after his mom died?* he wondered. *What did his mother think about it all? If she suspected her son might be involved, wouldn't she want him to confess to bring some peace to the missing women's loved ones? What was that family dynamic all about? Or was Cox just toying with everybody all along?*

Brian barely slept that night. Once he got up and went into the kitchen, he was surprised to see Booger at the table drinking coffee dressed in slacks, a sharp shirt, a tie and a sports jacket.

"Good morning, Booger. You're looking sharp," Brian said, rubbing his eyes awake. "What's the occasion?"

Booger didn't answer. He just smiled.

"Have you decided to write the story?" he asked.

"Yes, but first, I have some questions that I hope you can answer for me."

"Depends on the questions," he replied.

"The men that broke into the warehouse stole your evidence, hit you on the back of the head and started the fire. What about them?"

"I'm not sure I follow you."

"Well, how do you think they were involved?"

"With the Springfield Three, you mean? Your focus is too narrow. I've covered a lot of cases, remember."

"Wait, what? Are you saying this folder from the bunker, you know, the one I went back in your smoldering building for, might not have been what those guys were after?"

"Bingo."

"What then?" Brian said, confused and frustrated. "What did they want?"

"Calm down there. I can't be sure what exactly they were looking for. I thought it was likely they wanted the evidence I had gathered on the missing women, but I don't believe that anymore. Not since about an hour ago when Agent Moffitt got a phone call from the FBI's crime lab in St. Louis. They pulled up a print from my office and ran it through their criminal database. Last night they got a hit. It turns out that the people that broke into my office were pawns in a drug cartel that services the region, the same one suspected of killing the informant in my parking lot a while back. I guess they found out I was receiving information from him and wanted to get their hands on whatever I had."

"Damn, Booger. They could have killed you and me and Rose too."

"Nah, if they wanted to kill me, they would have done it that night. As for you and Rose, they didn't even know you were in the warehouse. Anyway, everything will be fine soon. The FBI is planning a raid. They'll pick up those boys and shut their operation down. In the long run, it won't make any difference. Cops will cut the head off the local snake only to realize it's a snake with twenty heads."

"So, we're all safe?"

"I think you were always safe, son. Me, they may have wanted to hurt because I've made some enemies. I've gotten myself too close to the sun a few times and been burned. Rose only mattered to them because she worked with me. Them leaving the GPS device in her house was designed to frighten her and to get me to mind my own business. I've never been good at that, though. You can go home whenever you want. Rose and I will be able to leave this safehouse as soon as the arrests are made. That'll give us some breathing room."

"Where are you going to go, Booger? They burned your office, and you won't be able to get back in your apartment for a while."

"Don't worry about me. I've always got someplace to go," Booger said. "As for this story of yours about the Springfield Three, what are you going to say?"

"The truth or at least as close as possible based on the facts we know them. I'm sure I'm going to have to conduct some interviews. This might be a long process, you know? I live in St. Louis now."

"Have you considered the families of those women? They've suffered a lot."

"I understand that. I don't want to cause them any more grief. But, if by writing this story, it results in additional leads, then it will be worthwhile," Brian said, followed by a pause where he was working out an idea in his head. "I've imagined that I would try to interview Stacy's mom, someone with the Levitt family, maybe the police chief or the spokeswoman for the department, but I might be going about this all wrong. I'm thinking like a reporter, and I'm not one anymore. Well, I'm not sure just what I'll do yet, but I'll figure it out."

"Look, before you write whatever it is, there is someplace we need to go."

"Where?"

"You'll see. Throw some water on your face and meet me outside. Rose is coming, too."

In the driveway was Booger's classic red Corvette convertible. It was freshly cleaned and glistened in the sunshine. It was a beautiful day, not a cloud in the sky, warm but not hot, with a light breeze that felt good. Booger had the top down.

"When did you get your car back? I thought it was still near the warehouse."

"Agent Moffitt got it for me. He even cleaned it up after they dusted it for fingerprints. Seemed someone had bugged my car," Booger said. "Go ahead and get in. Hop in the back so the lady can sit up front."

"Yeah, sure."

Booger went back in the house and got Rose. She was wearing a slim, pink and gray dress that looked like it was straight out of a late 60s fall edition of Vogue.

"I feel a little underdressed," Brian said, smiling at the two of them.

"Don't worry about it," Booger responded. "Ain't she a treat?"

"Yes, of course."

"Yes, I'm a treat, so put this top up, old man. We can wait. You're not about to mess my hair," she said, grinning, before she turned to Brian. "How are you doing this morning?"

"Fine, thanks. Just a little tired from reading those folders of Booger's."

"Yeah, well, the old man has a gift for gab," she said, glancing over at him, who was now putting the top on.

"I just thought it was nice today," he said, mumbling to himself.

The weather was perfect to ride with it down, Brian thought, unsure if that was bad during a pandemic. The fresh spring day was too good and clean for him to imagine the world was in the grips of a deadly disease.

"Are you comfortable, m'lady?" Booger asked Rose after he got in the car and began heading east into center-city.

"Yes, quite. Thank you for putting the top on. I don't think a scarf would have held this all together," she said, as she cupped her hair with her hands.

"Of course. It's lovely, and I wouldn't want to ruin it," Booger said, smiling.

Brian suddenly felt uncomfortable. "Wait, what is happening here? Am I the third wheel? So, where are we going again?" Brian asked aloud.

"Just hang tight, buddy," Booger said, as he refocused on

the road and adjusted his rearview mirror.

"Rose?" Brian asked. "Do you remember when you first heard about the Springfield Three?"

"Yes. It was on June 8. I was working at George's Steakhouse. A customer came in and said three women had disappeared from a home in Springfield. She said it was on the news. We turned the radio on and heard about their disappearance. The thing was that most people were curious about what happened but didn't seem concerned. That changed in the next few days. The longer the women went missing, the more anxious everyone was."

"Yeah," Booger chimed in. "A person could make a lot of money selling security systems or offering self-defense classes back then."

"Rose, I keep forgetting that's where you worked then. Did you know the lady who said she was sure the three women came in that night?"

"Yes. I don't know what she saw. She wasn't vocal about it right away. After a few days, she seemed to think the ladies had been there. I think she talked to the cops after a couple of weeks. As time went on, she became more certain, but nobody else remembers seeing them," Rose said. "I will say she wasn't the type to lie. I believe she told the cops the truth – whether that's what actually happened or not is different."

"Booger, what are you going to do after I leave?" Brian asked.

"You mean besides celebrate?" he said with a laugh. "I figure I'll rebuild the office and warehouse. Maybe make a few improvements to the bachelor pad."

"Dungeon," Rose interrupted.

"Hell, I might even add a few windows to it," he said, glancing over at Rose with a smile. "Then I'll go back to work. A man has to keep working, or he'll start dying."

"What if you were wrong, Booger? What if Cox didn't take

those women? What if I write the story the way you gave it to me, but Cox isn't the monster?" Brian asked, half serious, half joking.

"Son, trust me, Cox is a monster. Even if he's just yanking chains when he says he knows what happened to them, that's what a sociopath would do. He's locked in a cell, so why not mock the people who care about these women? That's his mentality. It's funny to him that people care about anything," Booger said, which left the car quiet for a moment. "Still, until he confesses or is convicted of the crime, there is always a small chance that I am wrong. It could be another monster, but I don't think I'm wrong."

"Then, do you think there was anything those women could have done to prevent it all?"

"Son, let me tell you something. People have a tendency to blame the victims, to assume that their behavior or their activities had something to do with becoming a victim. That is bullshit. Cox was a predator. Even if you don't think it was him, and I'm telling you it was, it was a pea from the same pod. Nothing was going to stop Cox that night. Those women did nothing wrong. He was the pervert, the maniac. He took everything from them. I've seen this before. People will ask, 'Why? Why did so-and-so do it?' I'll tell you why. The answer is always the same. He saw something beautiful in them that he couldn't have or understand. He wanted to spoil that. He wanted to ruin it. He needed them to feel the world was as dark as it was in his mind. Why? The man did it to be seen. He took the mask off, and by the time they saw him, the real him, they were already dead."

"Yeah, I didn't mean to suggest they did anything wrong," Brian interjected.

"Look, I get it. Yes, maybe if circumstances were different that night, we wouldn't be talking about Sherrill, Suzie, and Stacy now, but mark my words, we would be talking about someone else. That's how this works with these guys. If you want to blame someone, blame the Florida Supreme Court for overthrowing

Cox's murder conviction. He got a second chance, and he took full advantage. Or, better yet, blame whoever messed with him when he was young. I'd bet money someone terrified and abused that guy before he became what he was. At some point, the monster is like a coping mechanism. Then, the identities become blurred. Before you know it, the kid Robert was is gone. That's what happens. One day they turn left instead of right, and they're just gone like that," Booger said, snapping his fingers at the end. Brian and Rose were silent, unsure what to say. Feeling the tension, Booger said, "Yeah, but maybe I'm wrong. I'm just an old redneck. What do I know?"

The car slowed, and the detective pulled over to a curb just outside a flower shop. He said he'd be right back and then went inside. A few minutes later, he brought a bouquet of fresh flowers and a card with him. He handed them to Rose and drove away without saying a word. "Who are the flowers for?" Brian asked.

"You'll find out soon enough," Booger replied, then drove off.

"Why is it I never know what's going on?" Brian asked. The question went unanswered. Booger was heading south now past the Missouri State campus. "What's happened with the families since the disappearances?"

"Lisa, Stacy's older sister, got married. She was picking out a wedding dress the day the women went missing," Booger said. "She had planned for Stacy to be her maid of honor. She has a couple of girls now, named one Stacy after her younger sister. Janis McCall is a grandmother. She's active in church and still talks to the local investigators occasionally to see what's new. Bartt Streeter is still battling substance abuse, I think. He has been in rehab a few times and goes through periods of being sober but eventually relapses. That's par for the course. I suppose he's been through a lot. He had a strained relationship with his mom and sister, so he's likely had some guilt about that. Sometimes, they say, a tree gets bent before winter and then hardens into place. It's best not to judge. The Streeter family has a blog dedicated to Sherrill and Suzie. I guess you could say everyone is carrying on with their lives as best they can.

"Have you ever lost anyone close to you, son?" Booger asked.

"My grandparents," Brian said. "A couple of friends. I've been pretty lucky."

"Did you go see them at the funeral home? Did you get a chance to tell them goodbye?"

"Yes."

"Well, try to imagine the families in this case. For twenty-eight years, they haven't been able to say goodbye. Their family was taken from them without any warning. People, even strangers, ask them about their loved ones; they read articles, blogs and television programs about the case. They can't get away from it. They begin to heal a little, and then the wounds open fresh again."

Booger turned right into Phelps Grove Park. It was only then that Brian realized where they were going. It was a beautiful park full of tall, old oaks, budding cherries and a few willow trees. Life was returning to the Ozarks. Robins and cardinals were glinting from branch to branch as squirrels jetted in every direction nervously. Few people were there; it was still early in the day. It was peaceful and quiet.

Booger stopped the car across from the Victims Memorial Garden. The three of them walked the stone path leading into the memorial. To Brian, it felt like a perfect, solemn place to reflect, like holy ground. As they entered, everyone was lost in thought. Near the center of the garden and at the edge of the walkway was a marble bench next to bright flowers. The names were carved into the stone, along with their dates of birth. Underneath, the following words were carved into the stone: *Missing since June 7, 1992.*

Brian thought about that date. He was a junior in high school then. Will, his stepson, was five-months-old at that time.

Booger and Rose stepped forward, stood three feet from the bench and knelt down. Brian followed just behind them and kneeled, too. As he did, it seemed time slowed down. He thought about his other sons: Chase, Andrew and Mason. When the three women died, Stacy and Suzie were about his age. They were just a year older.

Rose began to recite the Lord's Prayer. "Our Father who art in heaven." Booger and Brian joined in. "Hallowed be thy name."

Brian imagined if he had died at Stacy and Suzie's age – just after graduation. He put himself in their shoes. *What could have been?* he thought.

"Thy kingdom come. Thine will be done."

He would have never met Valerie. He would have never raised Will. Chase, Andrew and Mason would have never been born. *Who were the babies those girls might have had and raised?* he wondered. *Who are the husbands they never got to meet and marry?*

"Give us this day, our daily bread, and forgive us our trespasses as we forgive those who have trespassed against us."

He was Sherrill's age now. She would have died with her daughter, trying to protect her. And he could only imagine her horror, her love, her fear.

"And lead us not into temptation. But deliver us from evil," Brian's voice cracked in the last sentence.

With tears welled up in his eyes, Brian stood up. "Sorry, I'm sorry. I got em-emotional." Tears streamed down his face, and he couldn't talk anymore.

Booger saw Brian briefly and averted his eyes to keep himself from crying too. "That's okay, bud." Rose grabbed Brian immediately, giving him a big hug, her own eyes red and puffy. "You come here you. I understand. We understand," she said, patting his back as she held him.

He was overwhelmed, struggling with the full gravity of the injustice, the waste of their lives. He couldn't help but imagine how many other Stacys, Suzies, and Sherrills the world had lost, how many other families were broken.

Inside the car, Booger just sat there before he began to drive, looking out into the distance as if he was being swallowed up in thought. Brian never saw him cry but thought for a moment he could see his upper lip tremble through the rear-view mirror. Brian also could tell Rose was watching him closely from the front seat, though she never said anything. The ride back to the safehouse was quiet. Not a word was spoken.

Once there, after he got out of the car, Brian said, "I think I'll head home today. I've been gone a while, and I need to check on my dad to see if he needs help from me at the office. Plus, I want to get started writing soon while everything is fresh."

"Well, you can't leave until after I make lunch," Rose said.

"Okay, thanks. I've got some packing to do anyway," Brian said.

"Good," Booger replied. "Rose, we'll be right in. I want to talk to the boy for a minute."

"Okay, don't be too long, you two. Lunch will be ready in thirty minutes."

"What's up, Booger?" Brian asked with just a hint of hesitation.

"Not much. I want to make sure you're okay."

"Oh, what? Back there? That was nothing."

"Well, there's nothing wrong with getting choked up, but I meant with your family. I don't know what's going on, but I know you've been going through some stuff."

"Oh, well, yeah. Valerie and I have been separated. I was

thinking about her and my boys at the memorial. I don't know what to say. It's complicated, you know?"

"Okay, well, I won't press you on it. You're old enough and smart enough to know what's valuable."

"Yeah, that's true. I do think this week has maybe helped that."

"Well, I guess we can go enjoy some wonderful lunch," Booger said with a laugh and a too-hard pat on the back.

"Yeah, but wait, though," Brian said, hoping to get past the laughter. "I was curious about the flowers that you left for the women. Do you do that often?"

"Oh, every so often, you know. Probably not as much as I should. In the winter, I try to leave a wreath or something, but since spring has sprung and you were still here, it felt like we needed to do this today."

"What about the other flowers that were there at the base of the bench?"

"I'm not sure. I understand both Stacy's mom and the Streeter family leave stuff from time to time. Every time I've been there, it seems like there's something new. I like seeing that, and it feels good to think I'm contributing a little something too. In June, it seems like a bunch of people go by there."

"Oh, sure. That's a good thing," Brian said. "I wanted to ask also, what was the card you left? What did you say?"

"It's a personal note that I write occasionally, you know? It's different each time – usually a prayer or an inspirational phrase. This one today had a quote from an unknown source I saw online."

"What did it say?"

"It said, 'Some things can never be fixed; they can only be carried.' I just want the families to know that someone is thinking about them, I guess," Booger said, scratching his head, thinking about more he wanted to say. "A few years ago, I saw Janis

McCall leaving flowers at the bench one day, just after sunrise. There was no one else in the park. She just sat there on the bench. I don't know how long she was there. She looked so peaceful. I wanted to go up to her to tell her I understood the pain she was in. But I didn't, probably better anyway, because no one could understand the suffering she was going through and had gone through for so many years. I lost my wife a long time ago, but that was different. She suffered a long illness. I had time to say goodbye to her. Janis McCall didn't have that time. When I saw her, it had been a while since I'd been back there. Longer than normal. Seeing her made me recommit myself to never go too long without stopping by. If I can give those loved ones any comfort, I feel like I've done something."

"I like that," Brian said before a long pause. He had another question to ask. "Booger, there is one thing that bothered me about pinning this crime on Robert Craig Cox."

"What's that?"

"It's the man driving home with his daughter about 3 a.m. the morning of June 7."

"Yes. What's bugging you?"

"Well, the timeline of what that witness saw makes sense."

"Yes, it does. And your point is?"

"Well, he seemed pretty certain he got a good look at the driver of that van, and he thought it had to be Gary Hall."

"Yes, that's what he said."

"Well, I don't know how he could be sure it was one twin versus the other at 3 a.m. while he's being driven off the road. Still, the bigger point I'm making is that he thought it was one of the Hall twins and not Cox."

"Look, you wanna know what I think? I think it was dark. I believe he was wrong. He only got a flash, a glimpse of the driver. It all happened in a second."

"Okay, but what about the evidence the police supposedly

found in Gary Hall's van?"

"What about it? They haven't released any information about what they took from the van, except for the piece of paper with Branson written on it, and it's a stretch to call that evidence. Yeah, there were two women assaulted in a park in Branson about the time of the disappearances and investigators looked at the Hall brothers for that crime. But there wasn't proof of anything. I've turned this case over in my head a hundred times. I wouldn't put much into that if I were you."

"Well, the other thing that bothers me is the area in rural Webster County where investigators used search warrants to retrieve evidence."

"Yeah, I've got to admit that has me puzzled before, but there is still a gag order on everything, though. Steve Garrison's statement that led police to that area seemed credible, at least credible enough for investigators to get three separate search warrants for that area. But until the order is made public, we'll never know exactly what the cops found."

"That's fair. It still feels off, you know? Look, I feel like it's probably Cox who's guilty, but there's that lingering doubt that maybe we're trying to fit a round peg into a square hole," Brian said.

"It's easy to keep doubt alive if you want to but consider the facts. There were inconsistencies in Steve Garrison's statements to police, enough that they later felt he was unreliable. Investigators may have gathered evidence with those three search warrants, but whatever they found didn't result in charges against anyone. For all we know, there was nothing valuable there, or at least, it may not have related to the Springfield Three. Don't overthink this. It's Robert Craig Cox. Give your mind some rest."

"Yeah, okay," Brian said, and with that, they went into the house. Brian felt they had done all they could do.

Shortly after gathering his things, Rose had lunch ready.

She had made more egg salad sandwiches before he could leave. "You always seemed to enjoy them so much, I thought you should have them one last time," Rose said.

"Oh, yes. Brian loves those!" Booger said, grinning ear to ear.

"Thank you," he said. He ate the entire sandwich without complaint.

When it was time to go, Booger said, "Let me know when your book is going to be released."

"Who said it would be a book?"

"It'll be a book," he said with a smile. "And stick to the facts as much as you can."

"I will, Booger."

Rose smiled and gave Brian a long hug. "We'll miss you, Brian. Next time you come to Springfield, be sure to stop in and visit."

"I will," Brian promised.

With that, he walked out of the door and got into his car. He glanced back as he pulled out of the driveway, already feeling a bit nostalgic. The curtains to the living room window were open, and he could see Booger and Rose embrace. Brian took his time pulling out, eyeing the window. Then, they were kissing. "I knew it!" he said out loud.

In the weeks and months that followed, something close to normalcy returned for Brian and Alan. The COVID-19 summer meant masks and social distancing anytime they were out and about, but business largely bounced back at the office. Alan called it their "new normal." When they had spare time, the son and father pieced together their story about the three women. This was one benefit of life slowing down a bit. Then one day, when their book was all done but the editing, the phone rang. It was Booger McClain. Brian picked up.

"So, how the hell are you? How's your pop doing?"

"Great. It's good to hear from you, Booger. I gotta tell you...."

Booger cut him off. "Son, I got some news for you. I received a call from Special Agent Moffitt today. They made several arrests on that drug case I was involved in. They think they found the people responsible for breaking into my office and setting the fire."

"Really, who were they?"

"Why do you know all the druggies?"

"Well, no, I just thought...."

"Just playing with you. Yeah, they had most of the information they'd stolen from my war room. They had an underground meth lab and a barn full of product ready to sell."

"Oh, okay. That's very interesting."

"You haven't heard the best part yet."

"What's that?"

"The drug operation was based out of a salvage yard in rural Webster County?"

"A salvage yard?"

"Yes. One of the agents on site noticed they had parts from an old '68 Dodge van, bumpers, windshield, and side panels. Guess what color those panels were?"

"No."

"That's right. They were moss green."

-THE END-

EPILOGUE

INTERVIEW WITH JANIS MCCALL

As the 30th anniversary of "Remembrance Day" approached, Janis McCall had two major heart attacks.

On June 6, 2023, the day before the 31st anniversary, I interviewed her for this epilogue. About a week earlier, I had asked if she wanted to write a foreword, and she graciously agreed. However, some of those same health issues from the year before had returned, so we pivoted to an interview.

"It's traumatic," she said of Remembrance Day. "It brings it all back. There's like a fluttering in my chest, and it feels tight – like everything is closing in."

I felt awful. I'd forgotten about the anniversary. I work with my father, Alan, in St. Louis, and our small marketing firm had been extra busy since Memorial Day. I hadn't thought about the date at all. Plus, edits had been delayed on the re-release. It was just a coincidence that we weren't finished at least a month earlier.

Regardless, if Janis had any reservations about speaking with me, I couldn't tell. It seemed our conversation wasn't about her. It was about something bigger.

From the beginning, Stacy McCall's mother had been the

public face of the case. She had done countless interviews over the years, always trying to keep her daughter's story alive and putting pressure on investigators to bring closure to everyone who cared about Stacy, Suzie Streeter, and Sherrill Leavitt.

"They're not really talking to us anymore," she said of the police.

Her frustration was evident as her voice cracked when I asked why she thought the case still hadn't been solved.

"I wish I knew," she said. "I think they focused too much on Robert Craig Cox. I think they put all their eggs in one basket."

She told a story of going to meet with investigators the Monday after the three women disappeared and being told at that time by one of the men in charge that there was no proof the women had been abducted.

"I didn't know what to say. Stacy didn't even have her car keys," she said, adding that her daughter didn't have her bathing suit or anything she was supposed to take to the waterpark in Branson. It was clear to Janis from the scene at Sherrill's home that none of the women had her their things.

Janis acknowledged there have been a lot of theories about what happened. She said she's wondered before if the person responsible for the disappearance could have been a cop or someone posing as an officer.

"We've all given fingerprints - the 15 to 18 people or whatever who were in that house so they could eliminate us [as suspects]," she said. "I just don't think they've pursued every avenue."

For all the years of not knowing and the lack of closure, and despite her health issues, Janis McCall is no victim. She has, time and again, done what she could to help investigators and engage with the media. At the end of the day, she's a fighter because she is a mother.

"Stacy was vibrant. She was beautiful. If you went to the

mall or something with her, you'd see heads turn," Janis said.

Before her disappearance, Stacy would model bridal gowns and participate in local fashion reviews. Her mom said she was very organized and planned to buy outfits for Rush Week at college.

"I remember she was making $68 a week, and she knew where every dime was going. She'd say, 'Mom, I want to get these flowered shorts or this skirt, and I don't think I'll have enough money,' and I'd say, 'Well if you need it, we can help you out," Janis said.

Stacy used to babysit quite a bit in their south-side neighborhood and loved kids, according to her mom. She was considering a career involving children or the healthcare field but hadn't made up her mind yet. She was an avid reader too. "She was always trying new words on us. I remember she once pronounced the word 'awry' as 'aww-ree,' and we laughed. We would call her Spacey Stacy."

I asked Janis about how difficult it must have been to see her daughter's picture on shop doors and billboards all over town in the days after the disappearance – a result of a community coming together to find three of its own. "There was a positive energy all around us, but I think I was in shock for a long time."

When the three women went missing, Stacy, it seemed, had the whole world in front of her.

"She was really happy," Janis said before she paused for a moment. "We have to keep the case open. Everyone deserves answers. Not just us. Everyone."

Brian Brown
June 7, 2023
Remembrance Day

Alan Brown grew up in the suburbs of Kansas City and graduated from Shawnee Mission East High School in 1973 and Avila University in 1979. Now he lives in a suburb of St. Louis, MO, with my wife and three daughters. He also has four sons that are grown and living outside the home. He enjoys writing about his experiences growing up, examining the fantastical and dark sides of a person's natural fears. All of his books are based on the reality in his life. He is a fan of Alfred Hitchcock. Like his stories, Alan Brown's will conclude with a twist, something he hopes will take the reader by surprise.

Author Brian Brown. I am a husband, father of four, and a former business and political reporter from Springfield, Missouri, currently living and working in the St. Louis area. I've written five books with my father, Alan Brown, and edited a sixth. All our novels involve our fictional detective, Booger McClain, in what we have dubbed our Ozarks' Noir style. I'm also an amateur photographer: @Bbrownspfd on Instagram. More information about our novels is available on our Facebook page (Alan and Brian Brown Write Stuff): https://www.facebook.com/profile.php?id=100064104282706

Made in the USA
Monee, IL
26 September 2023